# Taken
# by the
# Cowboy

Julianne MacLean

# Acknowledgements

Special thanks to my cousin and critique partner, Michelle Phillips (aka children's author Daisy Piper), for many years of shared creativity and editorial support. Also to Joyce David (aka Joyce Sutherland) and Lorraine Vassalo, who were among the first to read and critique this novel in its earliest form. Cathryn Fox, Anne MacFarlane, Bev Pettersen, Shawna Romkey, and Pat Thomas from Romance Writers of Atlantic Canada—your editorial contributions were invaluable. A special shout-out to Julia Phillips Smith for all the great support on your most excellent blog! And finally to Stephen and Laura, who make my world a happy place.

# Prologue

*Dodge City, Kansas*
*Present day*

Jessica Delaney sat in the waiting room outside the Operating Room, barely able to move, much less comprehend what had just happened to her brother. "How much longer?" she said to her parents. "He's been in there for two hours."

Jessica's mother blew her nose, while her father sat in silence, squeezing his wife's hand. "I'm sure they're doing their best," he said. "We'll hear something soon."

Jessica rose from her chair and walked to the edge of the waiting room to peer down the long hall at the surgery doors to the O.R. She thought of Gregory lying on the table under the lights, a team of masked surgeons working over him. What were his chances? Did anyone ever survive a bullet wound to the chest?

Feeling nauseous all of a sudden, she returned to her chair and sat down. She stared at a framed painting on the wall and wished this day had been different. Gregory didn't deserve to be lying on that table. He was too young, and such a good person.

At least the gunman was behind bars. The convenience store clerk had noticed the out-of-state license plate just before he called 911.

An orderly in a white uniform walked by pushing a cart stacked with folded blue hospital gowns. Jessica watched him while he steered the cart onto the elevator. When the doors slid shut behind him, she thought of Liam, her fiancée.

Should she call him and tell him they were still waiting for news?

Jessica chewed on a thumbnail and recalled their conversation hours ago, when she'd called him at work....

"Liam, something terrible just happened. Can you come with me to Dodge?"

"When? Now? I'm in a meeting. I can't just skip out."

She fought to keep her voice steady. "Gregory's been shot. He's on his way to the hospital. I need to go right now, and I'd really like you to come with me."

He was silent for a moment. "God, Jessica...is he going to be okay?"

"I don't know. That's why I need to go now—to be with Mom and Dad."

"Of course. You should go."

"Can't you come?"

She heard him sigh heavily on the other end of the line. "It's a really bad time, Jess. We've got clients coming in tonight. It could be a million-dollar deal. If I'm not there, it might cost me my job — and you don't know what kind of day it's been for me." He began to tell her about the mountain of emails and texts he still had to get through.

Jessica covered her forehead with her hand. She didn't want to hear the details. Not now.

She interrupted him. "Look, don't worry about it. I'll go alone."

"Let me know how he's doing. Call me later."

"Sure." She hung up without saying goodbye and drove from Topeka to Dodge alone....

The squeak of the surgery doors swinging open pulled Jessica from her thoughts. She stood up to look down the hall again and saw a doctor in O.R. greens walking toward them. His shirt was drenched in sweat. "Mom, Dad…someone's coming."

Her parents stood up.

The doctor, who looked to be in his mid-thirties, kept his eyes on Jessica as he walked the length of the hall. A terrible rush of anxiety exploded in her belly as he came to stand before them.

"Mr. and Mrs. Delaney," he said, "I'm Doctor Jake Spencer."

He shook her father's hand, while Jessica put her arm around her mother.

"I'm sorry to tell you this," the doctor said. "We did everything we could for Gregory, but I'm afraid he didn't make it."

Jessica stared blankly at the doctor, who kept his gaze fixed on hers. His eyes filled with empathy, while hers filled with tears.

Her parents said nothing for a moment, then her mother let out a sob. "Please, no."

The doctor put his hand on her shoulder. "I'm so sorry, Mrs. Delaney. The wound was deep. The bullet entered his chest and punctured a lung. It lodged in the wall of his aorta. We tried to stop the bleeding and put a graft in place, but it bled too heavily, and we couldn't stop it. We did all we could do. I massaged his heart to pump it manually, but…I'm very sorry."

Jessica's mother leaned into her husband and buried her sobs in his chest. All Jessica could do was stare at the doctor while she listened to her mother's weeping and the sound of her own blood rushing through her veins. She still couldn't believe what the doctor was saying.

"Will you be all right?" he asked. His voice was caring. Almost shaky. His green eyes were compassionate and sincere. He reached out and touched her shoulder.

Jessica managed to nod.

"If you need anything or have any questions," he continued, "you can contact me at any time." He handed her his card.

"Thank you," she replied.

He made a move to leave but turned back. He shook his head in frustration. "I'm sorry, Jessica. I did everything in my power to save him. I wish I could have done something to prevent it from happening."

His expression was tight with strain, as he bowed his head and walked away.

Her grief swelled as she stared after the doctor, until the doors to surgery swung closed behind him. She choked back a sob and turned to embrace her parents.

It wasn't until many hours later, after they left the hospital and went home to call their friends and relatives, that Jessica wondered how the doctor had known her name.

# Chapter One

*One year later*

Jessica shifted nervously in the driver's seat, her fingers like vice grips around the steering wheel. She'd driven for two hours, slicing through a rain-battered dusk, wishing that she lived closer to Dodge and her parents. If she did, she wouldn't have to spend so many hours traveling from one city to the other.

Maybe it was time to move home, she thought, for the tenth time that month. There wasn't much keeping her in Topeka anymore—not since she broke off her engagement to Liam.

She was self-employed and could write her fitness column from wherever she pleased. All she needed was a good pair of sneakers for running, her laptop, and wireless Internet at a nearby Starbucks. Her apartment was a sublet. She could give a month's notice and be out of there in a heartbeat. The change would do her good.

Not that she wasn't happy in her work. She loved what she did. There were no problems in that department, but everything else seemed so uncertain and unpredictable.

Her brother had gone out to buy ice cream after supper one night, and he never saw another sunrise again.

Jessica had imagined she'd be married by now with a kid on the way, but the man she chose for a husband turned out to be a self-absorbed child, and she was suddenly single again, paying off debt from a honeymoon she had no choice but take alone.

Yet, she was ever hopeful, waiting for a sign from above, a clue to suggest what she was meant to do with her life. There had to be some greater purpose.

Should she stay in Topeka, or move home to Dodge to be closer to her parents?

They weren't getting any younger and wouldn't be around forever. If she'd learned anything over the past year, it was to make the most of each and every day, because you never knew when it could all end — just like that — with no warning whatsoever.

Come on, destiny. Which is it? Topeka or Dodge?

A flash of lightning and an instantaneous thunderclap caused her to jump in her seat. Rolling her neck to ease the tension in her shoulders, she flexed her fingers on the steering wheel and repositioned her slick palms. The windshield wipers snapped noisily back and forth.

Another crash of thunder overlapped the last. Counting the seconds to keep her mind occupied, Jessica raked stiff fingers through her hair. She'd just finished a cup of bitter service-station coffee, and now her brain, whirling with caffeine, couldn't match the lightning with the correct thunderclap.

Maybe the radio would take her mind off things. She tuned into a fiddling festival, then tapped her thumbs on the steering wheel to "Oh! Susanna." Other vehicles passed her at dangerous speeds, their tires hissing through puddles on the slick pavement. She glanced impatiently at her watch, wondering how much longer she'd have to fight this storm.

Ahead of her, a white freight truck lumbered slowly up the incline. Knowing she'd have to pass, she glanced over her shoulder and signaled to cross into the passing lane.

She barely managed to gain any distance when her car suddenly hydroplaned and began to fishtail. Instinctively, she slammed her red stiletto pump onto the brake, realizing too late what she had done. Her heart pummeled her ribcage as she tried to regain control, but it was no use. The steering wheel was useless as the vehicle spun around in a dizzying circle.

Oh! Susanna, don't you cry for me....

The car whipped around and flipped over, bouncing across the pavement like a child's toy. The world spun in chaotic circles. Jessica's head hit the side window. Glass smashed, and steel collapsed like tin all around her.

Frozen with fear, she felt all her muscles constrict. Please, stop! Get me out of here!

Lightning split the ashen sky. The car lit up and sizzled with one electrifying pulse after another.

The light...it was too bright. She couldn't see. She squeezed her eyes shut.

All at once, the world became silent except for the echoed thumping of her heart in her ears. There was no pain, only blackness. She felt as if she were floating, detached from everything but the extraordinary quiet, the complete absence of all cares and misgivings. She felt no fear now. Was this death? Maybe she would see her brother....

Something wet trickled down her forehead and onto her eyelashes.

The distinct visceral sensation sucked her out of the tranquil beyond, and when her eyes fluttered open, she found herself lying on her back, gazing up at the dusky sky, watching silvery clouds roll and twist and turn in the most fantastic way.

Then real, conscious thoughts began to form in her brain.

She'd been in a car accident. She was lying in the grass. Her hair was wet. Was it blood?

Blinking in panic, she touched her throbbing temples but discovered the wetness was only rain. Relieved, she sat up and realized she was sitting in a puddle of mud. A damp chill rippled up her spine.

Had she been thrown from the car? She couldn't remember anything that violent. Of course, she had shut her eyes and blacked out. Or at least she thought that's what happened.

7

With trembling hands, she rose up on her knees and rubbed the side of her neck where the seatbelt had chafed her. Next, she touched her scalp, feeling a gritty, sandy residue. Shattered glass, she realized, as she studied the pads of her fingers. And her head—Good Lord. A bump was already sprouting at her temple.

Wondering if she had a concussion, she carefully tried to stand. She pressed her hand into the gooey muck to keep her balance and rose to her feet. Her stiletto pumps sank deeper into the puddle, right up to the ankles of her skinny jeans. She noticed that her favorite black belted jacket was ruined. A button was torn off, and the pocket was ripped.

She glanced around, searching for her car.

Where was it? And why couldn't she hear traffic from the road?

Bewildered, she scanned the rolling prairie for the vehicle. Surely it was somewhere.

She rested her hand on her stomach that churned with nausea. It was a normal reaction, she knew, after what she'd just been through. In fact, it was a miracle she was even able to stand.

But where was her car?

The only explanation she could come up with was that she must have been wandering around in shock for the last little while and had left it behind — along with her purse and cell phone. And the strange floating sensation.... That must have been some kind of dream state.

So where was she, exactly? To her left were miles of flat, green prairie. To her right, a small hill. She decided to climb it to see what was on the other side.

When she reached the top, she stepped onto a country road pocked with puddles and wet stones. She pushed her damp hair away from her face to look around, and her heart sunk.

More miles of prairie. In every direction.

How had she gotten this far? And which way should she go?

She stared transfixed at a distant flicker of lightning far off, just above the misty horizon. A quiet breeze fanned the odor of cow manure into her face, and nervous dread swelled inside her.

Something didn't feel right. She couldn't possibly have walked much of a distance. Could she?

Well, she thought, taking a deep, steadying breath and resolving to stay rational. There was no point standing around doing nothing. That road had to lead somewhere.

Off she went.

After walking a few miles on the dirt road through the pouring rain, Jessica wished miserably that she had worn her running shoes instead of her stupid "sexy-girl" shoes, but there wasn't much she could do about it now. All she could do was try to ignore the excruciating sting of the blisters—which felt like hot coals burning the balls of her feet—and walk with an awkward limp.

A short while later, she sighed with relief when the setting sun finally peeked through the thick blanket of clouds. Raindrops glistened like tiny diamonds as they fell, weightless and softer now. Lifting her wrist to check the time, she realized she'd lost her watch. Damn. It was brand new.

Reaching a fork in the road, she stopped to look at a dilapidated wooden sign that read: DODGE CITY. The sign pointed left, so with little choice, she limped in that direction.

By the time she spotted a town up ahead—unfortunately it didn't look like Dodge City—the rain had stopped and darkness had folded over the terrain. Though she felt like a drowned rat, she was relieved to have found some signs of civilization.

She couldn't wait to find a phone and call her parents. They were probably worried sick.

As she limped across an old plank bridge that led into the town, she heard the faint music of a brass band, and each time its cymbals crashed together, it was once too often for the pounding sensation in her head.

Then a horse-drawn wagon rumbled by.

She stopped abruptly and stared at it—what the heck?—then stepped off the bridge and walked up the wide main street. She glanced around for a phone booth, but found herself distracted by the buggies, the cowboy costumes on the men, and the music from inside a place that looked like an old saloon. A piano man played "Oh! Susanna," and a banjo plucked along with it.

That song again.

She stood shivering at the corner of two unpaved streets, looking left and right. Wide boarded sidewalks and hitching rails fronted the buildings; saddled horses and mules were lined up side by side.

Good God, there had to be at least six inches of slop underfoot and it smelled like horse poo.

What kind of place was this? Had she stumbled onto the set of one of those reality shows where they throw people into a historical time-period and watch how crazy they go?

When a couple of ragged looking cowboys staggered by, waving whisky bottles and revolvers in the air, Jessica decided to walk a little faster. She hadn't seen any women yet, only men, and she suspected this wasn't the safest place to be standing around, taking in the sights, because it all looked pretty sketchy.

Stepping up onto the boardwalk, she paused outside a bar called the Long Branch Saloon, which made no sense because the Long Branch was part of the Dodge City Museum—a re-creation of historic Front Street, mostly visited by tourists. But this didn't look anything like that. It seemed far more real. Almost too authentic.

She backed into a post to let a group of men in tattered cowboy costumes pass by, then glanced at the swinging doors. From where she stood, she could hear glasses clinking and dice rolling. There was a click and clatter of poker chips and billiard balls while a man hollered above the music, "Twenty-five-to-one!"

Her stomach churned again. She really needed to find a phone.

She decided to try the saloon, but shrank back when she glanced at the window. June bugs. She hated June bugs. When she was seven years old, her best friend's little brother had planted some in her bed during a camping trip and they'd given her the heebie-jeebies ever since.

Trying not to think about that anymore, Jessica shivered with disgust, pushed through the doors, and collided with a thick wall of cigar smoke. Her nose crinkled. Stifling a cough, she gazed uneasily over the crowd.

Most of the men wore hats and looked as if they'd just walked out of an old movie.

Focusing on what she had come in for, she approached the bar. "Excuse me. I've been in a car accident and I need to get to a phone. Do you have one that I could use?"

The bartender, who wore a white shirt with the sleeves rolled up, topped by a brown vest, stared at her while he polished a shot glass.

"Sir?" she asked again. "Can you at least tell me how I can get to Dodge City? The real Dodge City?"

"This is it, darlin'. You're exactly where you want to be."

Now this was getting ridiculous. "No, you don't understand. I've been in an accident and I need a phone."

"Don't have no phone, but I've heard about 'em."

Jessica stared at the man for an agonizing second, then turned on her heels and walked to the window. A snake handler wandered by carrying a lantern. Following closely behind him was a squealing pig.

She rubbed her throbbing temples and squeezed her eyes shut. Maybe she did have a head injury and this was all a hallucination, or maybe she was unconscious and dreaming.

She returned to the bar. "Is there a telephone anywhere in this town?"

"Not that I know of." He turned around and placed the polished shot glass on a shelf.

Enough was enough. Jessica pushed a damp lock of her hair behind her ear and took a deep breath to calm herself.

"Are you fixin' to buy a drink, ma'am," he asked, "or are you just gonna stand there and stare at me all night?"

Jessica glanced around the saloon at the rough and tough looking clientele, and held up a hand. "No thanks. I'll find help elsewhere." Struggling to keep it together, she walked out.

Squinting through the darkness, she searched for a friendly face or a shop with some lights on, but all she saw were those same two drunken cowboys flinging bottles, laughing uproariously and spitting tobacco.

Suddenly a shot rang out in the street. Panic exploded in her belly, and she ran back into the saloon. "Is there a police station nearby?" she said to the bartender. "I really need some help."

"You'd be looking for Sheriff Wade," he casually replied. "He's just over that way in the city clerk's office, not far from the depot and the water tank." He pointed a bottle of whisky toward the window.

"Is it far? I have to walk there by myself."

"Not far, but a young woman ain't safe roaming these streets alone during cattle season. These cowboys have been on the trail a while, and have a hankering for more than just the chuck wagon, if you understand my meaning." He leaned over the bar and glanced down at her skinny jeans and muddy red pumps. "They'll be takin' a shinin' to you, even dressed the way you are in those britches."

"I'll be fine." She turned and walked out the door.

She hopped off the boardwalk and down onto the street with a splash, groaning when she sank ankle-deep into the mud. No matter. She'd be at the sheriff's office soon enough, and this whole thing would be straightened out.

She stopped, however, when something tickled and buzzed behind her ear. She scratched and tousled her hair, then realized with a terrible surge of panic that a June bug was stuck in her hair!

Jessica shrieked. She tried to brush it away, but it was tangled in her long wet locks. She tossed her head around, flailed her arms in all directions, and jumped through the puddles to try and escape.

Boom! Another gunshot ripped through the night. Her heart exploded with fear, and she tripped backwards over a plank in the street. Down she went, splashing into a puddle on her backside. No sooner than her butt began to throb, she looked up to see a man falling out of a second story window!

He dropped onto the over-hanging roof and rolled straight toward her. Jessica scrambled to her feet and slipped through the slick muck, barely escaping the plummeting man's path. Just as she slid out of the way, he landed heavily in front of her, splashing muddy water onto her cheeks. A second later, a metal object dropped into a puddle beside her.

"Sir!" she hollered, dropping to her hands and knees to help him. "Are you all right?"

He was face down in the mud, and Jessica was just about to roll him over when the saloon doors swung open, smacking against the outside wall. Men and women poured out and gathered on the boardwalk to stare at her in shocked silence.

"What in God's name happened?" someone asked.

"This man fell out of a window," Jessica replied. "He needs help."

The stranger ran toward her and together, they rolled the injured man onto his back. Jessica stared in horror at his face. A clean bullet hole gaped between his eyes, and blood trickled down his nose.

"Dear Lord," the stranger said. He stood up and quickly backed away.

"Somebody call 911!" Jessica shouted. She pressed her ear to the man's chest to listen for a heartbeat. When she heard nothing, she knew there was no hope, but she still wanted an ambulance. A cop car, too.

If there was such a thing in this backward place.

"Will somebody call an ambulance?" she shouted in frustration.

"Now...just be calm, miss," the stranger said. "We don't want any trouble."

"What are you talking about?" she replied. "I don't want to cause trouble. I'm trying to help him. Doesn't anyone have a cell phone?"

That particular request was met with blank stares.

"I saw her wavin' a gun around like some kind of lunatic!" someone offered.

"I wasn't waving a gun," she explained. "I was trying to kill a June bug."

There was a series of 'oohs' and 'ahs' from the crowd as everyone backed away in unison.

Realizing she was quickly becoming a primary suspect in this man's murder, Jessica raised both hands in the air and stood. "Look, everyone needs to stay calm. It wasn't me. I was just trying to help him."

"Do you know who this is?" the stranger asked.

Jessica shook her head. "No."

"That's Left Hand Lou!" someone called out from the crowd.

Before Jessica had a chance to comprehend what this meant, people rushed over to get a look at the corpse.

"He's wanted in three states!" someone hollered. "You just killed the fastest draw this side of the Mississippi!"

What did they think she had done? She hadn't shot him! And what did they mean—the fastest draw this side of the Mississippi? This wasn't Gunsmoke, for pity's sake.

"Wait a minute," she said. "Seriously. There's been a mistake."

Just then, a deep voice cut through the commotion. "Can I ask what's going on in this little gathering of yours?"

Unable to discern from where the voice had come, she looked all around through the darkness.

"Ma'am? I asked you a question." The crowd parted, clearing a wide path for the inquiring man to approach. Jessica was finally able to get a glimpse at him, although the brim of his black hat shadowed his face from the dim lantern light spilling out of the saloon.

He moved slowly toward her, and she was taken aback by how handsome he was, with dark hair, blue eyes, and a fit, muscular build.

Closing the distance between them, he pushed his open black coat to the side. His purpose was clear as he rested his large hand on an ivory-handled revolver holstered to his leather gun belt.

His trousers—also black—were snug and worn at the knees, and his boots were spurred. Jessica hadn't actually looked at his feet, but as he walked, the sound of the spurs jingling alerted her senses to everything about him.

Someone moved aside, and a gentle stream of light reflected off the shiny star pinned to the man's lapel.

It read: Sheriff.

Thank God.

He angled his head and spoke in low voice – sort of like Clint Eastwood, but not exactly. "Ma'am, you look a little distressed. Can I be of some assistance?"

His observation, which couldn't have been closer to the truth, melted all her cool bravado in an instant, and she was so relieved, she could have grabbed hold of his shirt collar, pulled him toward her, and kissed him square on the lips.

"Yes, you can," she replied. "I'm so glad you're here. Thank you for coming so quickly."

He chuckled softly, but the smile in his eyes was cold and calculating.

"I wouldn't thank me just yet," he drawled, as he wrapped his big hand around her arm and tugged her closer. "Because by the look of things here, missy, you're gonna be spending the night in my jailhouse."

The crowd murmured approval, while Jessica glanced up at his ruggedly handsome features, bronzed by wind and sun, then cautiously lowered her eyes to the gun at his hip.

He shook his head at her, as if she'd been a very naughty girl, and said, "Tsk tsk tsk," while she paused to think carefully about the best way to handle this.

# Chapter Two

Wetting her lips and clearing her throat, Jessica managed to muster some dignity from somewhere inside, and proudly wiped her mud-splattered cheek with a finger.

Without a word, the sheriff reached into his pocket and handed her a crisp white handkerchief.

"Thank you," she coolly replied, while she proceeded to clean her face and wipe her hands.

"She just killed Left Hand Lou, Sheriff!" someone said. "Imagine, a pretty little thing like that—"

"I see what happened, Matthew," the sheriff said, without taking his eyes off her. "But I'd like to hear the whole story from the lady."

With calculated decorum, Jessica finished wiping the mud from her hands and passed the kerchief back to him. He shoved it into his coat pocket.

"Is that the gun that killed this man?" he asked.

"Yes, sir, it is," Matthew replied as he bent to pick up the revolver at her feet.

Proudly he raised the revolver for everyone to see, and there was no shortage of more 'oohs' and 'ahs' from the crowd as muddy water dripped from the barrel.

This was getting worse by the second.

"Hand it over," the sheriff said to Matthew. His inquisitive eyes studied Jessica with intentional detached interest as he took the wet revolver, shook out the excess water and shoved it into his belt.

"You haven't told me your name yet," he said.

"Jessica Delaney."

"Well, Miss Delaney," he replied, "I'm pleased to make your acquaintance. The name is Truman Wade." He tapped his thumb against the ivory handle of his gun.

It was clear he held the silent crowd's respect. Or maybe they feared him. Judging by the way Jessica felt at the moment, it was probably the latter.

"Are you going to tell me what happened here," he asked, "or am I gonna have to ask the dead man?"

Jessica turned to examine the corpse behind her. "You don't understand. There's been a mistake."

The sheriff's quiet laughter made her clench her jaw in aggravation. Wondering what the joke was all about—when a dead man lay two feet away—she faced the cool lawman again.

"You mean to tell me," he drawled, "you shot this man square between the eyes by mistake?"

The crowd jeered until Sheriff Wade cast his steely gaze in their direction. He turned back to her, an eyebrow raised as he waited.

"No. That's not what happened—"

"So you did it on purpose, then."

She shook her head, struggling to play it cool, and decided a casual chuckle might, in fact, be apropos. Glancing around at the nosy spectators, she tried to smile and said, "No, of course not. I don't even know how to shoot a gun. Honestly, I can explain."

His gaze slowly raked over her from head to foot. He scrutinized her long wet hair, her belted jacket, her skinny jeans and pointy-toed red shoes, which he stared at for quite some time. "I think folks around here will be mighty disappointed to hear your aim ain't as sharp as they think it is."

Jessica bit her lip and pushed her hair behind her ear. "Sheriff Wade, I don't appreciate your tone. I know my rights, and I want my phone call."

"Phone call," he repeated, as if it was the most ridiculous thing he'd ever heard.

Fixated on the subtle sexuality hidden beneath the Sheriff's half-crooked smile, Jessica glanced around at the others. Logic and self-preservation told her to be quiet and patient until she could speak to a lawyer.

"She said she was trying to kill a June bug," Matthew offered helpfully. "Whatever that is."

Wonderful.

The sheriff eyed her with curious interest. "Must have been an awfully big bug."

A number of onlookers mumbled with amusement.

Oh sure, this was all downright hilarious.

"Matthew, see that Lou gets looked after." The sheriff's smile vanished, and it felt as if the temperature dropped. "I think you better come along with me, Junebug. We're going to have a little chat in the jailhouse."

Jessica's stomach lurched with dread as he took hold of her arm and led her down the street, granting no opportunity for debate. They marched quickly, and it wasn't easy keeping up with the sheriff's long strides. He had to be at least six feet tall. But everyone seemed tall next to her tiny five-foot-four inch frame.

"Would you mind loosening your grip, Sheriff?" she said haughtily. "There's no need for police brutality. I'm not resisting arrest."

He let her go, but kept one hand on his weapon at all times as if he half expected a gang of outlaws to ride up out of nowhere and break her free.

Finally, they reached the two-story jailhouse, and he escorted her through the front door and into a jail cell.

"Hey, you can't put me in here."

Before she had a chance to say another word, he swung the bars shut in front of her face and locked her in.

Jingling the key ring in his hand, he gave her a quick look before hanging it on a hook across the room.

Jessica, reeling with frustration, gazed around the one-room jailhouse. She had expected to see a telephone, a computer and maybe some florescent lights, but even the law office was straight out of another century.

At that instant, her frustration turned to fear. "I need to speak to a lawyer," she said, gripping the cold iron bars. "And I need a phone."

"No phone here I'm afraid."

It was one brick wall after another. Her stomach muscles clenched tight, mirroring her desperation.

The sheriff sat on a messy, paper-covered desk, folded his muscled arms at his chest, and crossed one ankle over the other.

Growing increasingly anxious by the minute, Jessica pinched the bridge of her nose. She had to ask the question that had been niggling at her ever since the accident—the question she hadn't wanted to ask—and she needed to ask it in a way that wouldn't make her sound insane or delusional. "Sheriff, what's the date today?"

"June 29th."

She cleared her throat and felt some relief, because June 29th was the date she woke up that morning. "And the year is, of course...."

His dark eyebrows drew together. "Eighteen-eighty-one." He stared at her.

Jessica squeezed her eyes shut against the panic, and felt a crippling need to lie down.

"I need to speak to a lawyer," she said again, more shakily this time.

"Are you all right, Junebug? You look a little pale." His voice conveyed some concern, as if he finally noticed how unsettled she was.

She sat down. "No, I'm not all right. I was in a car accident. I almost died today, and I had to walk here from the wreck. And now I'm in jail! And don't call me Junebug."

He leaned forward in his chair and again looked down at her jeans and shoes, everything crusted in mud. "I didn't hear about any train wreck."

"No, not a train wreck. A car wreck."

He frowned.

Please tell me you know what a car is.

"Really, you have to believe me," she said. "I'm not sure how I got here. I can't remember what happened exactly, but I don't belong in this place." She swallowed hard over the panic and tried to beat it down, but it was no use. Her heart began to beat very fast.

Sheriff Wade opened a drawer, pulled out another clean folded handkerchief, stood up, and passed it through the bars. "No need to fret, darlin'. You're safe now."

Her pride bucked wildly as she glanced down at his offering, then she lifted her gaze to meet his and spoke with a hard edge of confidence. "I don't need a hanky, and I'm not your darlin'. What I need is to speak to a lawyer, and I won't say anything more until you bring me one."

He watched her for a moment. The fierce lines around his eyes softened, then he turned back to his desk. "You stay put till Deputy Dempsey gets here. I'll see if I can fetch Mr. Maxwell. He won't be happy about being disturbed after hours."

"Is he a lawyer?" Jessica asked, her hopes igniting.

"Yep." Without another word, Sheriff Wade turned and walked out.

Truman walked out of the jailhouse and stood alone on the dark, damp street. His shoulders heaved as he breathed in the cool night air.

He had an uneasy feeling in his gut. The woman he just tossed in jail… something wasn't right about her. It wasn't merely the strange things she said either—like talking about a car wreck.

Whatever that was.

No, it was something else. She had an odd fear in her eyes that didn't seem to go with her tough and plucky attitude. He wasn't sure how to describe it, and he was even less sure where it was coming from.

All he knew was that he'd felt compelled to leave the jailhouse to get her that lawyer she wanted- even though she wasn't in any trouble. She hadn't done anything illegal. All she did was bring in an outlaw who was wanted dead or alive, and now he was dead. Case closed.

Then why the hell was he holding her? he wondered uneasily, as he stomped down the steps to fetch Maxwell.

# Chapter Three

Jessica sat on the cot inside the tiny cell and tried to stay calm while she figured things out. What exactly happened to her when she blacked out in the car and woke up on the prairie? Did she really travel through time, or was this some freakishly elaborate hoax?

She looked around the room, searching everywhere for something that didn't belong in 1881. An electrical socket hidden behind the unpainted wooden table? A prop made of plastic, perhaps?

Unfortunately, after a futile search, she had turned up nothing. Everything seemed perfectly old fashioned and authentic—the tin wash basin, the desk, the WANTED posters on the wall.

Sitting back down on the cot, she ran her hand along the scratchy wool blanket beneath her. When she squeezed the mattress, the straw crackled inside.

Just then, the door opened and a young man entered the office. He wore a cowboy hat, brown trousers, and a beige shirt with a navy vest. Clearing his throat, he tugged at his collar to loosen it. He couldn't have been more than eighteen.

"Howdy, Miss. I'm Deputy Dempsey. They say you killed Left Hand Lou."

Jessica let out a sigh and wondered when this nightmare would end.

"Lou's been wanted for a year now," Dempsey said. "Sheriff Wade's been after him, offered a reward for his capture, dead or alive. I guess that'll be dead in your case."

Jessica stood and walked to the bars. "I'm going to get a reward? Is that legal?"

"Sheriff Wade nailed them posters up himself."

She decided it would be best to play along. "What am I doing in jail then, if I brought in a wanted man?"

"The sheriff's pretty thorough. I reckon he'll be askin' around to confirm who you are. Just to make sure you're not wanted by the law, too."

"Well, I can guarantee he won't find anything on me." And that was the truth, especially if this really was 1881. "How much is the reward?"

"You mean you don't know? Everybody knows about that reward. Lou was famous."

She hesitated and chose her words carefully. "I'm from out of town."

"Well then...." He smiled proudly. "It's five hundred dollars."

A nice tidy sum. It might come in handy if she was stuck here for a while.

"When will I get the money?" she asked.

"Wade'll have to talk to the governor. It might take a few days." He walked around the sheriff's desk, sat down in a creaky chair, and rested his elbows on his knees. "So, how'd it feel to meet Sheriff Wade in person? Most folks get all tongue tied and like to go home braggin' about it."

She sat on the cot. "Why? Is he famous or something?"

"Darn tootin! He can draw quicker'n you can spit and holler howdy. Lou was pretty good, too, but I would've put my money on Wade if I was a gambling man." Deputy Dempsey's face went pale. "But I suppose, you must be pretty good, yerself."

Jessica shook her head and looked down at the floor. If she wasn't up to her ears in anxiety, she might find some of this amusing. "How is it Sheriff Wade became so famous?"

"Well, nobody knows the whole story for sure. The way I heard it, he shot the outlaw who killed the old town marshal. There was a draw, and nobody even saw Truman go for his gun."

Dempsey drew his six-shooter. He clumsily twirled it around his index finger and dropped it back into the holster. "He was just like lightning they say. They elected him county sheriff not long after that. He also holds the office of town marshal. Dodge has been pretty quiet since then. Nobody wants to mess with him."

"That's it? He won a single draw?" Jessica said. "Could've been pure luck."

"Luck?" Deputy Dempsey's head drew back as if she had just said the sky was green. "No, he's never missed."

"You mean he's killed others?"

"That's what people say. He's only been here a year, and he hasn't killed anybody else in Dodge other than that one outlaw. Hasn't had to. People don't risk making him want to shoot them, I guess."

Dempsey stood up and sauntered to the window. "They say he used to be a hired gun and killed people for money. He won't talk about it, though."

All of a sudden, Jessica wasn't feeling too well. Ever since Gregory was shot, guns were not her favorite topic of conversation. Yet here she was, held prisoner by a man famous for killing people. For money.

She pressed the heel of her hand to her forehead as the ground started to whirl beneath her feet. That worried her because she'd had a few dizzy spells since the accident.

"I think I need to lie down." She put her head down on the pillow.

Dempsey quickly averted his gaze. "I beg your pardon, ma'am. I'll be outside if you need anything." He placed his hat on his head and left.

Jessica lay on the rickety cot, trying not to make any sudden movements that might cause her to hurl. She rolled onto her side and rested her cheek on her hands. The sheriff's face appeared in her mind, and something about his eyes sent her head into another spin. Maybe it was the unusual turquoise color of his eyes that struck her with such potency.

No, that wasn't it. There was something else....

Jessica sat up. Sheriff Wade was familiar. She was certain she'd seen him before. But where? She wouldn't forget meeting a man like that.

Just then, the door creaked open. Jessica rose to her feet.

"Miss Delaney?"

"Yes?"

Sheriff Wade entered the jailhouse with one thumb hooked in his belt loop and the other tipping his hat off his forehead. Those eyes gleamed in the lamplight, and for a flashing second, she forgot about the bed spins.

"Here's the lawyer you wanted," he drawled.

A portly middle-aged man wearing spectacles and a three-piece suit entered the jailhouse. A gold watch chain dangled from the pocket of his vest, and he carried a soft brown leather briefcase. The top of his balding head didn't quite reach the bottom point of Sheriff Wade's badge.

This was the man who was going to help her? She was hoping for someone...taller.

"I understand you are vehemently requesting a lawyer," he remarked.

"Yes."

"I'm Angus Maxwell." He crossed the room with his hand outstretched. She immediately put her own through the bars and gave him a firm handshake. He stared into her eyes for a moment.

"Why are you looking at me like that?" Jessica shivered.

"Sheriff, will you excuse us please?" Maxwell asked, turning. "I'd like some privacy with my client."

Wade nodded and disappeared out the front door with Dempsey. Mr. Maxwell set his briefcase on the floor.

"What is it?" Jessica asked again. The man's silence was unnerving. Something was wrong. She feared he was about to deliver terrible news.

"I understand you shot a man."

"No. That's what I need to talk to you about."

"Sheriff Wade also said you were in a car accident."

"That's right, but—"

"How long have you been in Dodge?" he asked.

"That depends on what Dodge you're talking about. This sure isn't the Dodge I know."

He narrowed his bespectacled gaze. "How do you mean?"

"You wouldn't believe me if I told you."

For a long moment, he squinted into her eyes, then looked down at her outfit. "Sheriff Wade got me out of bed to come here and talk to you. He said you were desperate, and I'd like to know why."

She thought hard about what she should say. "Is client confidentiality invented yet? I mean, you're sworn to secrecy, right?"

"I assure you, I am very discreet."

She paced back and forth in the cell. "Well, in that case...I'm going to tell you something that's going to sound a little crazy."

He quirked a brow. "Believe me, I've heard it all. Nothing you say will surprise me."

Jessica continued to pace, but watched his expression carefully as she began to explain.

"I think I might have...I know this sounds unbelievable, but..." She leaned closer and whispered. "I'm not from here, and I think I might have traveled back in time. In my world, it's 2011."

His stunned expression silenced her.

"You don't believe me, do you?" she said. "I knew it."

Mr. Maxwell cleared his throat, as if he had no idea how to respond.

"Nothing's the same here," she continued. "I'm used to telephones and lights and...well you probably wouldn't understand. Sheriff Wade just told me that it's 1881, and I'm having a hard time accepting it myself. Maybe I've lost my mind, or I'm hallucinating. I don't know. I just want to go home."

His eyes narrowed as if he were struggling to understand. "When did you arrive here?"

"About an hour ago, or maybe it was longer. I don't know. It was a bit of a walk, and I was disoriented."

"What happened to the car?"

"I have no idea. It seemed vanish into thin air, but I think I blacked out for a while. When I woke up, I was lying on the prairie."

He stared at her. "This is inconceivable."

Jessica turned away from him and crossed the cell to the crude square mirror that hung over the wash basin. She looked at her reflection carefully. "Tell me about it."

"But you don't understand..." he began to say.

Just then, the door of the jailhouse opened and Wade entered with Deputy Dempsey. Mr. Maxwell swung around to face them.

"You two about finished?" the sheriff asked.

Maxwell stepped forward. "Sheriff Wade, my client was doing her duty as a U.S. citizen. Her intention was to bring in Left Hand Lou in response to your advertisement."

Jessica opened her mouth to object, but Mr. Maxwell held up a hand to silence her.

"Fine," Wade said. "I'll arrange for the reward money in the morning."

Jessica stared at him in astonishment.

"But I want to hold her for a while," Wade added, "until I do some checking on my own."

"That's fine, Sheriff." Mr. Maxwell approached the bars again and whispered to Jessica, "Come and see me when he releases you. I'll provide you with a place to stay." He slipped a card to her with his name and address written on it. "And don't tell anyone what you've just told me. There's more you need to know first. I'll explain when I see you."

Turning away, he tipped his hat at the sheriff, and left Jessica standing there with her mouth agape.

Sheriff Wade unbuckled his gun belt and hung it on the hook next to his hat. "You can go home, Dempsey. I'll look after Miss Delaney for the night." He sat down in the chair and threw his long legs up onto the desk. Jessica looked at Deputy Dempsey for help, but he'd already disappeared through the door, which was bouncing on its hinges.

"Don't expect me to answer any questions without my lawyer present," she said.

Sheriff Wade studied her intently. "I've never met anyone so fixed on having their lawyer around."

"I know my rights."

"You certainly do advocate that." He looked down at her belted jacket and noticed the torn pocket. "Do you have any other clothes? You're covered in mud."

"No," she replied and gave a little shiver.

"I'll see if I can get something else for you to wear."

Wade rose from the chair and crossed the room toward the staircase. The flame in the kerosene lamp flickered as he passed by, and Jessica breathed a sigh of relief to be out from under his concentrated scrutiny.

A few minutes later, his black leather boots came tapping heavily down the stairs. Jessica stood up and watched him approach with a pale blue calico dress and some white cotton petticoats draped over his arm.

Just before he passed the garments to her, he ran his hand gently, almost tenderly, across the lace neckline. "This should fit," he said, "though it may need hemming. You're not as tall as...as my wife."

Jessica reached out to take the garments from him and pulled them carefully through the bars.

She noticed there was no corset, but he probably assumed she was already wearing one. "Your wife won't mind?"

He leaned one elbow on the tall cabinet and glanced out the window. "I doubt it."

Jessica held the dress up in front of her. It was like something out of an old movie. "I don't know about this. Look at this petticoat. Geez. I'm going to get all caught up in it. I'll be tripping all over the place."

"Put it on," he said. "At least you'll look like a lady, even if you can't sound like one."

"I assure you, Sheriff, I'm every inch a lady."

He gave her a quick once over from head to foot, as if studying all those inches she had just referred to, then he lifted the black hat from its hook on the wall, placed it on his head and buckled his gun belt around his hips.

Slowly, with a wildly sexy lawman's swagger, he walked toward her.

A dizzying current of heat shot through her veins, and she took an instinctive step back, forgetting for a moment that there were bars between them.

"Blue's your color," he said, his voice silky smooth.

Jessica tried to ignore the sudden rush of adrenalin that fired her blood. "I appreciate the compliment," she said. "But I have a question for you, Sheriff Wade."

He lounged casually against the bars and waited.

"Are you a gentleman?"

He paused. "I like to think so."

"Then how about looking the other way?" she suggested. "I'd like a little privacy before I unbutton my blouse, if you don't mind."

For a brief second, his eyes seemed playful. Then he chuckled. "Everybody wants privacy tonight. What a shame, in your case." He politely fingered the brim of his black hat, then turned to go. "I'll be right outside."

Jessica paused a moment, her mood softened by the warm blush of heat that rose to her cheeks.

Sheriff Wade was one seriously handsome man—and as she'd just discovered, a bit of a flirt, too.

She had best be careful around him, because she always did have a thing for gorgeous hunks in cowboy boots.

"No peeking through the window," she said.

"I'll try to restrain myself."

When Sheriff Wade stepped out, Jessica watched him through the open door. He hooked his thumbs in his belt and pushed back the long slicker. He looked up and down the street as if to ensure there were no vandals causing a ruckus, then shut the door behind him, and stomped down the stairs with those heavy black boots.

As soon as he was out of sight, Jessica quickly shed her twenty-first century clothing and slipped into his wife's dress.

Which fit perfectly.


"Good morning. Hope you slept well." Sheriff Wade lowered his legs from the desktop and slammed his black boots onto the floor.

Still half asleep, Jessica sat up and ran her fingers through her tangled hair. She felt like she'd slept for days. Remembering what had happened the night before, she shook her head in disbelief. Was this for real? Had she really traveled back in time?

If she had, she needed to find a way to get home. Her parents needed to know she was all right.

"How long have you been here?" she asked, smothering a yawn with her hand.

"All night."

He stood and jingled the keys in his hand as he made his way to the cell door. "Normally, Dempsey would've stayed, but I told him it wasn't necessary. You wouldn't be going anywhere."

"And what makes you so sure of that? How do you know I don't have a gang of outlaws waiting to break me out of here?"

He inserted the key into the lock and pulled the cell door wide open. "Hope you're joking about that, Junebug. Wouldn't want to change my mind about releasing you." He gave her a heated look that made whole body tingle.

"No need to change your mind," she replied, as she balled up her twenty-first century clothes and sauntered out of the cell.

"Your reward money will take a few days," he told her. "Do you have a place to stay?"

"Yes, with Mr. Maxwell."

"That's mighty neighborly of him." He crossed behind her, stopping there for a few seconds.

Jessica turned her head, wondering what he was doing back there – sizing up her derriere?—but in the space of a single heartbeat, he re-appeared in front of her. "You're free to go."

"Thank you."

She turned to leave, but Wade stopped her.

"I'd be careful if I was you. Folks'll be staring."

"Why?" she asked.

"There's a story about you in The Chronicle this morning. The editor must have been up all night setting that type. I doubt the ink had a chance to dry."

"Let me see it."

He gestured toward the newspaper on the desk. Jessica went to pick it up and began reading:

> Jessica Delaney, more widely known as Junebug Jess, fired the shot that killed Left Hand Lou, notorious bank robber. Known for her quick draw and deadly aim, Junebug Jess travels about the West wreaking fear and havoc. Folks say she's killed more men than she cares to count, but her blinding beauty keeps her out of the noose. While the usual plea for killing a man is self-defense, Miss Delaney travels with the story that a giant insect frightened her into

firing her gun by accident, hence her name. While Dodge City is tense with the presence of Junebug Jess, the citizens are relieved to learn that the notorious Left Hand Lou is no longer a threat.

Wade raised an eyebrow at her. "Care to tell me about anybody else you killed by mistake?"

# Chapter Four

Jessica's pulse quickened at the note of accusation in the sheriff's voice. "I didn't lie to you last night," she assured him. "I swear on my life."

His expression remained relaxed and casual, as if it were nothing at all for a person to gun down another in the street – as long as the victim had a reward on his head.

"I reckon that remains to be seen," Wade said, "so don't leave Dodge. I still have some checking to do on you, but I don't expect that to be a problem. You want your five hundred dollars, don't you?"

"Of course."

When he sat down at his desk, Jessica hesitated a moment. "What about the dress? When should I bring it back?"

His gaze lifted briefly—as if to look at the dress one last time. "Keep it," he said. Then he dipped his pen in an ink jar and set to work.

She wondered curiously what could have happened to his wife—if he was willing to give her clothes away to a stranger—but thought better of asking.

Once outside, Jessica squinted into the bright morning sunshine. A buckboard and team rolled by, its driver bouncing about like a Mexican jumping bean. She recoiled in disgust as the stink of pigs assaulted her nostrils. Two large, snorting hogs scurried past, but stopped to sniff a few randomly spread cow patties. Did they actually herd cattle through here?

She made her way down the stairs, carrying her only possessions from the twenty-first century—her blue jeans, her pink scarf, and her favorite jacket—then crossed the street and stepped up onto the boardwalk.

A large clock in a shop window ticked away the seconds. A display box contained a few publications, Peterson's Ladies' National Magazine and Harper's Bazaar. She searched longingly for a high color, glossy magazine with Jennifer Lopez on the cover, or wedding pictures of William and Kate. No such luck.

She walked on, stopping at each window along the way. A barber advertised a shave for five cents and a haircut for ten. This whole experience was far too real to be a hallucination.

Soon, Jessica reached the end of the boardwalk and had to step onto the street again. Retrieving Mr. Maxwell's card from her pocket, she stared at the address written in black ink. She was thankful to have somewhere to go, and asked a young woman for directions.

When she arrived a few minutes later, he welcomed her with a smile. "My dear, where did you get the dress?"

"Sheriff Wade gave it to me," she replied as she entered his house. "It belongs to his wife."

Mr. Maxwell frowned. "His wife? Sheriff Wade has never been married. Not that I know of."

She looked down at the skirt's tiny floral print against the blue background. "Why would he lie?"

"Who knows? Sheriff Wade keeps his personal life to himself, which is why I'm surprised he mentioned anything at all. But he can shoot straight—that's what counts. They say he's killed ten men."

Ten men.

"That's supposed to impress me?" Jessica asked.

He studied her intently. "I suppose not, but keep in mind, things are different here compared to what you're accustomed to."

She followed him into the parlor. "Doesn't anyone around here worry that he might be dangerous? Anyone who could kill ten men without thinking about it has to have some personal issues. And how do you know what I'm accustomed to?"

He didn't answer the question. Instead, he gestured for Jessica to sit down. "I've been here since Wade took the job, and I have no complaints," he said. "I like him a whole lot better than that Wyatt Earp fellow. Now there was a man who attracted all kinds of problems."

"You met Wyatt Earp?"

"Certainly did. He was deputy marshal in '76 and deputy sheriff as well. Would you like some tea?"

Jessica nodded. While he went to fetch it, she gazed around at the Victorian furnishings and paintings on the walls, and felt wildly displaced.

"I suppose you saw The Chronicle?" Mr. Maxwell shouted out from the kitchen.

"Yes," she replied, "and I know we said I killed Lou to get me out of jail, but I hate the idea of people thinking I killed a man. And what if someone else comes forward to collect the money?"

"I reckon they would have already done so by now," he replied. "I suspect whoever did it is an outlaw, too, and was long gone by the time Sheriff Wade got there." Mr. Maxwell returned, pushing a teacart into the middle of the room. "It would be foolish to change your story now."

"But we could try to prove I didn't do it."

He shook his head as he picked up the teapot and poured her a cup. "That would be pointless. They don't have pathologists to retrieve bullet fragments and prove you didn't do it. It's best if you stick with the story that you did it for the reward."

Jessica frowned up at him as she accepted the cup and saucer. "How do you know about pathologists and bullet fragments?"

He stared at her a moment, then shrugged.

"Ah, I get it," Jessica said, pointing a finger and smiling. "You're from the future, too, aren't you? That makes perfect sense."

He nodded. "I was wondering how long it would take you to figure that out."

Relief poured through her. She wasn't alone here, nor was she completely delusional.

"When did you get here?" she asked.

"Almost ten years ago."

Her relief went sour. "Ten years? Didn't you want to go home?"

"Yes, I did. I had a successful law practice back in the twenty-first century."

"Then what kept you here?"

He poured himself a cup of tea and sat down. "Jessica, I don't know how to tell you this, but there's no way back."

She shifted uneasily on the sofa cushion. "There has to be."

"There isn't. Believe me, I've tried."

A slow panic began to mushroom inside her. "Well, you didn't try hard enough. We managed to get here. We'll manage to get back."

There was no way she was staying here in this smelly old cow town. Especially with the sheriff thinking she was a killer.

"I've looked everywhere," Mr. Maxwell said. "I don't know how to do it."

"But how did you get here?"

"I had a car accident," he replied.

"Was there rain and lightning?"

"Yes, but—"

"The same thing happened to me," she told him, "so there has to be a connection."

He considered it for a moment, while he raised the teacup to his lips and took a careful sip. "Perhaps," he said at last, "but you can't just buy a ticket home. I don't know how to do it from this end. We don't have cars here."

She couldn't just give up. How could she accept never seeing her family again, or her dog, George? And what about her fitness column? She had deadlines.

Jessica stood up to pour herself another cup of tea. She took one step forward, but her stiletto heel caught in the petticoat beneath her skirt. She stumbled and nearly fell into the teacart. These long skirts would take some getting used to, she thought with frustration as she steadied the tray. In fact, everything here would take some getting used to.

Mr. Maxwell regarded her with sympathy. "You should get that hemmed and buy more practical footwear. Those shoes will attract far too much attention. There's a tailor not far from here. I could lend you some money until your reward arrives...if you'd like."

She managed a melancholy smile. "Thank you, Mr. Maxwell. I'd appreciate it."

"Call me Angus. I just wish I could do more for you."

"Maybe you can," she said. "Maybe we could work together to find a way out of here. Will you try to remember what happened to you when you came here?"

"I suppose. I could search the house for the things I was wearing. That might help, but don't get your hopes up. You may have to accept that you'll never get back."

Jessica sat down with her teacup, glanced out the window at the outhouse in the yard, and shook her head at him. "No, Mr. Maxwell, I could never accept that – because I'm not the sort of woman who can go long without indoor plumbing."

Jessica spent the morning with the tailor who hemmed her dress, then she went straight to Wright's Store and purchased a new pair of more sensible shoes. Afterwards, when she stepped outside with her red pumps packed in a box, the heat, mixed with the stench of cow dung, stifled her mood beyond comprehension. All she could think of was what Angus had said: There's no way back.

There had to be, she thought, as she walked past the saloon. She couldn't live the rest of her life without seeing her family again. She might as well have died in that accident. Or her entire family might as well have died. Lord, she didn't need this kind of pain again. None of them did. Not after losing Gregory last year.

Just then, a towering brute stepped into her path.

Jessica stopped. She stared at his belly, then looked up at his double chin and flaring, hairy nostrils. He smelled like a stale, sweaty barnyard, and was in desperate need of a shave.

"Excuse me." She stepped to the side, but he did the same.

She stepped the other way, but he blocked her again.

The stench of tobacco escaped his mouth as he spread his narrow lips over his rotten teeth and spit through the gaps. Jessica leaped back to avoid the stream of brown juice before it plopped on the ground at her feet.

"So this is the little lady that's got this town's ropes in a knot?" he bellowed. "She don't look like much to me. Why, she ain't even carryin' a weapon."

Laughter erupted behind Jessica, but she kept her eyes fixed on the jackass in front of her. "Move it, buddy. I need to get by."

He chuckled. "Not just yet, little lady. I want to buy you a drink." He motioned toward the saloon doors.

"Not interested." I'd rather stick needles in my eyes.

She made a move to continue on her way, but he blocked her again.

"I don't think you heard me, Junebug. You're comin' inside and havin' a drink and a meal." He glanced over his shoulder toward his drunken pals. "I'm so hungry, I could eat the arse end off a dead horse!" Laughter exploded all around them.

Jessica was beginning to perspire. What was it about this place that always turned her into a spectacle?

"It seems you know my name," she said, determined to stay cool and collected, "but I don't know yours."

If she could just get around his big fat ass....

"The name's Virgil. Virgil Norton."

"Well, Mr. Norton," she replied, "it's a pleasure to meet you, but I can't join you for a drink today. Maybe some other time."

She took a quick step around him, but he followed. Jessica quickened her pace, hoping that if she ignored him, he might simply give up, but his beefy arms snaked around her waist, and he lifted her up, squeezing the air out of her lungs until her feet dangled like two balls on string.

"Let go!" She dropped her parcel onto the boardwalk and struggled to pry his thick fingers off her waist.

Virgil carried her toward the saloon doors. "This here's a spirited filly!"

He kicked the doors open, so they banged against the inside wall, and hauled Jessica toward a table. Hopes of talking her way out of this in a polite manner began to vanish, especially when the men in the saloon began to hoot and holler.

As soon as they reached a table, a gunshot fired in the street, followed by some shouting. Virgil dropped Jessica onto the floor, and she landed hard on her tailbone.

It took a second or two to gather her wits and comprehend what had happened. Virgil was now storming through the swinging saloon doors, so Jessica scrambled to her feet and dashed outside to make her escape.

She stopped dead on the boardwalk, however, for perched high on his black horse in front of her, looking as gorgeous and intimidating as ever, was Sheriff Wade.

He looked down at Virgil suspiciously. "There a problem here, Virgil?" he asked, his blue-eyed gaze shifting instantly to Jessica. "You just can't stay out of trouble, can you, Junebug?"

She regarded him with frustration. "No, Sheriff. Trouble seems to find me wherever I go, but I'm not about to apologize to you, of all people, because this cattle town of yours is more messed up than my daddy's junk drawer."

She was surprised when a flicker of amusement touched the corner of his mouth. He was so handsome in the high noon sunlight, so dangerous and virile towering above her on that big black horse, that she nearly lost her breath.

To make matters worse, she was practically spellbound as he leaned back in the saddle, twirled the revolver in a few relaxed circles around his finger, and dropped it easily into his holster.

Ah, crap, she thought with a great wave of heated exasperation.

This is exactly what I don't need: a hot crush on a gorgeous gunslinger.

Somebody, just shoot me now.

# Chapter Five

"This ain't none of your business, Sheriff," Virgil said. "Me and the boys were just havin' a little fun. That's all."

"Yeah?" Sheriff Wade turned to Jessica. "The lady seems to think otherwise. She thinks this town is messed up, and that don't reflect well upon me."

Without a word, Jessica picked up her parcel and moved as far away from Virgil as possible.

"I think you boys better be gettin' along," Wade suggested. "I need to have a few words with Miss Delaney." He inclined his head at her and touched the brim of his hat. She hopped off the boardwalk and stood next to his horse.

"Just a minute there, Junebug," Virgil said. "I ain't finished with you yet."

One of the boys in his gang stepped forward. "Virgil, I think you oughta'—"

"Shut up, Lewis." Virgil hawked and spit into the street. "I said I ain't finished with you, Junebug."

Jessica was about to step up and give Virgil a few lessons in twenty-first century manners, but before she could utter a single colorful oath, Sheriff Wade's hand came down to rest on her shoulder.

'Let me handle this' was his message, and she received it loud and clear.

Casually dismounting, he moved to stand in front of her. Jessica rose up on her tiptoes to see over the broad shoulders of his coat, at the same time taking in his subtle, masculine scents—leather, a faint hint of shaving soap, and...horse.

"Go home, Virgil," he said.

A curious audience began to gather on the wide street. Two wagons had come to a full stop. The drivers sat forward with their elbows perched on their knees. A stray dog tilted his head to the side, watching while he panted in the hot sun.

Virgil's boys backed away.

Sheriff Wade pushed his slicker back to reveal his heavy gun belt loaded with bullets.

Jessica moved to the side, her uneasy gaze roving from his shoulder down to where he tapped his thumb against the ivory handle of the revolver.

"Listen fellas," she said. "Why don't we just call it a day? No harm done."

Virgil's cheek twitched. His beady eyes traced a path from the sheriff's steady trigger finger up to his clean-shaven face.

"You ain't so tough, Wade. I ain't never seen you kill nobody. I bet you never killed a man your whole life."

"Think what you like, Virgil, but you won't put another hand on this lady. She's a guest in this town."

Relieved that Sheriff Wade was finally laying the blame where it belonged, Jessica nevertheless took another step away from him.

Virgil slowly reached for his revolver. "I ain't gonna shoot," he said with one hand out in front, fingers spread wide.

Jessica glanced at the sheriff's angled profile, then down at his gun. He was still tapping his thumb on it.

The whole town fell silent. Folks cleared off the boardwalk and moved sideways and backwards to stand our crouch behind wagons or barrels or whatever else they could find. Sheriff Wade didn't move a muscle...except for that thumb.

Virgil set his revolver on a wooden barrel, then stepped off the boardwalk to face the sheriff. "Let's see how tough you are, Wade. Man-to-man. Without your gun."

"A lawman doesn't give up his gun," Truman replied in a slow, menacing drawl.

"Well, I'll just have to trust you not to shoot me then...while I'm whippin' your ass."

Sheriff Wade moved forward to stand nose-to-nose with Virgil. "Give it your best, Virgil, but be quick about it, because I got more important things to do than knock your drunken arse around Front Street."

Virgil's bushy eyebrows pulled together in outrage. Then he swung his arm back and threw a punch.

Sheriff Wade ducked, and his hat flew off.

The horse backed up at the commotion, while Wade pivoted on the spot, kicked his leg out and caught Virgil in the knee. The heavy brute dropped to the ground with a groan and a thump, holding onto his leg.

It was the fastest move Jessica had ever seen.

Sheriff Wade scooped up his hat, wrapped his hand around her elbow, and led her down the street. She followed, but glanced back at Virgil, who was still groaning and rolling around. One by one, folks popped up from behind hay bales and barrels, and scuttled into the street with caution.

"Sheriff Wade...your horse," Jessica said.

"He'll follow."

They hurried down Front Street, and Jessica had to scramble to keep up. When at last they turned the corner towards Angus's house, Truman finally slowed his pace.

"You all right?" he asked.

"Yeah, I'm fine." She brushed some dirt off her shoulder. "He was a real butthead."

Wade glanced at her with amusement again, and Jessica found herself staring at him in fascination, trying to understand what lay behind those deep turquoise eyes of his.

With the strong noon sun overhead, she was able to take in the finer details of his profile—the square, chiseled jaw and full lips over a dimpled chin, and the straight, patrician nose. Her eyes dipped to the gun belt at his hips and the loose fit of his black trousers, visible when the wind blew his coat open.

There was no point denying it. He was by far the most incredible man she'd ever met.

Or maybe that was just a reaction to the way he helped her back there. In a place where she had no friends or family to call upon, besides Mr. Maxwell, it was nice to know someone was watching out for her.

"You sure do like to call attention to yourself, don't you?" he said.

She sighed. "Yeah, well… I didn't start that. Virgil was the one looking for trouble."

"I'm going to have to ask you, Miss Delaney, to make a more sincere effort not to get people all riled up. I've worked mighty hard to keep gun firing to a minimum in this town."

Jessica halted. "Hey, I wasn't the one who fired the gun back there. You were."

He continued walking, as if he hadn't heard a word she said.

Thinking it absurd that she was capable of riling people up, Jessica stood for a moment and watched him walk, his spurs jingling with each uncompromising stride.

A gentle breath of a breeze blew her hair across her face. She closed her eyes briefly, then pushed the hair away, hoisted her skirt up to her knees, and hurried to catch up with him. "I can make it the rest of the way on my own," she said. "You don't have to escort me."

"Yeah, I do. I need to make sure you go straight home to Maxwell's, and I suggest you stay there until this gossip cools down."

The thought had crossed her mind that it would be far less dangerous to hide away in Angus's pretty blue parlor. But how would she find a way home from there?

"Look," she said, "I didn't start any of this. I did nothing wrong, so you have no authority to put me under house arrest, if that's your intention. Besides, I have some business to take care of, and it's important."

Wade stopped in his tracks.

Jessica continued walking until she realized he wasn't beside her anymore. "What's wrong?"

He approached and stared at her with narrowed eyes, then removed his hat and wiped his forehead with the back of his sleeve. "I'd like to know more about this alias of yours – Junebug Jess. How long have you had it?"

She practically laughed. "Are you kidding me? It's not an alias. The newspaper made that up."

Squinting into the sunshine, he placed his hat back on his head. "How about answering this, then? Where'd you come from? Home must be somewhere."

Jessica suddenly felt like the shopkeeper had tied the laces on her new shoes too tight. What should she tell Truman? She couldn't say she'd just arrived from the future. She'd end up in an asylum.

"I'm from Topeka," she casually replied and started walking again.

He walked beside her, watching her face the whole time, but she resisted the urge to look at him.

"So what are you doing in Dodge?" he asked.

"Just passing through."

"Where to next?"

She paused. "Not sure."

"You don't know where you're heading?"

The sun beat down on the top of her head, and she could feel her nose beginning to burn. The rest of her face, she guessed, was growing redder by the second. How did these people live without sunscreen?

Wade looped his thumbs through his belt. "It's a bit odd for a young woman to be traveling alone, ain't it?"

She removed a handkerchief from her reticule and dabbed at her forehead.

"You don't have a horse, and you don't have any money," he pressed. "How did you expect to pass through here—by flapping your arms real fast?"

"No, I—"

"You needed the money so you killed Lou. You were pretty darn sharp with your aim. Who else have you killed?"

"I told you! Nobody!"

How was she supposed to answer a question like that? Sheriff Wade was wasting his time, and more importantly he was wasting hers. She needed to get the heck out of this stupid century, and if he would just leave her alone—go sign up for a high noon showdown or catch a crazy cattle rustler or something—she might be able to make some sense out of this situation.

Head spinning, she cleared her throat and loosened her collar.

"Relax, Miss Delaney," he said. "You're not in any real trouble. At least not today."

Jessica tensed immediately as he moved closer and removed a blade of grass that had blown into her hair. She stood very still until he flicked the blade onto a passing breeze.

Dust swirled up around them. Jessica moistened her lips, realizing she hadn't blinked or breathed while he had his hands in her hair. Finally, she regained her composure and transferred her parcel from one hand to the other.

"What are you keeping in there?" he asked.

"My old shoes. I bought new ones."

"Ah, that's right. You were wearing some strange footwear last night. Your feet looked like weapons." After a pause, he added, "You all right, Miss Delaney? You look flushed."

"I'll be fine."

But she didn't feel fine. She felt sick to her stomach. These dizzy spells were beginning to worry her.

She reached for her handkerchief again, to dab at the perspiration on her forehead.

"Let's sit down for a minute," he said. "This heat can sneak up on a person."

Wade led her to the shady side of a storage shed, removed his coat, and spread it on the grass. He gestured for her to sit down.

She knew if she didn't, she might faint into his arms, which was most definitely out of the question.

Hoping she wouldn't have to stick her head between her knees, she dropped her parcel onto the grass and settled down in the shade.

She rested her back against the wall of the shed and shut her eyes, praying for the dizziness to pass quickly.

"Ah," she sighed.

"Feel better?" He rested his hands on his hips as he looked down at her. "Need some water or something? There's a pump across the street."

"No sir, not necessary. I'll be fine in a minute."

A horse and wagon rumbled by in the street. "Howdy, Sheriff!" the driver shouted.

Wade touched the brim of his hat, then sat down beside Jessica and leaned against the shed, his knees bent. "Wonder what the good folks of Dodge will say when they hear about their trusted sheriff lazing about in the shadows with the infamous Junebug Jess?"

She opened one eye to peer at him briefly. "You know as well as I do that I'm not what the paper said I am."

"I can't say I do know such a thing. I reckon you're keeping something from me."

Jessica shut her eyes again and wondered if he'd always possessed such a keen instinct or if she was just a terrible liar.

"I told you before. That story was completely false." She moistened her lips and squinted across the yard at two clucking chickens pecking at the dirt.

"False," he replied. "So you keep saying."

His eyes held a cool hint of suspicion that unnerved her. Or was it concern she saw in those blue depths? Either way, he was onto her. He knew something was off its axis, and he wanted to know what it was.

Why? So he could lock her up again?

Or did he want to help her? To make it all better?

If only she could tell him the truth, but she couldn't possibly. Who knows what he would think?

Feeling the dizziness begin to subside, she opened her eyes and squinted at him in the sunshine. "Sheriff Wade, what are you going to do about Virgil? That gun of his looked like it could put a hole in Moby Dick."

Wade adjusted the brim of his hat. "Don't worry your pretty little head. He couldn't hit a bull's ass with a handful of banjos. Most of the time he keeps to the saloon, gambling. Occasionally he takes one of the saloon girls upstairs—"

Jessica quickly raised a hand. "Too much information. And don't say pretty little head."

He laughed. "Don't go wakin' snakes. I was just gonna say he likes to play the fiddle for them. That's probably what he wanted to do with you. He's pretty harmless."

"Well, I don't trust him," she replied. "Did you ask him where he was when Lou was killed?"

Sheriff Wade regarded her intently. "Lou was wanted dead or alive, and now he's dead. You've accepted the reward, so there ain't no more questions to be asked. Unless there's something else you haven't told me, which I suspect there is."

Recognizing her blunder, Jessica pushed a lock of hair behind her ear. She could feel him searching her face for the truth again.

"I'm feeling better, now," she said. "We should go."

Wade stood, offered his hand, and pulled her to her feet. While she brushed off her skirt, he gathered his coat and flapped it in the wind to shed the grass, then picked up her parcel. A beam of sunlight reflected off his gun and blinded her momentarily.

As they started walking again, Jessica wondered about that shiny weapon and the action it had seen. "Mr. Maxwell told me that since you've been sheriff in Dodge, you haven't had to shoot anyone. Is that true?"

He spoke with a heavy edge to his voice. "I didn't realize folks were keeping tabs on my gunshots."

"There's a rumor going around that you killed ten men."

Wade shook his head. "No, not ten."

She wasn't sure if he was quiet all of a sudden because she'd gotten the tally wrong, or if he was simply annoyed at her for asking. "How many, exactly, did you kill?"

"Six."

His spurs clinked a steady, ominous rhythm as they walked.

"Six men," she replied. "Holy crap."

Truman shot her a surprised look, then stopped and removed his hat. Combing his fingers through his dark, wavy hair, he said, "Look, Junebug. I don't like to share details about my personal life. Not with you or anyone else, and I sure as hell ain't trying to impress you with my killing record." He started off again, walking faster this time.

"Trust me, I'm not impressed."

When he didn't look back, she hurried to catch up. "What I meant to say is, have you ever talked to anyone about..." —How could she phrase it?— "the things you've done?"

He frowned at her. "What do you mean—talked to anyone?"

"Well, you know...really talked about it."

She might as well have suggested he stick his head in a brick oven.

"Why would I want to do that?"

"Sometimes it helps."

He patted his six-shooter. "I got all the help I need right here."

Jessica continued to hurry along beside him.

When they reached Angus's gate, he held out Jessica's parcel. She slipped her fingers under the tight string just as a sudden gust of wind lifted her skirts.

"Geez! Close your eyes, Sheriff, before you get an eyeful."

Slapping her free hand on top of it to hold it down, she felt the sheriff's curious eyes on her, and reluctantly looked up.

"I know you're hiding something," he said in that low voice that had a way of making her melt into a loose puddle of infatuation. "And your meddling questions and flying skirts aren't gonna distract me from finding out what it is. In fact, the way you're asking about my shooting record, Miss Delaney—if that's your name—is beginning to make me suspect the worst." He drew his eyebrows together and rested one hand on his gun. "You're not itchin' to put my name on one of your bullets, are ya?"

It was a ridiculous question and Truman knew it, but he wanted to shake her up a little. Apparently, it was working. She looked like he'd just flung her into the middle of next week.

"Now that is just plain ridiculous," she replied. "I'm not even going to dignify that with an answer."

She turned her back on him and struggled with the gate latch, jiggling it to and fro. Clank, clank, clank!

If he didn't do something soon, she was going to damage the hardware. He reached around her to release the latch, and breathed in the clean scent of her chestnut hair, just as she grew frustrated with the latch and bumped him twice - fast and firmly in the pelvis - with her soft, sweet bottom.

"Oh!" She whirled around. Then she surprised him yet again by laughing infectiously. "You're certainly getting your jollies with me today, aren't you, Sheriff?"

Hell and damnation. What a smile she had.

He took full advantage of her enticing nearness by allowing his gaze to wander over her creamy complexion, her tiny sunburned nose, and those full, cherry lips. He loved the way she smelled and wondered how long it had been since he'd enjoyed rubbing and bumping up against an attractive woman like her.

What the hell was he thinking? He knew exactly how long it had been.

Adjusting his hat on his head, he took a step back. "Just trying to be of assistance." He leaned forward again and effortlessly unlatched the gate. "Gently next time."

Miss Delaney turned and entered the yard. "Thank you, Sheriff," she said with a proud, exaggerated lift of her chin.

Truman rested his hands on his hips and watched her walk up Angus's porch steps, wiggling her little bottom as she went. He had half a mind to follow her in and ask her some more questions-like why she wore her hair down long and loose like that without a single pin, much less a hat or a bonnet.

Or why she always bit her lower lip just before she lifted her right hand to push her hair behind her ear. He'd seen her do it at least four times since he'd met her.

And what a mouth on her....

The things she said....

Truman exhaled sharply when the front door slammed shut behind her.

If he had any brains in his head, he'd beat himself to a jelly for getting all hot and bothered by her cute little backside, because the last thing he wanted to do was get all tangled up with a tempting fireball like Jessica Delaney and repeat past mistakes.

If he was ever going to heed his own advice and avoid getting into a barrel of trouble, now was the time, because this particular fireball was quite possibly a killer, and at the very least, a liar.

Lucky for him, she was a lousy one.

Bringing his fingers to his lips, he whistled hard. A few seconds later, Thunder came trotting up the street.

# Chapter Six

The next day, Jessica walked into Sheriff Wade's office and dropped the Wednesday issue of The Dodge City Chronicle onto his desk in front of him.

"Miss Delaney," he drawled. "What a surprise."

He sat with his long legs stretched out on the desk, a battered tin coffee cup in his hand. The instant Jessica met his devilishly handsome blue eyes, she forgot the function of that important organ inside her head and had to work hard to remember the reason for her visit.

Ever since yesterday's titillating encounter by the gate, she'd been in a constant state of frustration, for immediately after learning that Sheriff Wade had killed six men in cold blood, all she'd been able to think about were the naughty little thrills that had wracked her body when her rear end collided with his manly parts.

How could she blame herself, though? Really. He was a gorgeous hunk of manhood, in every sense of the word - a hottie from all perspectives, and he had a way of switching on her engine lights every time he spoke.

He lifted the paper and read the headline aloud. "The Shocking True Tale of Junebug Jess, Famous Gunslinger and Killer of Soft-shelled Insects." He set it down again and inclined his head at her. "Let me guess. You're here to file a complaint."

Jessica - distracted briefly by the hand-stitched designs on his black leather boots - somehow managed to meet his gaze head on. She noticed a flirtatious glimmer in his eyes this morning - the kind of look that makes a woman check to make sure all her buttons are fastened – and she felt a stirring of satisfaction.

"Yes," she replied. "That is exactly why I am here. This is getting out of hand."

Sheriff Wade finished his coffee and set the cup down on the desk. "Now, now. Don't get your knickers all in a twist. There's no harm done."

"No harm done? Not a shred of this is true, and my knickers are not in a twist."

"At least they got your name right," he mentioned. "And look - they even managed to spell Virgil's name correctly."

Jessica sighed. "They didn't even mention you. They said I fired the gun and scared Virgil off. I wasn't even armed." She picked up the newspaper, crumpled it in her hands, and threw it into the empty waste can. When she looked up, Wade was leaning back in his chair, watching her with narrowed eyes.

"Is there nothing you can do?" she asked, finally. "I don't want any more trouble, and I don't want people thinking I'm a killer, especially if I end up staying here a while."

He dropped his long legs to the floor. "I thought you were just passing through."

"Well, I'm not sure yet," she said. "I hope to be on my way soon."

Wade tapped a finger on the desk. "What does it matter what's printed in the paper anyway? It's just a few details they got wrong. It'll all be forgotten by tomorrow."

"But people think I drew a gun on Virgil when I wasn't even carrying one. It says I sent them all scattering like a flock of frightened chickens. What if this causes more problems for me? I can't imagine Virgil will be too pleased when he reads it. If he can even read."

"The editor just stretched the truth a bit, that's all," he replied. "Besides, folks in Dodge don't care about a minor incident like this. It's just another ruckus to them."

"Minor incident? There was gunfire...and running and screaming."

He chuckled. "Now who's stretching the truth?" Wade stood and walked to the window. "Nobody pays much attention to this paper anyway," he said. "The editor's a strange one. Folks around here read The Times for the real news."

Jessica sat down on the edge of the desk. Wade glanced at her briefly, then looked down as if he mulled over what to do. "I'll tell you what-I'll talk to Gordon today. I'll see that he gets his stories straight about you from now on."

"Thank you, Sheriff," she replied, rising to her feet. "And while I'm here," she added, not quite ready to leave just yet, "has my reward arrived?"

She wasn't sure how long it would take to find a way home, and some ready cash would come in handy.

"Not yet. It'll take a few more days, at least."

"You'll let me know right away?"

"Of course."

Wade crossed the room and began sorting through some papers on a small wooden cabinet. His long fingers moved one page aside, then another. Jessica found herself staring transfixed at those big, rough, callused hands. She knew they were a killer's hands, yet at the same time she remembered how gently he had stroked the lace on the dress she was wearing.

Jessica lingered a moment, watching him work, then noticed a few bullet holes in the wall over his head. "How did they get there?" she asked, pointing at them.

He glanced in the direction of her outstretched finger. "Left Hand Lou."

"The man who was shot?" She quickly corrected herself. "I mean, the man I shot?"

Those clever blue eyes fixed intently on hers. "The same."

"What happened?"

Wade carried the papers to his desk and sat down. "I had him locked up, but one of his pals came in and busted him out. He fired three shots. Two bullets hit the wall, and the other got me right here." He pointed to his left side, just below his rib cage. "Don't remember much after that. They got away, and I woke up on a table at Doc's place." After a pensive pause, he added, "You did me a favor. I was tracking Lou for a while."

"Is that how you usually thank someone for doing your dirty work?" she asked. "By locking them up?"

His lips inched into a slow, tantalizing grin that made her go weak in the knees. "Tell me, Junebug…how did you want to be thanked?"

She squirmed inwardly at the wild rush of excitement. "You could have been nicer."

"Nicer."

"Yes." She raised an eyebrow.

He leaned forward over the desk. "If I had locked you up 'nicely,' you would have been happier with me?"

She considered it for a heated moment. "Well, maybe not. My point is you didn't have to lock me up at all, because I didn't do anything wrong, and you knew it."

After a long pause, he frowned and asked, "Who are you?"

Her mind swam with the disturbing implications of that question. In 1881, she was no one. She didn't even exist.

"I've already answered that." Focusing her gaze on the bullet holes again, she decided it was high time to steer the conversation back to a safer topic. "Is that the only time you took a bullet?"

"No," he answered flatly.

"When was the other time?"

Wade shuffled a few papers around on his desk. "I thought we agreed you wouldn't ask me any more questions like that."

"I was just making conversation. And I never agreed to stop asking questions. You just said you didn't like it."

He shuffled through some more papers. "I have work to do."

Clearly he wasn't in the mood to share. He slid his chair forward and began writing.

Jessica watched his hand glide across the page. He paused, dipped the pen in an ink jar, then began writing. The only sounds in the room were Jessica's breathing, the clock ticking, and the fervent scraping of metal on paper.

It was just as well. Learning too much about Sheriff Wade could lead to a problem she would do better without. If she wanted to keep her eye on the ball and find a way back home to the future, she couldn't afford to become besotted with anything here in the past. Or anyone.

"Good day, Sheriff," she said as she turned to leave.

"Good day, Miss Delaney," he replied. "And try to stay out of trouble today, if at all possible?"

"I'll do my best."

# Chapter Seven

After leaving the sheriff's office, Jessica decided to visit The Chronicle and talk to the editor herself. Perhaps once he met her, he would consider printing a retraction even before Truman came to see him.

Bells jingled as she closed the door behind her. A scrawny little man with thinning hair was seated at a large oak desk strewn with papers. He looked up when she entered.

"Miss Delaney," he said, rising quickly to his feet and nearly knocking over his chair. He regained his balance and pushed his wire-rimmed spectacles up the length of his nose.

"Are you Mr. Gordon, the editor?"

"Yes."

She approached his desk with purpose. "I'm here to object to the stories you've printed about me. They were false, and I want a retraction."

The color drained from his face. "But I get my information from a very reliable source."

Jessica narrowed her unwavering gaze. "I'm sorry to be the one to break it to you, but your source isn't as reliable as you think it is."

Mr. Gordon pulled a white hanky out of his pocket and blew his nose. His spectacles slipped down again, and he pushed them back up. "Miss Delaney, you don't think I made it all up, do you?"

She tilted her head to the side and tried to size him up. "Someone made it up at some point," she asserted. "Who told you those things about me?"

"I' m sorry, but I can't reveal my sources."

Jessica considered this for a moment. "You know, you'd have a much better paper and earn more respect if you were more accurate and reported the truth."

He stuffed his hanky back into his pocket. "People like the stories I print. They sell because they're colorful."

Jessica drew in a frustrated breath, thinking that, when it came to sensational newspapers, things hadn't changed much in a hundred-and-thirty years.

"Why don't you just print a retraction?" she suggested, spreading her arms wide. "See for yourself. I don't even carry a gun."

"I'm afraid I can't do that. How do I know you're not lying to me now? It's your word against the word of my source, and my source didn't shoot a man point blank between the eyes two nights ago."

Jessica sighed heavily. She couldn't blame people for thinking she killed a man. She'd flat out admitted to it.

"What about yesterday?" she asked, not ready to give up on her reputation just yet. "Sheriff Wade was the one who fired the shot in the street and knocked Virgil out, not me. Lots of people saw what happened. Ask any one of them."

Mr. Gordon began to chew on his thumbnail. "Are you sure you're not carrying a gun?"

A cynical laugh escaped her. "I think I'd know if I were."

He raised both hands in the air, a clear demonstration of fear and submission.

Jessica pinched her nose in defeat. Nothing she said to these people seemed to do any good. She was obviously wasting her time here—time that would be better spent trying to find a way home. What did it matter what they thought anyway?

"Look," she said in calm, collected voice, "if you want to print something interesting, print the truth. I'll give you an exclusive interview."

He sat down and shook his head. "That's very generous of you, Miss Junebug. I mean, Miss Delaney. But I think I'll stick to my sources. They haven't steered me wrong yet."

She glanced around the office at all the clutter and decided she'd spent enough time here. She had more important things to do.

"Fine," she said, "but if you cause any trouble for me, Mr. Gordon, I swear I will slap you so hard with a law suit, you won't even know what hit you."

He stared at her in bewilderment.

"Good day," she politely said as she strode out the door.

Truman walked out of the jailhouse and locked the door behind him, just in case Miss Delaney decided to backtrack and ask him more questions. He led Thunder over to Hoover's Saloon, tethered him at the rail, and found comfort standing at the bar with a full bottle of whisky. A drink didn't pass his lips often, and things had to get pretty bad before he gave in to that urge. But little Miss Junebug was making things about as bad as they could get.

Truman filled his glass and tossed back a bitter swig. He arched his back to release the tension and ache of old wounds, then rolled the glass between his palms and clenched his jaw as he thought of her.

Why did she insist on making him remember things he damn well wanted to forget? He felt as if she knocked things over in his mind. Spilled things, was making a mess in an otherwise tidy place.

Since she arrived in town, he'd been thinking about Dorothy again, trying to believe her death wasn't his fault. Of course, he had done his best to care for her those last few months. He'd tried to make her happy. He'd given up bounty hunting the day he spoke his vows in front of the preacher, just like she'd asked. He'd even tried to make a go of it on their meager parcel of land. But when she got sicker and sicker, everything started to die. He'd promised her he wouldn't try to collect any more rewards, but there came a day when they needed the money, and it was the quickest, easiest way. He was only going to be gone a few days....

Truman wrenched his thoughts out of the past and took a second drink. Or was it the third? He reached for the bottle and tipped it to pour another, but his steady hand slipped when a ruckus outside caught his attention.

Ah hell, not again...

Laughter and cussin' came sailing through the air. The saloon doors swung open, and in came five dirty, tobacco-chewing, card-cheating, horse-stealing thugs. They whistled, laughed, and howled as they headed toward the rear of the saloon. Judging by their smell, they needed baths something awful, and their language was about as foul as their gone-off odor.

Truman covered his badge and kept his head bowed low under the brim of his hat as they passed by. None took notice of him, but they sure did take notice of Wendy, the young barmaid. He suspected they hadn't seen a woman since last oyster season.

"Hey, pretty thing," one of them yelled as he sat down at a table. "Why don't you come on over here and cook us up a drinkin' contest?"

Truman slowly turned to keep an eye on things as Wendy carried her tray to their table.

"What can I get ya'?" she asked, spitting in an arc toward the nearest spittoon. The girl had pluck.

"I can think of only one thing." The stockiest member of the gang grabbed hold of Wendy's arm and pulled her onto his lap.

Struggling fiercely, she dropped her tray onto the floor. It rolled like a dime toward Truman and stopped at his feet. He made no move to pick it up. He simply watched the situation, hoping it would work itself out before anyone got hurt.

"Now, now, don't be a baby," the man cooed. "I'm just tryin' to make friends with you, that's all."

"Let me go, you disgusting brute."

The others laughed raucously.

"My name's Bart," he said, undaunted, "and this here's Corey. Corey wants to know what you're doin' later tonight."

"I'm busy," she said. "Now let me go, and I'll get you some drinks."

"Give me a turn, Bart!" Corey pleaded. "I want her on my lap next."

"Don't be greedy, Corey. I saw her first."

The gang froze when a gun cocked in Bart's ear. Corey's words were sucked down his throat as his eyes widened in panic. He sat back in his chair as far from Bart as possible.

"I think you better let the lady go, Mister," Truman drawled.

Bart slowly lifted his hands like a bank teller in a holdup. Wendy bolted, taking cover behind the bar.

"And who might you be?" Bart asked, still holding his hands high over his head.

"You're the one who oughta' be answering that question," Truman replied, "before I take your ear off."

Bart cleared his throat. "Didn't you hear me introduce myself to the lady? The name's Bart. Now why don't you put that gun down, friend, and have a drink with us?"

"I ain't your friend," Truman said, "and I've had enough for today." Keeping his revolver tight against Bart's cheek, Truman flexed his fingers around the ivory handle.

"You gonna stand there all day with that thing pointin' in my face?" Bart asked, growing more and more fidgety by the second.

Truman considered how long he wanted to stand there, then eventually lowered his gun and holstered it. As he did so, he pushed his coat aside to let the shiny star reflect into Bart's eyes.

"Damn. You're Sheriff Wade, aren't ya?"

"What's it to you?"

Bart grinned, revealing a gap-toothed smile. "This is quite an honor, ain't it, boys? Hell, we've heard all about you." Bart lowered his hands, then slowly reached two fingers into his pocket. He took out some tobacco and chewed off a hunk.

Truman took a good look at each of the five men, but one in particular caught his eye. The man wore a brand new Stetson on his head and a red bandanna around his neck. He had a common face, nothing unusual about him, and yet he looked familiar. "Any of you boys been in Dodge before?"

They all glanced at each other, while the familiar one rolled a cigarette. "Don't reckon we have," he said, without looking Truman in the eye.

"You gentlemen are just passing through then." It wasn't a question, but rather a very strong suggestion.

Turning back toward Truman, Bart sported a glare that would stop a train. He spit tobacco onto the floor next to Truman's boots.

"You better be careful where you spit, Mister," Truman warned him. "I'm likely to get insulted by your stinkin' mouth."

Bart slowly rose from the chair and showed off his size. He was a buffalo, complete with the foul odor and unsightly hump on his back.

In the flash of a second, one man at the table drew a weapon. By the time his gun went off, it was flying through the air, riding on Truman's bullet, which lodged in the wall behind them. Dust floated from the ceiling onto the man's hat, and his gun landed in a spittoon. He swallowed hard, then looked at Bart with eyes wide as saucers.

Truman cocked his weapon again. Corey's jaw clenched. He drew and fired. Half a second later, Corey's revolver was spinning on the floor behind him.

Truman was getting tired of this game. He pointed his six-shooter at each man at the table, daring anyone else to draw. No one did.

"Okay, Sheriff," Bart said. "You've proved your point. That's enough boys. We don't want any more trouble." Bart sat back down and waved at Wendy to bring a bottle.

Truman backed away from the table. "I expect you boys'll be leavin' town first thing?"

"We'll be gone before you know it," Bart replied, without looking up.

Turning to leave, Truman flipped a coin toward the barkeep, who caught it in his hand. He pushed through the saloon doors, hopped off the boardwalk, and freed Thunder from the hitching rail.

Just then, Wendy came running out of the saloon. "Sheriff Wade!"

He paused, still holding the reins.

"Those men in there…" she said. "Do you know who they are?"

"They look like a bunch of ignorant horse thieves to me. Other than that—"

"They used to ride with Left Hand Lou."

Truman glanced back into the saloon and suddenly remembered where he had seen the one who was rolling the cigarette—sleeping in a jail cell once, a couple of years back.

Truman laid a reassuring hand on Wendy's shoulder, then turned away and hoisted himself up into the saddle.

"Aren't you going to arrest them?"

"Can't."

"Why not?"

"No time to explain now. Let me know if they cause any more trouble. There's something I gotta do."

Wendy backed away, and Truman galloped off. He had something to tell Miss Delaney, and he had to tell her now.

\* \* \*

From the second story bedroom window of Mr. Maxwell's house, Jessica saw a horse and rider galloping up the hill, leaving a cloud of dust in its wake. She recognized that black hat and black coat sailing on the wind. It was Sheriff Wade.

She watched him ride up to the house and dismount, then take Mr. Maxwell's front steps, two at a time, to the top. A quick second later, rapid knocks sounded at the door. Jessica's heart began to race. Something was definitely wrong.

Before she had a chance to put on her shoes, the screen door swung open and Wade barged in. "Anyone here?"

Jessica called out to him. "I'm upstairs!"

His heavy boots pounded up the stairs, and suddenly there he was, filling her bedroom doorway with his striking, black-clad form. He halted when he caught sight of her, as if he'd just walked in on a naked lady.

"Whatever it is, I didn't do it," she said, as she struggled to calm her raging pulse.

Wade glanced at the brass bed. He went speechless for a second, as if he realized, only then, the impropriety of where he was—but he recovered quickly, and his eyes caught hers.

Boldly, he strode into the room.

"What's happening?" she asked.

"You can't stay here."

"Why not?"

Tension simmered behind those compelling blue eyes. "Because you're going to need some protection."

Without another word of explanation, he led her toward the stairs.

"Tell me what's happened," she said. "I need to know."

They descended the stairs together, and when they reached the ground floor, he moved to the parlor window and peered out onto the street. "Someone wants you dead."

The words reverberated off the walls before they finally settled into her consciousness. "Who? What are you talking about?"

"That outlaw you gunned down had some friends," he explained, "and they decided to pay a visit to Dodge."

She shook her head, refusing to accept what he was suggesting. "Maybe they just came to pay their respects. Lou's funeral is tomorrow."

"Men like them don't have much respect for anything," Wade argued. "You're the reason they're here. I'll put money on it."

She moved closer. "You mean they want revenge?"

"That would be my guess."

A terrible dread exploded in her belly. She sank down onto a chair and cupped her forehead in a hand. "God, if you're listening—this isn't funny. Please get me out of here."

Sheriff Wade frowned at her. "Where exactly would you like Him to send you?"

She looked up and found herself staring at that shiny star again. "I have to tell you something," she said. "I didn't kill Lou. Honest. Someone else did."

He shook his head. "That ain't gonna work, Junebug. You can't go changing your story now."

"But I'm telling the truth!"

He paused for a moment, then looked out the window again. "We don't have time to argue about it. We have to go." He made a move toward the door, but Jessica remained seated.

"If we tell them I didn't do it—"

"Nobody's going to believe that," he told her. "Lou's death was worth five hundred dollars. You trying to tell me somebody else killed him and didn't bother to collect the reward?"

"Yes! I don't know why, but that's what happened. I didn't kill him."

Wade studied her warily, and she wondered if he'd ever believe anything she said.

"We don't have time for this," he replied at last. "We have to get you out of here."

"But where will I go? They'll find me."

He strode closer and held out his hand, gesturing strongly that she accept it. "I'll see that they don't."

"But what makes you so sure you can keep me safe? There's only one of you."

He stared at her intently, then knelt down and took both her hands in his.

"I promise I won't let anything happen to you, but you have to come with me now."

He was so close, she could smell his clean, outdoorsy scent, and those hands—those killer hands—were so warm upon hers.

"Okay."

She was always such a sucker for a man who asked nicely.

Something faintly reassuring sparked in his eyes as he rose to his full height, and Jessica felt a sudden charge of connection, an inexplicable bond between them.

"Do you need to pack anything?" he asked. "You may not be back here for a while."

"How long is a while?"

"Hard to say."

She looked down at her dress. "I don't really own anything else, other than my jeans and jacket. I was going to buy another dress when I got the reward money."

He inclined his head, as if confounded by her reply, then started for the door. "Let's go, then."

"But wait. I should leave a note for Angus."

She ran up the stairs and pulled a sheet of paper out of his desk.

After tacking the explanation of her whereabouts to his bedroom door, she took one hurried look around her room, then headed for the stairs. She stopped dead at the top, however, when Sheriff Wade shouted up at her.

"Jessica! Stay where you are!"

"Why?"

"There's a rider coming, and he's got a gun."

# Chapter Eight

Jessica hurried back into her room, slammed the door shut and locked it. She dashed to the window. Outside, a man on a brown horse reached into his saddlebag, withdrew something that looked like a baseball, and pitched it. Glass smashed in the other bedroom. Jessica ducked down and hit the floor, afraid the rider might see her and fire a shot.

A frantic moment later, she heard him gallop away. The blinding terror of the hoof beats faded into the distance.

Barely able to breathe over the crazy velocity of her heart, Jessica got to her feet and sank into the wing-backed chair, resting her hand on her heaving chest, listening numbly to Sheriff Wade's boots tapping up the stairs.

"Jessica!" The knob turned and the door rattled. "Open up. It's me. He's gone."

She rushed to let him in. "He had a gun."

"I know." Wade pulled her into his arms and held her. "You all right?"

Resting her cheek on his chest, Jessica listened to the heavy rhythm of his heart. His hand cupped the nape of her neck, and she slid her arms around his waist.

"I thought he was going to come in here and shoot me," she said.

He rubbed his chin over the top of her head. "I won't let that happen."

Suddenly conscious of the emotion rising up within her, she drew back slightly, gripped his coat lapels in her fists, and looked up at him with parted lips. She wanted him to kiss her. She wanted it very badly.

He frowned—as if he were angry that she had lured him, against his will, into holding her like this and caring about her safety.

She opened her mouth to say something, but he gently pushed her away before she had a chance to speak.

"I heard a window break," he said.

She pointed. "The other room."

He took her by the hand and led her down the hall to Angus's room.

Sharp slivers of broken glass covered the floor. Sheriff Wade stepped carefully across the braided rug, while Jessica waited in the doorway, still shaken by her fear and the unexpected intimacy they'd just shared.

Crouching down on his hands and knees, he reached under the bed and pulled out a large stone with a note tied around it. He read the note, then frowned at Jessica.

"What does it say?" she asked.

Without a word of explanation, he handed her the note as he passed by her on his way out of the room.

She stood in the doorway, reading it with eyes that refused to stay focused.

HAND IT OVER OR DIE.

"Sheriff Wade!" She quickly followed him down the stairs. "Where are you going?"

He was already halfway out the door. "I should be strung up and left to rot."

"Why?" She followed him out onto the porch.

"You just lied to me again, didn't you?" he asked as he untied the leather reins from the bottom post. "About not shooting Lou."

"No!" she insisted, feeling the sting of his words more than she cared to admit. "I don't know what this note means. You have to believe me."

He looked up. "Think hard. They want something you have. What is it?"

She was more confused now than she had been the night she arrived. "I don't know! Maybe the reward money? Maybe they killed Lou."

He bowed his head so that she couldn't see his face under the brim of his hat. "I don't know when to believe you, and when not to. It feels like you're always hiding something."

She knew she couldn't continue to lie to him, because it was pointless. He could see right through her.

"Okay," she admitted at last. "I am keeping something from you, but it's not what you think."

His shoulders lifted noticeably.

"But I can't tell you what it is," she added, picking up her skirts to move down the steps.

"Why not?"

"Because you'd never believe it anyway. All I can say is that my secret has nothing to do with Lou. Honestly, I didn't shoot him." She approached Wade and laid her hand on his arm, hoping to keep him from riding away from her when at that moment she needed him more than ever.

"Why'd you say you did, if you didn't?"

"Because I wanted to get out of jail," she explained. "Angus said it was the simplest thing to do."

Sheriff Wade removed his hat and raked his fingers through his hair. "Either way, you lied to me, and it's not so easy to trust you now."

"Please trust me," she pleaded, "at least about this. I didn't kill Lou or anyone else for that matter. I swear it on my life."

He stared at her a moment while he considered it. "I know this much at least. Lou's gang didn't shoot him."

"How can you be sure?"

"Because these guys have a keen appreciation for easy money. They would've come forward for the reward, and everyone knows you don't have it yet."

"But they're outlaws, aren't they? Maybe they didn't want to get arrested."

He shook his head. "They're not wanted for anything at the moment. The governor gave them a pardon for trading information about Lou a while back."

She regarded him keenly. "So they were his enemies… Doesn't that give them a motive, and make them suspects?"

"Maybe, but it still doesn't explain why they didn't come forward for the money right away if they were the ones who shot him. Besides, they only rode into town this afternoon." He took the note she still held in her hand and read it again. His eyes lifted. They glimmered darkly with resolve. "I won't help you unless you tell me the truth. What is it they want from you? Whatever it is, I reckon it's mighty important."

She shrugged helplessly. "I already told you everything I know. I didn't kill Lou, and I have no idea what they're after."

He looked away toward the stockyards as if sorting through everything in his mind. Then at last he faced her.

"All right," he said. "I'll help you, but to do that, I have to take you away from here."

She breathed deeply with relief as he placed a booted foot in the stirrup and hoisted himself up into the saddle.

"You coming?" He held his hand down to her.

Jessica took an uneasy step back. "Uh, I've never been on a horse before."

Looking more than a little surprised, he leaned forward and crossed his wrists over the saddle horn. "Now you're just toying with me, aren't you?"

She shook her head.

He studied her for a moment, then leaned back. "Well, the way I see it, you can either get up here and ride with me, or you can wait for that plug-ugly border ruffian to come back." He thumbed his hat back off his forehead as he scanned the horizon. "I sure as hell ain't waitin' around."

Jessica shifted her weight from one foot to the other, while her stomach rolled with anxiety. "What's his name?"

71

"Thunder." Wade stroked and patted the horse's neck. "He's as steady as they come."

She let her gaze roam over Thunder's muscular neck and strong legs.

Finally, with no choice but to surrender to her fate, she offered her hand, and Truman pulled her up behind him. She wrapped her arms around his waist and squeezed her eyes shut.

"Relax and hold on to me," Wade said, as he clicked his tongue to urge Thunder into a slow canter.

They crossed a few back streets, and Jessica slowly adjusted to the rhythm of the horse's gait. It was nerve-racking at first, but she soon caught on, opened her eyes, and marveled at the impossible circumstances of her life. Here she was, riding across a prairie town on the back of a horse, to escape a gang of outlaws in the Wild West.

Not to mention the fact that her arms were wrapped around a gorgeous gunslinger's waist, and she could feel the firm bands of muscle at his torso where her forearm was resting on his revolver, and she was overwhelmingly aware of his appealing strength and masculinity.

He was unlike any man she had ever met. He wasn't addicted to texting or Tweeting, and he would never brag about the label on his suits or care about a spot on the leather interior of his luxury car.

Truman Wade had more important things on his mind. Like preventing violence.

And he smelled so…

Outdoorsy.

She fought to distract herself from the intoxicating aroma of his rugged appeal, to focus on more critical matters.

"Where are we going?" she asked.

"Back to the jailhouse."

Jessica lifted her chin off his shoulder. "But isn't that right in the middle of town? Are you sure that's wise?"

"Leave the decisions to me, Junebug. I know what I'm doing."

They rode up to the back door of the jailhouse, and he dismounted and lifted her down. Then Wade tethered Thunder to a post.

Dempsey met them at the door. "I heard about Lou's gang. Wendy told me. She said they left the saloon talking about scaring somebody."

"Yeah, well, they did a pretty good job," Wade replied. "They delivered this note to Miss Delaney." He handed the wrinkled sheet of paper to Dempsey as he escorted Jessica into the office.

"What do they want?" Dempsey asked, following them inside.

Wade sat down at his desk. "We don't know yet."

At least he seemed to believe her for once, Jessica thought, as she took a seat on the stool near the far cabinet.

"Did Wendy hear anything else?" Wade asked Dempsey. "Did they say where they planned to spend the night?"

"No, but Bart has kin at the Triple T Ranch. Maybe they're riding out there."

Wade nodded, leaned back in his chair, and stroked his chin thoughtfully. From clear across the room, Jessica heard the sound of his rough fingers brushing over his whiskers. "I think I'll ride out there myself and have a friendly word or two." He stood and stretched, as if his shoulders were stiff.

Dempsey grinned gamely. "You gonna arrest them, Sheriff?"

"Not tonight. They're not wanted for anything."

"But what about breaking Angus's window?" Jessica suggested.

He removed his hat and set it on the desk. "If I see the man who did it, I'll fine him. I got a good look at him."

"Is that all you can do?" she asked.

"For now. In the meantime, we'll just have to wait for them to try something else."

Jessica sat forward. "Wait for it? You mean I'll have to sit here in your office—like bait?"

He cocked his head to one side. "Relax, darlin'. I'll do my best to get them to leave town." He stood up, placed his hat back on his head, and moved to the door with a swagger that made her want to jump his bones right then and there. "Dempsey, get Miss Delaney out of here. This is the first place they'll look."

"Where should we go?" Dempsey asked.

"Wait till the sun goes down, then take her to the boardinghouse, and ask for Wendy. Tell her I sent you, and that I need a favor. She'll know what that means, and it'll do till I get back."

Jessica stood up and followed Wade out the back door. "Wait a minute," she said, but he was already mounting his horse. "Those men are dangerous. You'll be careful?"

He wheeled Thunder around and spoke with hardnosed confidence. "Relax, Junebug. If anything happens to me, Dempsey will take care of you."

That wasn't what she wanted to hear.

"Stop calling me Junebug," she said.

His eyes glimmered with amusement. "What would you like me to call you?"

"Jessica."

Thunder stomped impatiently and tried to turn away, but Wade wheeled him back around.

"Jessica…" he said. "That's a right pretty name."

"Thank you."

He didn't leave, however, and she could feel her body start to burn with desire as their eyes remained trained on each other.

"If we're getting cozy, maybe you should stop calling me Sheriff," he suggested.

She gave him a playful look. "What would you like me to call you?"

He trotted closer until Thunder relaxed and snorted, then he leaned forward and crossed both wrists over the saddle horn. "Truman."

Jessica gazed up at those mesmerizing blue eyes while she stroked Thunder's nose. "That's a right pretty name."

"Not as pretty as yours." He leaned back.

A moment later, he galloped away, and Jessica stood in a besotted haze, listening to Thunder's hoof beats until she couldn't hear them anymore.

No sense worrying, she tried to tell herself as she headed back inside. Truman was an expert gunman, and maybe he would come out of this unscathed, even if it turned into something serious.

Better yet, maybe those dumb-ass outlaws would cower in fear and ride out of Dodge altogether.

Sitting down at Truman's desk, she glanced up at the bullet holes in the wall and hoped that tonight everyone's bullets would stay locked inside their gun chambers – which was exactly where they belonged.

# Chapter Nine

Jessica stood at a window in Wendy's boardinghouse, watching and waiting, while Wendy slept peacefully on the bed.

"What do you think is taking so long?" she whispered to Dempsey, who sat in a chair reading a dime novel in front of the unlit fireplace.

"Don't rightly know, Miss Delaney."

"He said he'd be right back. Do you think anything could have gone wrong?"

"Doubt it. The sheriff is a legend. I reckon he'll be just fine."

Jessica recalled Wendy's tale of how Truman had put a stop to the ruckus in the saloon that afternoon.

Wendy seemed a bit smitten with him – just like everyone else in Dodge. They all seemed to regard him as the undisputed hero of the West.

Jessica couldn't deny feeling more than a little smitten herself. In fact, that particular word didn't do justice to her passions—because she was ready to drag that crazy-hot sheriff right out of his saddle, rip off his shirt and gun belt, and take advantage of him in the worst possible way – in ways that would surely shock and scandalize the good old-fashioned folks of this city.

*Jessica, you incorrigible slut.*

She chuckled to herself, then paced for a while on the narrow strip of carpet.

All was quiet outside except for the distant sound of music from the saloon down the street and occasional laughter from drunken cowboys. Jessica sat down in the rocking chair and continued to wait.

Startled by the whinny of a horse, she rose and moved to the open window, praying that Truman had returned. She poked her head out.

"Thank God," she whispered, watching him dismount and tie Thunder to a hitching rail. "He's back."

Dempsey closed his book.

A few minutes later, Truman's boots came tapping up the stairs. Jessica hurried out to meet him in the corridor.

"What took you so long? I was worried."

"You didn't have to wait up." He passed her without so much as a hat tip or hello. He entered Wendy's room, and Jessica followed him in.

"I couldn't sleep," she replied. "There's a gang of outlaws trying to kill me, remember?"

His eyes met hers. "You were perfectly safe here. Dempsey knows how to use his six-shooter." He removed his hat and coat and hung them both on the bedpost.

Wendy stirred and sat up. "Sheriff, you're back. What happened?"

"They were just where you figured they'd be," he said to her. "At the Triple T Ranch. We had a few polite words, and they promised to leave Dodge at sunrise."

Jessica inhaled a deep breath of relief, but didn't feel completely off the hook yet. "What will we do until then?"

He turned to Dempsey. "Why don't you ride out there now and keep an eye on things? I want to make sure they leave town like they said they would."

Dempsey stood. "Will do, Sheriff." He pulled out his gun, opened the chamber to check the bullets, clicked it shut, and re-holstered it.

"Stay low," Truman said. "Don't let them catch you spying."

"I'll be quiet like a mouse."

After Dempsey left, Truman locked the door and sat down in the chair. Wendy settled back into bed and closed her eyes again.

"You're going to stay?" Jessica asked him.

"Yes, ma'am." He picked up Dempsey's dime-novel and examined the cover. "Heroes of the Wild West." He chuckled quietly, then opened it to the first page.

"But how are Wendy and I supposed to get any sleep?"

"I don't mind him being here," Wendy added helpfully. "I can sleep through fireworks on the Fourth of July."

"I wish I had that talent." Jessica glanced at Truman's long muscled legs as he lounged back in the chair and felt another fiery stirring of attraction that she couldn't possibly ignore. "I think maybe I'll stay up for a while."

"Suit yourself." Wendy pulled the blanket up over her shoulders. "You don't mind if I..."

"Not at all," Jessica answered.

For the next half hour, Jessica sat in the rocking chair without uttering a word while Truman read the dime-novel, then she finally tipped her head back and closed her eyes.

She opened them, however, when Truman rose and stretched his arms over his head. While he stood with his back to her, she let her eyes roam appreciatively down the length of his finely sculpted body, his broad shoulders down to the gun belt buckled around those beautiful hips, then farther south to his muscular backside beneath the worn black trousers.

The sight of him in all his rugged, manly glory burned into her consciousness and robbed her of any hope of sleep. She simply couldn't take her eyes off him.

All at once, a rush of relief passed through her—relief that he had returned safely.

When he turned around, she met his gaze.

"I thought you'd be asleep," he whispered.

"I'm a little on edge."

For more reasons than one.

"No need to be," he replied. "You're safe for tonight." He strode to the window and looked out.

"How can you be sure?" Jessica found herself trying to memorize every contour of his body in the moonlight, so that when she returned to her own time—if she ever returned—she would be able to recollect every detail.

"Because I'm here," he replied. "Besides, Dempsey would be back in a flash if the gang left the ranch."

"I suppose." A cool evening breeze blew in through the open window, and Jessica closed her eyes, breathing in the distinct cow-scented aroma of the Kansas prairie.

She tried to imagine lying in her own bed back home with her dog George at her feet and nothing to worry about but waking up the next morning to make coffee and come up with a new column idea....

"You married, Miss Delaney?"

Her eyes flew open. "You're supposed to call me Jessica," she reminded him, not unconscious of the fact that it was the first time he had asked her anything personal without sounding like a prosecutor. "And no, I'm not. I was engaged once, though."

Leaning back against the windowsill, he crossed one booted ankle over the other and tucked a thumb into his belt. "What happened?"

It wasn't something she enjoyed talking about, because she was embarrassed to describe her stupidity, but for some reason, she wanted Truman to know. "I broke it off. I realized he wasn't the kind of man I wanted to marry."

"What kind of man was he?"

Coming up with the right words took a little thought. "He lacked integrity," she said. "He was very self-absorbed and didn't care if he stepped on people and crushed them while he tried to get ahead."

Jessica glanced down at her hands clasped together in her lap, remembering her decision to break off the engagement.

It had been difficult back then to admit to herself, and everyone else, that she'd made a mistake by letting things go so far with Liam—that she hadn't been able to see what kind of man he was beneath all the charm and success.

To make matters worse, after they broke up, she learned that all her friends and family had seen it, but no one wanted to say anything. They all just kept waiting and hoping she would come around on her own. Which she did, thank God.

Her self-confidence hadn't recovered from it, however. When it came to men, she wasn't sure she'd ever be able to trust her judgment again.

"Was he an outlaw?" Truman asked, and the question seemed almost comical.

Jessica looked down and smiled. "No, he worked for a collections agency. He threatened businesses with lawsuits and usually pushed them into bankruptcy. The problem was, he enjoyed it too much. It was like a competition for him. Eventually I began to see that aspect of his personality in other things, too. Bringing someone else down made him feel good. Even if it was me." She glanced up at Truman. "It was a mistake to fall in love with him. I still don't know how I could have been so blind."

"You weren't blind," Truman said. "You had the sense to end it before you spoke your vows."

"I suppose. I just wish I'd discovered that sense sooner, instead of spending two years of my life believing he was the one."

Truman narrowed his eyes. "I'll wager he was on his best behavior for at least the first full year. There was no way you could have seen what he was until he let down his guard, and that just took some time. You did the right thing in the end. That's what counts."

Jessica nodded, because he was right. Liam was perfectly charming in the beginning. He was handsome and successful. Superficially speaking, he was any woman's dream come true. She thought she'd won the lottery to be dating him, and her parents liked him—at first.

Truman turned to look out the window. A dog barked somewhere far away.

Jessica stood up to join him. "What about your wife?" she asked. "Where is she?"

He continued to look out at the quiet street and spoke in a voice that betrayed almost no emotion. "She died a few years back."

"I'm very sorry to hear that."

He met her gaze with an intensity that nearly knocked her over. "I've been alone ever since."

A sudden rush of empathy, mixed equally with attraction, ignited within her. She wanted to touch him and pull him close, to tell him again how sorry she was. Then she would touch her lips to his and offer a very different sort of comfort....

She fought the urge, however, because she was unsure of so many things – like how long she would be stuck in this century. Kissing Truman Wade would be a very dangerous game to play.

But Truman had different ideas, and she nearly lost her breath when he pushed a lock of her hair away from her face. Within seconds, his intentions became clear as he ran a thumb across her cheek, then slowly lowered his mouth to hers.

The kiss was reserved at first, experimental, and she knew that if she wanted to stop it, she would have to do it now. But his mouth – so soft and delicious and warm upon hers – obliterated all her prudent thoughts. He was so impossibly gorgeous. She couldn't resist the need to part her lips and let her tongue mingle wetly with his.

A tiny moan escaped her, and she slid her hands up over the tops of his shoulders to the back of his neck, where she ran her fingers through the warm locks of his thick, dark hair. The lush heat of his mouth caused a flame of arousal deep in her core, and she trembled with impulsive desire.

How long had it been since she'd been kissed like this? She couldn't quite recall....

His chest, tight and warm against her breasts, heaved in a steady rhythm; the buckle at his belt pressed against her belly.

Wendy stirred, but Jessica was too overcome by her passions to even worry about that. Truman's hands opened and closed over the fabric of her dress, stroked her back, and his inquisitive mouth explored the open warmth of hers. His breathing quickened. Jessica buried her hands deeper into the hair at his nape.

It was all too wonderful, but foolish at the same time. Jessica wasn't supposed to be here. She didn't belong here. She didn't want to become a permanent part of this place.

"I don't think this is a good idea," she whispered in his ear as she dragged her mouth from his, and he kissed down the side of her neck.

She didn't want to stop, but there were a hundred reasons why she shouldn't be kissing him.

"You're right," he replied, laying more kisses across her shoulder. "I'm supposed to be protecting you."

Truth be told, that was the last thing on her mind.

Truman held her close for another shuddering moment before he finally stepped back. "I told you I was a gentleman, didn't I?"

"Yes, and you are."

"This was my fault."

"No, it was mine," she argued.

And it was. She had wanted this. Desperately.

Then why did she stop? Was it good sense or fear?

"Get some sleep," he said, moving to the corner of the bed to pull on his coat. "I'll keep guard from the window in the hall."

"You don't need to leave."

"Oh, yes I surely do." He donned his hat and walked out.

Jessica sucked in a quick breath and sank down onto the rocking chair. She tried to remember how she felt with Liam in the beginning when he'd first kissed her. It was exciting, but not quite like this. There had never been anything forbidden about Liam. He'd seemed perfect on the surface, and she had let herself tumble willingly into the courtship, only to find out later that he was not what he seemed, that she'd made a terrible mistake.

Hadn't she learned anything from all that? If she had, what was she doing kissing a former bounty hunter who had killed six men?

# Chapter Ten

The early sunlight beamed into Wendy's boarding house room and woke Jessica from her slumber. The first thing she saw was Truman sitting at the desk with his back to her, reading the morning paper.

She watched him for a moment and wondered what they would say to each other after what happened last night. Would there be an unspoken intimacy between them now? Or would they pretend the kiss never happened?

Jessica sat up on the bed and rubbed her eyes with the heels of her hands.

"Morning," Truman said without turning around.

"Good morning. Where's Wendy?"

"She went downstairs to fetch some breakfast."

Jessica tried to gauge his mood. "Did you sleep at all?"

"Not a wink."

She presumed, based on his aloof tone, that he wanted to forget about their smokin' hot kiss, which was probably best.

But hadn't she already resigned herself to the fact that when it came to Truman Wade, she was an incorrigible slut? Maybe she should just hop into his lap, rip his clothes off, and be done with it.

"I take it nothing went wrong, then?" she asked.

"You take it right."

Oh… these nineteenth century manners. It was going to take some getting used to.

She stretched her arms over her head and let out an operatic yawn. Truman gave her a strange look.

"Sorry," she said, dropping her arms to her sides. "Always was a loud yawner."

Just then, a knock sounded at the door. Truman stood up, moved to stand beside it, and cocked his weapon. "Who's there?"

"It's Wendy, and Deputy Dempsey is with me."

Truman lowered his gun and let them in.

Wendy brought in a tray of fragrant warm bread, eggs, sausages, and a pot of coffee. "I hope this will be enough for everyone."

It smelled good enough to kill for.

Truman turned to Dempsey. "What are you doing here? You're supposed to be keeping an eye on Lou's gang."

"I watched them ride out of town this morning," he explained.

"Are you sure they're gone? All of them?"

"Positive. I followed them for more than an hour."

Truman holstered his gun and glanced at Jessica with a word of warning. "That sounds reassuring," he said, "but I wouldn't relax just yet if I were you. They're a slippery bunch."

Truman walked Jessica as far as the Front Street intersection, but stopped abruptly when she touched his arm and gave him a flirtatious look.

"You don't need to walk me home," she said sweetly. "Deputy Dempsey said the gang rode out of town, so I'm sure I'll be fine. Besides, I have a few errands to run in town."

She gazed up at him with those bewitching green eyes, and he knew something was up.

Jessica stuck out her hand. "Thank you, Truman. It was a pleasure." She paused. "Well, some of it was, and I'm sure you know which part I'm talking about."

He couldn't help but chuckle. Dang, she was a sexy piece of work. Of course, he knew what she was referring to, and her provocative words cost him a fresh rush of exhilaration.

He took hold of her hand and shook it. "I believe I do."

The air between them sparked with attraction, then she grinned mischievously and walked off toward the hardware store, wiggling her cute little bottom as she went.

He struggled to maintain an appearance of casual disinterest as he watched her turn into Zimmerman's. People passed him on the boardwalk, saying hello, bumping elbows with him. He nodded in return, barely aware of who he was acknowledging, and knew full well that he should be at the city clerk's office by now, but he needed to keep an eye on Jessica.

Besides, last night's kiss was still clanging like an alarm bell in his head, and he couldn't seem to silence it.

Ever since Dorothy was taken from him, he hadn't felt much need for a woman. Not until Jessica came to town. And last night she had looked up at him with those alluring green eyes, and he experienced a shock of arousal from his head to his nether regions that still had him reeling with desire this morning. All he wanted to do was follow her home, carry her upstairs to a bed – any bed would do—and plant himself firmly and snugly between her thighs. Over and over and over.

With a frustrated shake of his head, he leaned against a post and watched the goings-on in the street, while he kept an eye on Zimmerman's.

A few minutes later, Jessica walked out and started up the boardwalk again in the other direction. He expected her to turn up the street toward Maxwell's place, but instead, she turned down Second Avenue toward the bridge and disappeared.

Wondering where she was going, Truman went into Zimmerman's and approached the counter.

"Morning Sheriff," Fred said. "Beautiful day."

"Yep, it's something else. Tell me, did you just wait on a young woman, about so high with dark, reddish hair?"

"Sounds like you're referring to Junebug Jess. Pretty little thing, ain't she? I don't believe a word of what the papers say. That girl wouldn't hurt a fly."

"Yeah...well. What did she buy?"

"Nothing. She sold me something."

Truman's eyebrows pulled together in a frown. "What was it?"

Fred reached into the glass display case and withdrew a necklace. "I don't usually deal in this type of thing, but I couldn't pass it up. Look at the size of that diamond, and she sold it for a song."

Truman examined the silver chain and single sparkling stone. It was the biggest diamond he'd ever seen in his life, at least half an inch in diameter. It was no small trinket. Why was Jessica selling this? Something worth that much money would have to be a family heirloom. Unless, of course, it was stolen. Maybe this was what the gang wanted from her.

Had she lied about that after all? Something tugged hard in his gut, and he wished he'd never kissed her. It was only going to complicate things, because he still wanted to do it again.

"Thanks, Fred." Truman walked out of the store and crossed the street.

He spotted Jessica at a distance, crossing the bridge and heading onto the open prairie where the herds were grazing. Without a horse or buggy, she wasn't going to get too far. There wasn't much out there except for grass.

Maybe she was going to meet someone.

Truman decided to follow. He fetched his binoculars from his saddlebag, left Thunder tethered at the water trough, then crossed the bridge, maintaining a safe distance behind Jessica and crouching down in the tall grass.

About a mile outside of town, she stopped and moved to the edge of the road. Truman scanned the horizon for company, but saw no one, so he hunkered down behind an old upturned wagon to keep watch.

From where he was kneeling, he could see her quite clearly through the binoculars. She paced back and forth on the road, as if searching for something. Truman lowered the binoculars and squinted through the summer haze while insects buzzed all around him.

After a moment, Jessica trudged down a grassy bank into an irrigation ditch, then stretched her arms out to the side and began to spin around. She ran in circles, flapping her arms like a bird attempting to fly.

"What the devil…?" Truman raised the binoculars and watched her whirl and dance around. She pulled her skirts up over her knees – she wasn't wearing any stockings—and hopped up and down like she was plum out of her mind.

Refocusing the lenses on those suntanned, smoothly muscled legs, Truman's hands turned clumsy and he dropped the binoculars. Jessica continued to spin and jump, and all he could do was stare.

Just then, she stopped spinning and staggered sideways. She toppled over and fell into the grass.

Truman quickly stood. He remembered Dorothy collapsing….

Gathering up his binoculars, he took off in a full run across the prairie to reach her.

Jessica lay flat on her back, blinking up at the sky.

Why hadn't it worked? All she'd managed to do was make herself dizzy and give herself another headache.

She pressed her palm to her forehead and tried to shut out the world, which was still spinning around and around.

What would it take? If only she could remember all the details of the experience.

Gazing up at the topsy-turvy sky, she pondered the fact that the fluffy white clouds were no different from the clouds back in the twenty-first century. She could be home for all she knew.

But it wasn't likely. She couldn't hear any traffic, only the gentle whisper of the wind through the tall prairie grasses and the sounds of grasshoppers and bees.

She sat up and wondered if a rainy day would do the trick. Maybe it was the lightning.

Suddenly she heard someone call her name. She glanced toward town and saw Truman running toward her. Thank God it was him, but how long had he been watching her?

She collapsed onto her back again, relieved and mortified at the same time. He had seen her, she knew it, and any moment now, he was going to arrive and ask her if she'd taken leave of her senses.

His boots whisked over the grass and came to a halt beside her. "Are you hurt? What are you doing out here? Are you okay?"

Jessica sat up. "I think the more relevant question is what are you doing out here?"

"I followed you."

She laughed. "Well, that's quite obvious, but something tells me you weren't concerned for my safety. Otherwise, you simply would have made your presence known."

Truman ripped off his coat and tossed it onto the ground. "You didn't answer my question, Jessica. I asked what you were doing out here."

"It's none of your business."

"No? I saw you walk into Zimmerman's, and I know you pawned a necklace. That wouldn't be what Lou's gang was after, would it?"

"No!"

"Then why didn't you tell me about it?"

She laughed with disbelief. "You never mentioned you wanted an inventory of all my worldly possessions."

He shook his head. "It was more than a worldly possession. You parted with a fortune this morning, and you seem to be taking it pretty lightly. You could've at least gone down the street for a better price. Why were you in such a hurry to get rid of it?"

Jessica wasn't sure if she should tell him that the stone was a cubic zirconia that Liam had given her for Christmas. She explained that it was a fake to the clerk, but she doubted he'd revealed that to Truman.

"I just needed some cash," she told him. "I didn't want to keep borrowing from Mr. Maxwell."

"So you practically gave away something worth a fortune? Makes me think you didn't care much about that necklace. I'd hate to think you got it through some unscrupulous means."

Jessica frowned. "You think I stole it?"

"I didn't say that."

"Good, because it's not true. If you must know, my ex-fiancé gave it to me, and it really wasn't worth very much."

Truman paused. "You didn't give it back to him?"

"No. He didn't want it. The necklace was a fake, just like everything else in our relationship."

Truman raked his fingers through his hair. "A fake?"

"Yes."

He sat down in the grass beside her and said nothing for a long time.

"When was the last time you saw him?" Truman asked.

"It's been a number of months."

He looked at her intently. "Do you plan on seeing him again?"

She laughed bitterly. "Trust me, with the way things are going, it's not likely to happen. Not in this lifetime."

She and Truman sat quietly on the grass while Jessica considered the situation. With all these personal questions about her fiancé, she was beginning to wonder if he was as obsessed by last night's kiss as she was.

Part of her was excited by the possibility, but another part of her didn't want anything to distract her from finding a way home.

"There's one question you still haven't answered yet," Truman said.

"What's that?"

"You haven't told me what you're doing out here."

She searched through the chaos in her mind for a reasonable reply. "I just wanted to go for a walk."

"A walk... Then what was all the dancing and spinning?"

Jessica began to smile. "I suppose I looked quite outrageous." She couldn't help but laugh.

Truman regarded her with puzzled dismay, then shook his head in resignation and lay back in the grass. "I give up. You are crazier than a waltzing pig."

She chuckled at that. "So why were you following me?" she finally asked.

He tossed his arms up under his head. "I wanted to know where you were going."

"Why? I'm not your prisoner. I'm free to leave town if I want to."

"Is that what you were doing?" he asked with suspicion. "Leaving town?"

"No. I wasn't sure I could even get out of here."

His chest heaved with a sigh. "You don't always make a lot of sense, Junebug."

"I'm quite aware of that," she replied, squinting toward the horizon.

"Are you also aware that when you're cryptic," he said, "it only makes me more suspicious? More intrigued?"

She didn't answer. How could she? She didn't know if he was speaking professionally or personally, or if it was a good thing or a bad thing.

"Well..." He rose to his feet and offered his hand. "Time to head back."

She was eye level with his belt buckle. She gazed at his hips and muscular thighs, and was half tempted to ask him to stay a while longer and talk. She might not always like his questions, but she did enjoy the anticipation she felt whenever she was alone with him.

"Coming?" he repeated.

Jessica shook herself out of her infatuation and accepted his hand. He pulled her to her feet, and she lifted her skirts and hiked ahead of him through the tall grass toward the road.

"Jessica!"

Heart thumping a rapid rhythm in her chest, she stopped and turned. "What is it?"

He glanced at her feet. She looked down and realized she was holding her skirts clear above her knees.

Knowing a thing or two about the times, she guessed Truman had never seen a woman do that. She quickly dropped the skirt and shrugged, as if to say, 'what does it matter anyway?'

"You're different from most women," he said.

"I know."

He stared at her for a long moment, then kept this eyes trained on the ground as he walked past her. "And you ain't easy to be around."

"I know that, too," she casually replied.

While they walked side by side back to town, they talked about simpler matters – like Dodge City's cattle trade and the occasional scuffle that kept Truman busy in his job.

When they reached the bridge, Jessica cleared her throat. "Truman, I hope from now on you won't waste any more time trying to investigate my past. I guarantee there's nothing to find."

"Model citizen?"

"You could say that."

Truman's gaze roamed leisurely down the length of her body, and she felt another stirring of excitement as she remembered the kiss, and wanted very much to do it again.

"I'll tell you what," he said in a low, husky voice. "I'll stop trying to dig up your past, if you promise to keep a close watch over your shoulder."

A surge of apprehension moved through her. "Why? Do you think the gang will come back?"

"Don't know. But if you didn't kill Lou, somebody else did, and there's probably a damn good reason why they haven't come forward for the reward." He leaned even closer and whispered hotly in her ear. "And I don't want to see you get hurt."

She thanked him politely, but inside, she swooned.

# Chapter Eleven

In the days that followed – while Jessica waited for a rain and lightning storm so that she could go back out onto the prairie and try spinning again—she saw Truman only once. Passing him on the boardwalk, she smiled politely after he tipped his hat at her, and when he was gone, she had to fight a hot and lusty compulsion to chase after him, grab him by the hand, drag him home to her bed, and get naked in a frenzied hurry.

If only she could conquer those heady urges. She was lonely; there was no denying that. There was also no denying that she was lonely for her home and family. The thing that worried her, however, was the sense that Truman could make it hurt less if he made wild, passionate love to her for about ten days straight without stopping, except to eat and take short naps. Together of course.

That evening she tried to sweep thoughts of him and her family from her mind by focusing on dinner preparations for Mr. Maxwell. She wanted to cook something delicious for him in return for his many kindnesses, so she prepared a hot supper of roast beef, turnips and gravy, and cherry pie for dessert.

After dinner, they retired to the parlor to sip apple brandy.

"Jessica," Angus asked, "is Wendy as nice as she seems?"

"Yes. She's a lovely person."

"I thought so." He looked down at his crystal glass. "She always looks happy. Will she be going to the circus next week?"

"I have no idea."

"Will you be going?"

"I'm not sure." A wagon rolled by outside, and Jessica could hear the driver talking to his mules. What she wouldn't give to hear the sound of a modern day police siren or the ring of her computer to let her know that she had email…

She waited until the wagon passed. "Would you like me to invite Wendy to go with me?"

Angus's face lit up. "Would you?"

"Of course. We can all go together." She finished her brandy and stood to go to bed, but stopped in the doorway when that sinking feeling returned. "Angus? Do you even care if you ever go home? Do you miss it at all?"

He sighed heavily and with obvious compassion. "Not much anymore. It's been so long. I've grown used to this place. It would be very strange to go back now."

"What about your family? Don't you miss them?"

He gazed wistfully at the window. "Of course I do, but I suppose I've learned to accept that I won't ever see them again."

"But how can you just accept that? I don't think I ever could. It would mean giving up."

His eyes glimmered with sadness, or maybe it was simple wisdom. "It's no different from losing a loved one," he said. "You grieve, but then you have no choice but to go on living your life. You find a way to be happy again. It's not impossible. You just have to decide when you're ready to accept that they're gone."

She nodded and understood that after ten years, Angus had grown comfortable in this century and wasn't as eager as she was to find a way home.

As she climbed the stairs, she decided that she was going to have to stay on top of this, before she grew too comfortable herself.

\* \* \*

Two days later, Jessica knocked against the jailhouse door until her knuckles burned. When no one answered, she cupped her hands to the window and peered inside. The cabinets were locked, there were no troublemakers in either of the cells, and the coat rack was bare of hats, gun belts, and coats.

Turning to face the street, Jessica heard a hammer cracking, a man's deep voice shouting orders, and a dim yet constant screech of monkey laughter. It then occurred to her that the circus was setting up in town. Perhaps that's where Truman was this morning.

She picked up her skirts and walked along the railroad tracks, past the windmill spinning steadily in the breeze and the water tower beside it. She walked up Railroad Avenue where she stopped to watch a gigantic white tent blooming like a flower from the ground. Its sluggish movement resisted the push to rise as the wind blew hard against the tarpaulin. Men tugged and shouldered the poles to launch them to an upright position as the canvas billowed and fought against their thrust. It was a magnificent sight against the bare, flat prairie beyond, where everything seemed still and lifeless.

She drew in a breath when she spotted Truman lending a hand. This morning he wore a white shirt with the sleeves rolled up and a brown vest. His dark hair was blowing in the wind.

He gripped a corner post and tested it to ensure it stood firmly.

Slowly she approached, watching him the entire way. Each time he checked a post, the muscles in his forearms tensed and relaxed. Jessica stopped not far away, staring at those bronze, sinewy forearms. He took a step back, looked everything over, and wiped the sweat from his brow.

All around him, others milled about—men and women, dogs and chickens. Large cages rolled by containing tigers and giraffes, but Jessica watched only Truman. He stood alone at the far side of the tent, his eyes following the broad side as if surveying it for weaknesses.

Jessica rested a hand on her belly to quell the nervous knots. She hadn't spoken to Truman since the day they parted on the prairie, and she woke this morning knowing she had a good reason to see him again—for the reward – and she'd been looking forward to this moment more than she cared to admit.

Long, eager strides carried her across the windy prairie toward him, and she was only halfway there when he looked up from his work and met her gaze. He watched her for a moment, then released his grip on the post, wiped his hands on his trousers, and headed in her direction. They met in the middle of the circus yard, not far from an elephant.

"Mornin' Junebug," he said.

"Good morning Sheriff. I see you're busy."

"I reckon so." A drop of perspiration rolled down the side of his neck, and she watched it until it disappeared beneath the collar of his shirt.

"I guess this circus is a pretty big deal, huh?" she said, laboring to make polite conversation.

"You could say that. It's one of the few things around here that gets the Front Street rowdies and the finer folks of Dodge all under one roof. You going?"

"Yes. I might ask Wendy to go with me. And Angus of course."

Truman pointed toward the tent. "Normally Wendy would sit on that side with the rowdies, but if she's with you and Angus, she'll sit on this side."

He faced her again. His eyes were so blue they outshined the sky, and Jessica had to struggle to remember why she had come. "The reason I'm here, Truman, is—"

"You want your reward money."

"Yes. How'd you guess?"

"It arrived this morning. It's at the bank."

Jessica knew it was time to leave, but her feet were glued to the dirt.

She stood a moment, fiddling with the heavy cotton fabric of her skirt, then took a deep breath and said, "Would you walk with me?"

"I'll get my hat," he replied, needing no further bidding.

Truman couldn't help thinking that Jessica looked different today. She'd pulled her hair up like the other ladies in town. At the same time, there was nothing in her appearance that could compare. Even from a distance, she was a strikingly handsome woman, her chestnut hair contrasting sharply with her creamy white skin. Add to that a pair of full red lips the color of ripe raspberries and those legs he had been fortunate enough to observe through the binocular lenses, and he had to work hard to keep from pulling her behind a monkey cage and behaving quite unlawfully.

They walked together into town, talking mostly about the weather and other mundane things. It was nice for a change, Truman thought—to be discussing normal everyday things instead of his work, because few folks wanted to talk to him unless they had something to complain about. A broken window. Too much noise on a Sunday morning...

When they reached the bank, Truman held the door open for Jessica, then accompanied her to the wicket. Mr. Webster, the banker, stood behind the bars. He was a fat, balding man, and his suit bulged at the buttonholes. Truman said a silent prayer that Jessica would keep her mouth closed, not because of what she might say, but in case one of those stressed buttons decided to spring off Webster's vest.

"Sheriff Wade," he said. "You're here to pay out that reward, I presume?"

"That's right. This here's Miss Jessica Delaney."

"Ah, yes, it is an honor indeed," he said. "I'll be right with you." The banker finished writing something on a slip of paper, placed it a drawer, then went hunting through another drawer for the reward information.

Truman turned his back on Webster, leaned both elbows on the counter and looked out the window. He felt Jessica's arm next to his, and a sudden ripple of sexual awareness rushed through him, but he did his best to focus on the wagons rolling by in the street.

"Would you like to open an account, Miss Delaney?" Webster asked.

"Uh, no. I'd like to have it all in cash."

Truman suddenly lost interest in the morning traffic. "You're not planning to carry that around with you, are you?"

"No, I'll keep it at Mr. Maxwell's."

"It would be safer here at the bank."

"But I don't know how long I'm going to be staying in Dodge," she replied. "I may need to leave town on a moment's notice."

Mr. Webster peered at them over the gold rims of his spectacles. "Perhaps I'll give you two a moment to discuss it in private while I go fetch the money." He turned to go into the back room.

"What's the hurry?" Truman asked. "Is Dodge not good enough for you?"

"It's not that," she replied. "It's just not my home, that's all."

"Home." He studied the green hue of her eyes. "Topeka, right?"

"That's right," she firmly substantiated.

Truman shook his head. "You oughta' know I did some checking, and there ain't no record of any Delaney's in Topeka. I sure as hell would like to know where you really come from."

"Is that why you haven't talked to me in the past few days? Are you mad about that? And I thought we agreed you'd stop trying to investigate my past."

Truman wanted to kick himself for having promised the impossible, and wished he didn't care either way, but he had no excuse to give. He was a hot-blooded man who hadn't been with a woman in three long years, and Jessica was a spirited creature with a voluptuous figure and legs like he'd never seen – smooth, contoured and golden from the sun. He wanted to do things to her that he shouldn't even be thinking about, because he was a lawman who had enough commotion in his life.

He really needed to stop thinking about her legs.

And stop checking into her past.

"I'm not investigating," he said. "I'm just making conversation."

Maybe it was a good thing she wanted to leave town.

Jessica began to twirl a silver ring around on her middle finger. Truman stared down at her tiny pale hands, then followed the line of her narrow wrists covered by lace cuffs, upward to her arms and gently rounded shoulders, then to her face. His blood grew hot with the shock of wanting her, and it annoyed the hell out of him.

She sucked in a breath as their eyes met.

Mr. Webster returned and counted out five hundred dollars. Truman shifted his gaze to the window again.

Jessica shoved the money into a blue velvet pouch and drew the string. "Thank you, Mr. Webster. Have a very nice day."

She turned and walked to the door, leaving Truman in the bank, leaning against the counter. As soon as the door swung shut behind her, he quickly followed.

Jessica stood on the boardwalk, waiting for him. "Truman, I know you don't believe a word I've told you about anything, but the truth is, I have secrets, and it's going to have to stay that way."

He chuckled with disbelief. "That was about the worst thing you could have said to me. Now I'm obsessed."

She stared at him for a moment while her skirt billowed and flapped in the wind. "Please trust me," she continued. "I've never done anything dishonest or illegal, but there's a reason why I can't tell you these things, at least not yet. I wish you could just leave it be until I'm ready to tell you."

"Sorry darlin'," he said.

Jessica tucked her upswept hair behind her ear. "Why not?"

"Because." What a damned stupid answer. In a moment of weakness, he said, "Why won't you just tell me where you're going after you leave Dodge? In case I want to find you."

She scoffed. "Because you wouldn't believe me."

"Then tell me why it's so important for you to leave."

For a long time, she struggled with that question, then said simply, "You'd think I was insane." She turned and hurried down the street.

"But I already think that!" he shouted after her.

Truman moved to follow, but thank God, he was able to restrain himself. He removed his hat and combed his fingers through his hair.

"Jessica!" Wendy greeted her at the door of her boardinghouse room. "What are you doing here?"

"I went shopping." Jessica held up a large box on a string. "I like to shop when I'm confused."

Wendy stepped aside, and Jessica entered the sunny room.

"I got my reward money and bought a ready-made dress," she explained. "Why I bought it, I have no idea. With any luck I'm leaving town soon, and where I'm going, this is very passé." Jessica set the box down on the bed.

"Can I look at it?"

"Of course. I'm going to wear it to the circus tonight."

"You're going?"

"Yes," Jessica replied, "and that's why I'm here. I would love for you to join Mr. Maxwell and me."

Wendy sat down on the bed. "Mr. Maxwell, the solicitor? Goodness, I don't know about that."

"Oh, please come. I need some female companionship. There's way too much testosterone in this town."

"Testos..."

Jessica sat down, too. "It means there are too many men waving their pistols around."

Wendy nodded gamely. "I think I know exactly what you mean."

Jessica smiled. "So will you come with us?"

Wendy crinkled her nose. "I don't think it would be right. You two will be sitting on the west side. Those folks up there on the hill...they think I'm... Well, you must understand."

"Oh, that's a load of bull," Jessica said, waving a hand through the air. "I've told Angus you're a fine, upstanding young lady. And you know, where Angus and I come from, just about every girl has waited on tables at some point in her life. Half the waitresses in the summertime are college students."

"Really?" She frowned skeptically. "That seems odd. Waitresses are going to college?"

"Yes!"

Wendy glanced down at the dress folded in the box. "Are you sure?"

"Absolutely."

There was a pause. "Well... I suppose," she reluctantly replied.

Jessica flopped down onto her back next to Wendy. "Great. Now I need to ask you a favor."

"What is it?"

She leaned up on an elbow. "Could you come over to Angus's house early and help me get ready? I haven't got a clue how to fasten this corset by myself."

Wendy laughed, looking curiously at Jessica. "You don't know how to fasten a corset?"

Jessica tried to backtrack. "Well, this particular one is complicated. I've never worn one quite like it."

Wendy sat back. "Sounds interesting. I'll come over to help."

"Five o'clock?"

"I'll see you then."

\* \* \*

That evening, Wendy helped Jessica dress in her new gown. It was dark red plush velvet, trimmed with satin pleats along the bottom. More satin was draped across the front—from hip to hip—and it cascaded down the back, over a small bustle. The fitted bodice had long sleeves and a buttoned front opening with a high neck. It was like nothing Jessica had ever worn in her life.

Wendy stood behind her, straightening the pleats and drapery. "He's clever, isn't he?" she asked.

Jessica presumed she was referring to Mr. Maxwell. "Very."

Wendy stood behind her, fluffing and poofing. "I don't think I've ever talked to anyone as clever as him. I'm not sure what to say. What if I bore him?"

"Don't be silly," Jessica replied. "He's very knowledgeable when it comes to legal matters, but other than that, he's just a regular man. I don't know anything about the law, but we hardly ever talk about that. There are so many other things to talk about."

"Such as?"

Jessica hesitated, wondering how, if ever, she would explain the conversations they'd had about daytime talk shows, processed foods, and all the other things Angus missed about the twenty-first century, like airplanes and toilet paper.

"We talk about the weather," she said ridiculously. "What goes on in town, who's on the front page of The Times and what they did."

"I can talk about that," Wendy said. "I read the paper today."

"So did Angus. There you go. You're all set."

After fixing each other's hair, Jessica and Wendy left the house and walked down the hill toward the circus grounds. They met Angus outside the main entrance to the tent.

"Angus, may I present Wendy Burchell?" Jessica said, introducing them formally.

"It's a pleasure Miss Burchell," Angus replied.

They smiled warmly at each other, so Jessica decided to enter the tent first and let them get acquainted.

She stopped just inside to look up at the tall peaks of white canvas. Bleachers lined both sides of the three hundred foot long ring, and both sections were filling quickly. The other side was glutted with cowboys, bartenders, and colorfully dressed women who made their presence known with whoops and hollers.

Jessica led the way to their seats, high at the top. Looking across the ring, she scanned the crowd for Truman. Her stomach fluttered with nervous anticipation at the mere thought of seeing him, and for the first time she was thankful for the distraction – for if there truly was no way home, letting loose with a man like Truman Wade would be a fine consolation indeed.

Maybe that's why she was here, she thought suddenly. Maybe he was her true soul mate, and there were other cosmic forces at work....

At that moment she spotted him. At the far corner of the tent, he stood leaning against the side of the wooden stands, watching everyone enter and cross in front of him. Jessica grew suddenly warm under her tight corset, flustered by her body's intense reaction to one man in a room full of hundreds.

Could this possibly be her destiny? she wondered with unquenchable desire. Maybe Angus was right. Maybe all she needed to do was simply surrender to it and accept that this was where she was meant to be.

# Chapter Twelve

From the far corner of the tent, the ringmaster entered and turned a slow circle until the audience hushed. "Welcome! To Ed Roper's Strictly Moral Circus!"

On the west side the crowd cheered, whistled and whooped. On the east side, they applauded politely.

The entertainment began with elephants circling the ring, followed by giraffes. A woman named Marla Peru walked blindfolded on a tight wire, one hundred feet above the ground. Another was hurled three hundred feet across the tent by what they called Ancient Rome's War Engine Catapult. She emerged unharmed, and the crowd cheered, but Jessica couldn't have been more preoccupied than she was by Truman's presence on the other side of the tent.

Later, after the circus performers took their bows, Jessica, Wendy and Angus followed the parade down Front Street, where a crowd gathered around a crackling bonfire. A young cowboy filled the night with music from a fiddle, and another cupped his hands around a harmonica and joined in. Soon everyone was dancing and Jessica was interlocking arms with strangers, twirling around, and kicking up her heels.

Perhaps she could live this life. Perhaps it wouldn't be so bad.

A short while later she stepped up onto the boardwalk under an overhang to watch Wendy and Angus, who were holding hands as they danced a jig. Jessica smiled and clapped her hands.

"Enjoying yourself, Junebug?"

Jessica started at the sound of Truman's quiet, sultry voice behind her. He was leaning against a wall in the shadows with a thumb hooked into his gun belt, his black hat dipped low over his forehead.

"Hi," she casually said, while her body erupted with heat. She wondered how long he had been standing there and if he had been watching her the entire time.

Truman's spurs clinked softly as he moved to stand beside her. "You look pretty tonight."

His gaze slid down the length of her body, and she felt it like a soft caress over her skin.

"Thank you."

"Is that a new dress?"

"Yes, I bought it with some of the reward money."

He glanced at her approvingly. "I'd call that money well spent."

She warmed at the compliment. Then a waltz began.

While cowboys took partners and the merchants danced with their wives, she gazed up at the full moon against the black velvet sky.

"Will you dance with me?" Truman asked, his voice close to her ear.

Gooseflesh tingled deliciously over her body. "I'd love to."

Did he know what she was feeling? Could he see what he did to her?

His hand came to rest on the small of her back, and a pleasurable shiver of awareness rippled up and down her spine as he escorted her off the boardwalk to the center of the crowd.

He placed one hand on her waist and held the other out to the side. She stepped into the waltz and was careful to keep her elbows high, which helped to maintain a safe and proper distance between them, while their eyes remained locked tightly together.

Jessica was vaguely aware of the townsfolk taking notice – for Truman was their trusted, single sheriff, and she was a single woman, a stranger in town, not to mention a possible outlaw.

None of that mattered, however, for her body was reeling from the rapture of being held in his arms and losing herself in his eyes.

Slowly, inch by inch, he closed the distance between them until their bodies touched and their hearts throbbed together. The sensation ignited something desperate within her, and she longed for so much more. She wanted to dash off into the shadows and kiss him passionately until he whisked her back to his bed and made love to her until dawn.

When the waltz ended, they did not let go until a polka began.

Truman let go first, and Jessica stepped back, feeling half-dazed with giddy, overpowering desire. They faced each other without speaking a word, while the townsfolk danced around them. Someone bumped Jessica's shoulder.

"Come and sit with me," Truman said.

He closed his hand over hers and led her toward a long wooden bench on the boardwalk. People wandered past them, laughing and talking, some staggering, but Jessica was aware of little else but Truman's sleekly muscled leg touching hers in the most innocent way.

"I take it you haven't heard from Lou's gang," he said.

"No," she replied. "Do you think I will?"

"Hard to say."

"It's been four days."

"Yeah, but don't get too comfortable, Jessica. Men like them are hard to predict."

A lot of things in her life were hard to predict these days.

"Don't look so discouraged," he said, meeting her eyes. "If they come around again, I'll be here."

Just then, a shot rang out from the saloon across the street, and some of the women shrieked. Truman jumped clear off the boardwalk. The music and dancing ceased, while everyone in town watched Truman bolt toward the gunshot. He disappeared into the saloon.

A few minutes later, the saloon doors flapped open and a cowboy came flying out. He tumbled across the boardwalk and down onto the street, where he crouched on his hands and knees, wiping a spot of blood from his mouth.

The saloon doors swung open again, and three men burst through. They grabbed the cowboy by the collar and hauled him to his knees. Truman strolled out of the saloon, twirled his revolver around his index finger and dropped it into his holster. The men held the cowboy until Truman thanked them. He took the drunken troublemaker by the arm and dragged him down the street toward the jailhouse.

"He's quite a sheriff, isn't he?" Angus said, stepping onto the boardwalk with Wendy on his arm.

"He certainly is," Jessica replied. She watched Truman until he disappeared from sight. "Are you having a good time?" she asked Angus and Wendy.

"We sure are." Wendy patted Angus on the belly. "This one's a real gentleman."

"Would you like to dance again?" he asked.

Wendy glanced at Jessica. "Maybe we shouldn't leave her by herself."

"I'll be fine." Jessica waved a glib hand. "Really. Go have fun."

Wendy and Angus returned to the dancing, while Jessica stood and watched.

Later, she spotted Truman on the other side of the street, talking to a woman in a low-cut lacy gown. She wore dark red lipstick and her hair was the color of a ripe tomato.

He nodded and laughed at something. Then he removed his hat and ran a hand through his hair while the woman smiled and fingered his badge.

Any fool could see she was flirting with him, and in this day and age, she could only be one type of woman—the kind who earned her living on her back counting ceiling tiles.

Truman glanced around, as if to make sure no one was watching. Jessica took a quick step back behind a mule. When she peered out again, Truman was reaching into his pocket. He withdrew some money and placed it in the woman's hand. She shoved the payment into her deep cleavage, then wiggled her hips in the other direction.

"What was that?" Jessica whispered.

She didn't want to feel jealous without knowing what it was all about, but how could she help it? The mere thought of Truman with a woman like that made her feel nauseous.

Deciding it was time to go home, Jessica returned to the dance to find Angus. She stopped in the middle of the crowd and looked all around.

Before long, unfamiliar faces glared at her, winking and smiling to reveal missing front teeth. Most of them were drunk and rowdy. Jessica covered her nose with one hand, all at once aware of the smell of cows and pigs and the droppings they left everywhere.

She suddenly felt very displaced and desperate for her family and home and all the modern conveniences she missed so much. If only she could pick up a phone to call her parents and ask them to come and get her. They'd be here in a heartbeat—if only it were possible.

A horse bucked as a cowboy tried to mount him, then they galloped past Jessica, swirling up a cloud of dust. Coughing and waving her hand in front of her face, she swung around, her eyes still searching the darkness for Angus or Wendy.

She looked around for Truman too, but couldn't find him anywhere. No one seemed to know where he'd gone, but one drunken cowhand offered to escort her into the dance hall to keep her entertained while she waited.

It was time to go. She'd walk home and wait for Angus on his front porch if she had to, but she no longer felt comfortable at the dance, and wanted to get out of there.

Swiping at a pesky fly, she walked through the crowd and kept her eyes lowered. The music grew distant as she walked on, and soon she was far enough away from the business district that she could hear the crickets again.

Blinking her weary eyes, Jessica stopped and looked up at the sky. It was a comfort to think that in some other dimension, her family could be admiring the same sky and glittering stars.

Who really knew how this worked? Maybe Jessica was still living her life back home. Maybe she was alive there, everything was normal, and her family had no idea she was living a parallel life in another century.

As she considered it more, however, she decided that the most likely scenario was that she had died in that car accident, and her family had already buried her. Maybe this was purgatory. Or hell. But why the Wild West of all places? If God really wanted to punish her, He could have put her on The Bachelor.

She took in a deep breath and wondered if destiny's blueprints were written up there somewhere, and if a doorway back to her own time even existed.

All at once, a distant clamoring interrupted her thoughts. The ground rumbled beneath her feet. Stampede. She felt a surge of panic.

Straining to see through the darkness, all she managed to make out were the gloomy shapes of buildings and abandoned wagons. An angry dog barked somewhere down the street.

Then, from around a corner, they appeared like living shadows.

Hooves thundered toward her. Dust rose up from the ground. There must have been four, maybe five horses approaching, and Jessica's heart began to race. She felt like she was standing on a boat, rocking back and forth on a series of swells while she tried to keep her footing. Please, let them ride right by. But her prayers were in vain.

She hurried to the side of the road, but they skidded to a halt in front of her. She backed up and bumped into a white picket fence at the edge of someone's yard. Two of the men dismounted while the others, scowling down at her, remained astride their horses. The tallest man approached.

He was difficult to make out in the darkness, but Jessica could sense, simply by the manner of his stride, that he was big and strong and he meant her harm.

"Looks like we found her, boys." His face sagged into a vile frown. "Your sheriff ain't here to protect you now, is he, little darlin'?"

# Chapter Thirteen

Jessica glared up at the man's brute size and took in the foul stench of his clothes. She clenched her jaw and demanded, "What do you want?"

He stroked her cheek with his knuckles. "You sure got soft skin."

Jessica jerked away from his loathsome touch.

"She's shy, boys!"

Another approached and cocked his head to the side. "She sure is pretty, Bart. What do ya' say we take her for a ride?"

"Sounds like a fine idea, Corey. Then we can search her." The others laughed. One of them hawked and spit tobacco onto the ground.

"If you lay one hand on me…" Jessica threatened through gritted teeth.

"Yeah?"

"I swear you'll wake up tomorrow and wish you were dead."

He scowled. "I don't think you'll get a chance to take your revenge out on me, Junebug. Not when we're through with you."

The one named Corey grabbed her wrists, but she kicked the leader in the shin. He groaned and crouched down, while Corey shoved her up against the fence pickets. The point dug painfully into her skin beneath the fabric of her dress and forced her into submission as he brushed his lips over her ear. His foul breath sent shivers of revulsion down her spine.

"Now, listen here," Corey said.

"Help!" she screamed, but he quickly covered her mouth with his clammy hand while he clamped both her wrists in the other.

Jessica bit him. He hollered and let her go. She took off toward the dance, shouting for help. The other three followed in quick pursuit.

"Someone, help me!" she screamed.

It wasn't long before one of the gang members threw himself into a tackle and knocked her down. Her ankle twisted as she tried to keep from falling, but she fell anyway. The gritty dirt scraped into her palms, and her chin hit the ground. She bit her tongue. Pain shot to her temples.

Scrambling to her hands and knees, she crawled away from him, but he wrapped his arms around her waist. He flipped her over onto her back and straddled her.

"Get off me!" she hollered.

Corey and the leader, Bart, came running, out of breath, watching her with amused expressions while she squirmed and wriggled helplessly beneath the heavy brute. Where was Truman?

She quit fighting when a gun cocked in front of her eyes. Paralyzed with fear, she stared down its long, black barrel.

"Now, calm down, Junebug. We ain't gonna hurt ya'." Bart knelt down next to her and held the weapon steady. The cold barrel brushed over her eyebrow. Jessica squeezed her eyes shut.

"Now, where is it?" he asked.

"Where is what?"

"Ah, come on. You know what I'm talkin' about."

She shot him a fierce glare. "No, I don't. Let me go."

"Think hard, sweetness."

Jessica glanced sideways at the gun, while searching the far corners of her mind for an answer. "You mean...the reward?"

"Hell, no."

She shook her head quickly. "Then I don't know what you're looking for."

Bart squeezed her cheeks together in one hand so her lips puckered like a fish. "That's an awfully pretty face you got there. I'd hate to see it messed up."

"Just tell me what you want!" she pleaded.

"You know what we want! Where is it?"

Somewhere, a door opened and smacked against the outside wall of a house. A skinny, little old man in a white nightshirt, partially silhouetted by the light shining through the open doorway behind him, stepped onto his porch and aimed a shotgun.

Bart's gaze darted wildly toward him. "You stay out of this, mister!" he called out.

"You let the lady go, ya' hear?" the little man replied.

Bart's eyes burned with rage. "I said stay out of this, you old coot!"

Just then, voices called out from the bottom of the hill, accompanied by the welcome clatter of speedy footsteps.

"Let's go, boys," Bart said.

The gang took off like a pack of wolves.

Jessica rolled over onto her hands and knees, then rose unsteadily to her feet. Limping toward the side of the road, she leaned on a wagon and looked up to see a crowd of townsfolk running toward her.

Bart and his gang were long gone.

Barely able to support her weight on her twisted ankle, Jessica hung onto the side of the wagon.

"Miss? You all right?" someone asked.

She looked up at a worried face. It was the little old man with the shotgun. He must have leaped out of bed to come to her aid, for he wore no shoes.

"I'm fine now," she said. "Thank you so much. I don't know what I would have done."

"I think you better come and sit down." He helped her to a rocking chair on his covered porch. The anxious group of rescuers followed and began to ask a confusing mix of questions.

"Do you know who they were?" someone asked.

"How's your foot?" The boy looked really worried.

"What's your name, Miss?" another asked.

She wished all these people would just slow down.

Jessica rubbed her temples and squeezed her eyes shut. "I think someone better get the sheriff."

"I'll go!" The young boy bolted back to the main street before anyone else had a chance to offer.

The old man knelt beside her. "Can I get you anything? I got whisky."

"Yes, please."

He went inside, leaving her in the protection of the crowd.

"I can't thank you enough," Jessica said, wiping the blood from her lip. She wasn't sure whose blood it was at first, until she felt the sting and swelling when she ran her tongue across the inside of her mouth.

A few minutes later, she heard the rapid beating of hooves approaching.

"It's Wade!" someone yelled, and Jessica felt a swirl of anger rise up within her.

'I'll protect you,' he had said. If he hadn't been so distracted by that red-headed, big-breasted harlot, he might have been paying closer attention.

The crowd parted as Truman dismounted and shouldered his way through. He leaned forward, but Jessica turned her cheek away when he tried to touch her swollen lip with his thumb.

"Bastards," he whispered, straightening.

In a flash, he hopped off the porch, his spurs chinking as he landed in the dirt. "Which way did they go?" he asked, heading for his horse.

"That way, Sheriff!" someone answered.

He mounted and said, "Take care of her!" Then he clicked his tongue and took off at a gallop.

Jessica watched the cloud of dust that swirled up in his wake. As it faded into the darkness, tears filled her eyes. Cupping her forehead in a hand, she silently cursed this God-forsaken place and wished like hell there was a fast plane out of here. If there were, she'd be on it, and wouldn't look back.


"I saw you dancing with Sheriff Wade," Wendy said an hour later, sitting at the foot of Jessica's bed in Angus's house. "It looked like you were having a nice time. Why did you leave?"

Jessica turned her eyes toward the dark window. "Because I couldn't find you or him, and I didn't feel safe among all those drunken cowboys. Besides that, I saw Truman talking to a prostitute tonight, and I suppose I was a little miffed."

Wendy touched her hand. "It doesn't mean anything if they were just talking."

"But I saw him give her money."

Wendy paused. "Well...we don't know that it was payment for anything...immoral. He's a gentleman, Jessica. Ain't no man finer than him in this town. Except maybe Mr. Maxwell."

Leaning back against the headboard, Jessica regarded Wendy keenly. "Why are you so concerned with what I think of Sheriff Wade anyway?"

Wendy shrugged and stood up to open the window. A light breeze blew in and lifted the white linen curtains.

"He just seems different these days, that's all. His scowl is gone."

"What scowl?" Jessica didn't understand what Wendy was getting at.

Wendy returned to the bed. "He's always had this real intense look about him, like he's concentrating real hard. He never stops to chat, but over the past week, he's been saying hello to people. Sometimes he smiles."

"That's not so strange."

"I think he likes you more than you know."

Jessica couldn't help but chuckle at that. "Likes me? You think he likes me because he's not scowling?"

Wendy wagged a finger. "You two looked nice together when you were dancing."

"Just because two people look good together doesn't mean they're meant for each other."

Yet she couldn't stop thinking about how wonderful and exhilarating it felt just to be in his presence. The whole time she was dancing with him, her body was on fire with excitement, and she hadn't wanted it to end.

Nevertheless, she searched her mind for a non-committal answer. "He's a good dancer."

"I never saw him dance before."

"Not even with his wife?"

Wendy cocked her head to the side. "Sheriff Wade's not married."

"He used to be."

Wendy leaned forward. "Are you sure?"

"Yes, he told me she died."

Wendy let out a breath. "I had no idea. What happened to her?"

"I was hoping you would know."

She shook her head. "I don't think anybody in Dodge knows about it."

Jessica and Wendy stopped talking when they heard a horse gallop up to the house, followed by footsteps up the walk, and a knock at the front door.

"Sheriff Wade, come in," Angus said from downstairs.

"Maybe he caught the gang," Wendy whispered, as they tried to listen to the conversation, but couldn't make out much of anything.

A minute later, Angus's footsteps tapped up the stairs, and he knocked at the bedroom door. "Jessica? Sheriff Wade wants to see you."

Her heartbeat skyrocketed. "Tell him I'll be right down," she answered through the closed door.

Wendy wrapped a blanket around Jessica's shoulders and helped her to the top of the stairs. Jessica then limped down on her own while Truman watched from the parlor. He stood quickly, holding his hat in his hands.

Truman hadn't expected Jessica to be wearing a nightdress, or to be barefoot. As she descended the stairs with the light of a bracket lamp flickering behind her, he saw her toes peeking out from under the white hem, and the bandages around her ankle. Then he looked up at her face.

What he saw there, in the compelling depths of her eyes, in the curving line of her lips, was an emotion he didn't want to see. Disappointment. She was upset that he hadn't been there to keep her safe.

It reinforced every doubt he had about his ability to keep any woman safe. He shouldn't have made that promise. He, of all people, should have known better.

"You all right?" he asked.

She limped to the sofa and sat down. Angus and Wendy went into the kitchen. "I'm fine."

"Your foot…."

"I sprained my ankle when they knocked me down."

He wrestled violently with a sudden strike of fury when he imagined those ruffians man-handling her.

"This was my fault," he said. "I shouldn't have left you alone."

The next thing he knew, he was moving closer, taking a seat beside her….

He wrapped his arms around her, and she responded by kissing him lightly on the lips, then resting her cheek on his shoulder.

His blood quickened at the nearness of her, at the softness of her flesh beneath the thin fabric of the nightgown. He cupped the back of her head, then ran his hand down the length of her silky hair to the small of her back, felt her breasts tight against his chest, and couldn't seem to curb the intensity of his desires.

He tried to tell himself he shouldn't be falling in love with her. He was a lawman. He should be suspicious. Skeptical. On his guard. But all those instincts were lost to him now—long gone and irretrievable. If she was lying about what the gang wanted from her, he didn't care. All that mattered was keeping her safe and to continue holding her like this.

"Where were you?" she asked. "I tried to find you before I walked here, but no one knew where you went, and the gang came out of nowhere."

The trembling in her voice cut him like a blade. "It won't happen again."

"That's what you said before."

"I know. But this time..."

He looked down at her swollen lip. Ghastly images of what those animals could have done to her slashed through his mind. He imagined what might have become of her had she not been rescued when she was.

No thanks to him.

"I don't know what they're after," she said. "They think I have something that belongs to them."

He stood up and walked to the fireplace.

Though she admitted openly to keeping secrets from him, every instinct told him to believe her about this.

"Think back to the night Lou was shot," he said. "Do you remember anything at all? Anything unusual?"

"No, I don't think so. I walked into town only minutes before."

"And you say you didn't kill Lou, but if his gang thinks you did, that would explain why they think you have whatever it is they want."

"Yes." She slouched back on the sofa.

He had no idea if he was doing the right thing or not, but he needed to go with his instincts. It's all he had. "They're a dangerous bunch. You won't be safe here."

"If not here, then where?"

"Get your clothes," he said, barely able to believe what he was about to suggest. "We're leaving right away."

# Chapter Fourteen

"Where will you take her?" Angus asked. "If you try to leave town, you'll be seen."

"It's best if you don't know where she is," Truman replied.

Wendy moved forward. "When will we be able to see her?"

"Can't say for sure."

Jessica, wearing the clothes she had on when she arrived—her skinny jeans, white blouse, and black, belted jacket—took the leather satchel Wendy handed her, which contained the only two gowns she owned from this century, along with her red stiletto pumps.

She couldn't imagine ever wearing those shoes again. The thought made her sigh with regret.

"Don't worry," Angus said. "The sheriff will take good care of you."

Jessica hugged them both, then limped out the front door and down the steps in her sensible shoes. She refused help from Truman until it came time to mount Thunder. Then she let him assist her into the saddle. He remained on foot to lead the horse down the street.

Jessica watched him walking out front. There was a certain absurdity in the fact that she had not yet gotten her mind around his earlier conversation with the redheaded prostitute.

She had entertained a number of theories, of course, regarding his whereabouts when she was attacked. Most of them involved a lewd image of the prostitute's squeaky bed and a few wrinkled dollars, which made her want to spit.

They headed down the street, and Jessica hoped Truman knew what he was doing. Those thugs could be watching them at this very moment. Her stomach churned with anxiety. Thankfully, she saw and heard no one.

Eventually, he led Thunder between two buildings and toward the back entrance of a saloon.

"Truman? What are we doing here?"

He ran a hand down Thunder's sleekly muscled neck. "This is where you'll be staying until I get things straightened out."

Her eyes scanned the outside wall of the building. "But this is a saloon."

"You won't be staying in the saloon."

She looked up at the windows on the second floor. "Then where are you taking me?"

Truman reached out to help her off the horse. Her feet touched the ground and pain shot up her leg. She stood on her good foot, teetering back and forth to keep her balance, despising the fact that she was in such a weakened state.

"You'll be sleeping upstairs," he explained.

A tremor of aversion tightened her nerves as she came to understand what this place was....

Before she could utter a single protest, Truman scooped her up into his arms like an impatient groom on his wedding night.

"Are you out of your mind?" she blurted out.

"Probably."

"Is this a whorehouse?"

"Yep."

Though more than a little disgruntled, she tried to ignore the casual amusement in his voice so she didn't attract attention.

"You can't just carry me up there like this," she said between clenched teeth.

"I reckon you've got a point there. Rosalie usually collects in advance."

"How would you know?"

He stopped at the back door and glanced briefly at her. "You're going to have to keep your voice down, Junebug."

"I am keeping my voice down, and stop calling me that. You know I don't like it."

The corner of his mouth curled up a little. "I'll take you through the kitchen and up the back stairs," he quietly explained. "I don't want anyone to see us."

Jessica breathed a sigh of frustration as she was shuffled about in his arms like a heavy sack of turnips.

He struggled to open the door with two fingers, but she kept her arms around his neck, enjoying herself far too much while she watched him toil awkwardly at the task.

Finally, she reached out and opened the door herself.

"Thank you," he said with a hint of sarcasm.

"There's no need for you to carry me," she said. "I can walk just fine."

"I'm sure you can."

Jessica began to squirm in his arms. "Oh, just put me down. For pity's sake. You're making me feel like some silly cartoon damsel."

Truman set her down on the floor inside the empty back room of the saloon. She kept one hand on his shoulder for support.

"What's going to happen when you get me up there?"

His eyes sparked with curious interest. "What did you have in mind?"

She had a number of things in mind as she gazed into his irresistible eyes, but she kicked all those raunchy images away. "Just how long do I have to stay here?"

He rested his hands on his hips in an impatient fashion, then pinched the bridge of his nose. "I don't know yet."

After some thought, she decided it might be wise to simply do as he said and stop thinking about how frustrated she was, in more ways than one.

Truman started up the back staircase. "Are you coming with me, or do you need me to come back down there and toss you over my shoulder?"

Chuckling inwardly at how aroused she was by that particular suggestion, she followed him up.

The narrow, enclosed staircase veered to the right after the fourth step. It was dark, and she had to move carefully on her sore ankle, and run her hand along the wall to judge where she was going.

When they reached the top, a long hall stretched in front of them with a railing that overlooked the saloon.

"Stay here," Truman whispered before he knocked on the first door and quickly opened it.

After he ensured the room was empty, he gestured for Jessica to follow. She glanced over the railing into the saloon where only a few gamblers and drinkers sat around square tables. It was quiet, except for the sound of some rolling dice at a far table.

Once Jessica was safely inside the room, Truman shut and locked the door behind them. The floorboards creaked as he moved to inspect the lock on the window and check inside the wardrobe. A single kerosene lamp burned in the corner next to the wrought iron headboard.

"You're not to leave this room," he instructed, kneeling to look under the bed.

"What am I supposed to do? Just sit around and stare at the wall?"

What she would give for her laptop and a wireless Internet connection.

"I'll get you a book," he said dryly.

Jessica limped to the chair, sat down, pulled off her shoe, and began unwrapping the bandages.

"What are you doing?" he asked, rising to his feet. "Those should stay on."

"I need to fix it."

He approached and knelt before her. "Then let me help you."

With skillful fingers, he took hold of the bandages and rewrapped her ankle. It was another one of those moments when she found it difficult to imagine him shooting anyone.

After he tied the bandage, he looked up at her. "Is there anything else I can do for you?"

Yes, you can slide your hand up my leg, and it wouldn't hurt to kiss me like you did in the boardinghouse.

"No, I'm quite fine," she replied.

"Then get some sleep." He stood up and held out his hand to help her to the bed.

But she didn't want his help – not like that. She wanted something else, and she didn't want to be alone.

"Will you stay with me?" she asked.

A muscle flicked at his jaw while he looked down at her.

"No," he finally said. "I can't do that. But I'll be in the saloon, where I can watch your door all night. Dempsey will be outside, keeping an eye on your window."

It wasn't quite what she had in mind, but he had a job to do, so she resigned herself to the fact that it would have to be enough.

A few agonizing seconds ticked by, then Truman turned to leave.

All at once, before she could stop herself, she stood up and limped across the room to block his exit.

"Don't go," she said. "Stay." The air between them sparked with electricity. "I don't want to be alone."

"Jessica..." He looked so uncertain.

Knowing it was a mistake to play with fire like this, she moved closer and laid her open hand upon his chest. "Just for tonight."

He drew back to look into her eyes, and his Adam's apple bobbed.

God, how she ached to slide her hands inside his shirt and slowly peel it off him....

"Don't do this," he said in a husky voice, heavy with arousal.

"Why not?"

"Because you'll make it too hard for me to protect you. And resist you."

She pressed her body close. "Then don't resist me. I don't want you to. I just want you to stay for a while." She slid her hand around his waist. "That's all I need."

An undeniable surge of passion rose up between them, and she felt his breathing grow fast and ragged. Then he cupped the side of her face in a hand, looked down at her lips with ravenous hunger, and roughly pulled her to him, as if he were still trying to fight the potent attraction that pulsed in the air. At last he took her mouth with an almost brutal intensity, smothering her gasp with the delicious, intoxicating flavor of his kiss.

She met it recklessly, running her hands through his thick hair as he braced her up against the door. Their tongues mingled quickly and hotly, sending a feverish sexual yearning into her blood.

He kissed the side of her mouth, then buried his face in the crook of her neck and shoulder, kissing the sensitive flesh at her collarbone.

Jessica tipped her head back while he stroked his thumb along her cheekbone and held her body tight, cupping her buttocks in one hand, thrusting his hips firmly up against hers. As she lifted her knee to stroke the outside of his leg with her inner thigh, she bumped into his leather holster and felt the barrel of his gun.

In that moment she remembered the situation, and looked down.

"This isn't right," he said, as if waking from a dream.

He dragged his mouth from hers, while her heart, pounding violently in her chest, felt the loss.

After a moment or two of agonizing indecision, he stepped back and raked his fingers through his hair.

"Don't do this to me," he said, a muscle flicking at his jaw. "I have a job to do, and you're not helping."

She couldn't miss the heightened level of his displeasure. "I'm sorry." She moved away from the door and sat down in the chair. "It was my fault."

"No. It was mine, but you should know to keep away from me. Don't tempt me like that." He reached for the doorknob.

"Why?"

"Because I'm not someone you should get to know real well. I'm bad luck, and I don't need this. I don't want this. You shouldn't either."

He pulled the door open, walked out, and shut it behind him.

Jessica listened. She could hear his boots pounding quickly down the hall.

She stared at the door, heart racing, breaths coming hard and fast.

Rising to her feet and limping to the bed, she flopped down and buried her face in the scratchy wool blanket, feeling utterly rejected and frustrated – both sexually and emotionally.

He said he didn't want this, but she knew that he did. He desired her. There was no question about that. Something else was holding him back, and whatever it was, she wanted very badly to conquer it.

But maybe he was right. This whole situation was spinning out of control so quickly. They were two vastly different people from different worlds and different times. He was a gunfighter, a man of violence who lived in a lawless place. She was a woman from the future who loved technology, hated guns, and considered the sexual revolution an historic event.

She could never resign herself to the idea of hiding her ankles and giving up the right to vote. Besides those things, she couldn't be happy knowing that she would never see her family again.

This magnetic pull she felt toward Truman was a powerful distraction, and it was preventing her from finding a way home.

If there even was a way. What if there wasn't?

Truman hadn't gambled in years, but since a drink was out of the question, tonight he was going to lay his money on the table.

Because of the late hour, there were only a few gamblers in the saloon, so he walked up to the card table and waved the dealer over. He sat at an angle to keep Jessica's door in view and waited for the first card to be dealt.

"Didn't take you for a gamblin' man, Sheriff," the dealer said, as he sat down and shuffled the cards.

"I ain't."

"Feelin' lucky?"

"I wouldn't put it that way."

"How would you put it, then?" the dealer asked, snapping each card down.

"I'd call it deserving of punishment." Truman leaned back in his chair, every so often glancing up at that door.

"How's that now?"

"It ain't worth talking about."

The truth was, Truman hadn't talked about anything personal to anyone in the full two years since Dorothy's death. It just seemed easier to keep it secret. If no one knew what happened, maybe he could forget it too. Pretend that part of his life never existed. He could even forget he'd been married.

But Jessica—with all her questions—had been pushing him to remember things. She'd been digging up the past. Rousing him when he didn't want to be roused.

Was it just physical? he wondered broodingly. It certainly felt that way – like his body was thawing out and yearning for the kind of pleasure he'd not enjoyed in a very long time.

He was a man, after all. He supposed he couldn't deny that forever.

But was that all it was? His body's aching need for sexual release and nothing else? If he satisfied it, would that be the end of it?

Truman played a card without thinking, then leaned forward to rest his elbows on the table. He glanced up at Jessica's door again, wondering what she was doing in there. Had she undressed and gotten into bed? Was she thinking about him at all, wishing he'd come back and pick up where they'd left off?

Clenching his jaw, he played another card. He could feel it again—that deep sexual need, the ache to hold her and feel his bare skin heating up close to hers. He hadn't enjoyed that kind of sexual pleasure in a long time. He wanted it now.

No, he didn't want it.

He wanted her, and the whole thing made his head pound with the searing knowledge that no matter how hard he tried, he was going to lose this battle. Maybe he should just yield now, go back upstairs, and get on with it.

He laid his cards down on the table and nodded at the dealer.

When Jessica pulled the covers back, she took one look at the sheets and doubted they were changed since the last guest—or guests—had slept there, so she unpacked her bag and decided to sleep in her clothes on top of the covers. She'd use her dress to keep warm.

Turning the key in the lantern, without extinguishing the flame entirely, Jessica snuggled down and closed her eyes, but they flew open at the sound of thumping in the next room. Wide awake now, she couldn't help but listen.

The bed next door squeaked and bounced. An occasional grunt alternated with giggly moans from a loud-mouthed woman.

Jessica sat back on a heel. She draped an arm over her other knee and cupped her forehead in her palm. What next?

It was impossible not to listen. She couldn't help herself. And with this being a whorehouse, the racket was probably going to continue all night.

Jessica waited for it to stop – thankfully it was over pretty quickly—then lay back down and pulled her dress up to her chin. A peculiar thought occurred to her, but she fanned it away. She was being ridiculous. Just then, the bed next door started squeaking again, faster this time. It thumped and whacked against the wall so hard, dust flew onto Jessica's bed. Anger boiled inside her until she sat up and swung her feet to the floor. She considered pounding against the wall to shut them up, but under the circumstances, she knew she had to keep quiet.

That ridiculous thought occurred to her again. It wasn't Truman, was it?

Don't be so foolish, Jessica.

The woman next door screamed out in pleasure. You'd think she just won the lottery. Jessica could feel her blood pressure rising.

Sliding off the bed, she limped toward the door. Maybe she could take a brief look downstairs. It would set her mind to rest if she could see Truman. Then maybe she could get some sleep. She stopped pacing and stared at the doorknob. Just one little peek....

As she moved closer to the door, the squeaking and groaning stopped. Jessica stood listening, frozen in her spot as the door to the other room slowly creaked open. Slow footsteps tapped along the hall. Jessica's heart began to race as the footsteps approached.

She stared at the brass doorknob. Please, let them pass by, she thought, stepping back.

The knob turned. She placed her hand on her chest to try and calm her breathing, preparing to scream for Truman.

Or scream at Truman.

Then the door slowly opened.

# Chapter Fifteen

All of a sudden, screaming didn't seem like the proper thing to do. Sneaking into Jessica's room and closing the door...was a woman.

Jessica examined the tattered looking pink lace and black stockings. The woman turned to face her with eyes that were darkened with kohl smeared thickly under her lower lashes. Jessica also noticed the woman's familiar red hair. She was the prostitute Truman had given money to on the street.

"You must be the secret guest," she said.

Jessica watched her carefully through narrowed eyes. "Yes, and who are you?"

She chuckled. "Don't worry, honey. I ain't your enemy." The woman crossed the room to the bed. "I just came in to make sure everything was to your likin', that's all." She leaned forward and pulled the covers back. "Hmm, sheets aren't too clean."

"I didn't think anyone knew I was here," Jessica said, her voice quiet and controlled.

"Yeah, well... your secret's safe with me." She looked Jessica up and down. "Truman said you were a real spitfire, but you don't look like much to me."

Being insulted had a funny way of shaking Jessica's senses into a workable order. "What do you want?" she asked, wishing the woman would state her business and leave.

"I wanted to get a look at the famous Junebug Jess, up close." She wandered casually to the window, pushed the curtain aside, and looked out onto the alley. Letting the curtain fall closed, she lifted her skirt, reached up to her garter, and retrieved a cigarette.

"What's your name?" Jessica asked.

"Rosalie." She took a match from the box on the bedside table, struck it, and lit her cigarette. The fresh scent of sulfur drifted across the room as Rosalie inhaled deeply.

"I'm Jessica."

"I know."

"Did Truman tell you my real name?"

"Nah, he just said he needed a room for a woman to use, and I wasn't supposed to tell anyone. It just so happens I know about Lou's gang bein' in town, and it ain't hard to figure out why you're hidin' out here. Folks have been talkin' about nothing else since you killed little Louie."

The woman's casual manner of speaking struck Jessica as odd. "You knew him?" she asked, raising an eyebrow.

Rosalie flicked ashes into a dish on the bedside table. "Let's just say, he was a very special customer of mine."

Jessica flinched. "I see. Well, I'm sorry about that. It was kind of an accident. A misunderstanding."

Rosalie smiled sardonically. "You don't have to give me that story, honey. I know what kind of man he was. You probably had a real good reason to shoot him."

"I told you it was an accident," Jessica said, growing increasingly impatient. She didn't enjoy pretending she killed Lou any more than she enjoyed talking to this woman.

"Whatever you say." Rosalie sauntered toward Jessica and blew smoke into her face.

Jessica fought a cough.

"What kind of danger are you in anyway?" Rosalie asked.

"Lou's gang wants something from me."

"Then I recommend you give it to them, Darlin'. I don't care who you are. It ain't too bright makin' enemies out of them boys."

"I'd give it to them if I knew what it was."

"They didn't tell you?"

"No."

The tip of Rosalie's cigarette glowed red as she took another drag. "Looks like you're in a whole lot of trouble. Those boys...they don't mess around. I'd watch your back."

"Thanks for the tip."

They stared at each other in silence.

"Well," Rosalie said in a bored way, "I better get back to work. I'll send someone in with some clean sheets." Just before she left, she turned around with one last word. "By the way. You're supposed to be my sister. Truman's orders."

Jessica clenched her jaw as she watched the door close behind her. Truman's orders. And in what scenario had he been giving orders to a prostitute?

The following morning, Jessica woke to an incessant knocking at her door and the rank smell of stale whisky, smoke, and body odor.

Quickly, she sat up, staring at the boot she had wedged under her door last night to prevent any more unwelcome visitors.

"Is that you, Truman?"

"Yes, open up."

"Just a minute." She scrambled out of the bed, forgetting her sprained ankle until it hit the floor, causing a searing pain to shoot up her leg. After a brief recovery, she limped to the door. She bent forward to pull the boot out from under it but felt a sudden shock when the door burst open and hit her in the head.

"Ouch!" she cried, stumbling back.

Truman stepped inside. "Sorry. I didn't know you were there."

Jessica rubbed her head. "I wedged the door shut. What did you expect?"

"I told you I'd be downstairs. If anyone so much as looked at your door, besides Rosalie, of course—"

133

"Okay, okay." Jessica, still half asleep, limped back to the bed and sat down. "Wow. I need coffee."

"Breakfast will be here soon," he replied. "And I've sent for Dempsey to watch over you today. I'm going to try to track down Lou's gang before nightfall and find out what they want." Truman yawned and sat down in the rocking chair.

"That would be good, because I'd hate to have to spend another night here."

"Believe me, if there was any other way..." He yawned again.

"Didn't you get any sleep?" Jessica asked.

"Not a wink."

"What did you do all night?"

"I lost most of my pay at the keno table."

Jessica watched him for a moment. She glanced down at his manly hands and muscular thighs and recalled how he had braced her up against the door last night with his strong, hard body and kissed her senseless.

"What would you have done if the gang had broken in here?" she asked in a desperate effort to distract herself from the thrill of that memory. "Would you have shot them?"

"If I had to," he flatly replied.

She regarded him keenly. "Doesn't that ever make you feel guilty?"

"Which part?"

"Killing a man."

He stared at her intently for a long time. "Most of the men I shoot are in bad need of killin'." Then he closed his eyes and leaned his head back as he rocked.

His casual comment made Jessica's ears prickle. She couldn't resist satisfying her curiosity another minute. "Tell me about the men you've killed."

He kept his eyes closed as he spoke. "Murderers. All except for one, but I didn't take too kindly to what he was guilty of."

"And what was that?"

Truman opened his eyes. "He did some unspeakable things to a lady. Hefty price on his head, too. The woman he assaulted was the wife of a governor." Truman stopped rocking and kneaded his eyelids with the heels of his hands. He yawned again and stood, moved to the bed and lay flat out on his back—beside Jessica. Crossing one boot over the other, he added, "I would've taken him down for free, though."

For a long moment, Jessica watched Truman in the morning light.

He had just revealed far more than usual about his past, and she wished he would say more, but unfortunately, he was falling asleep there beside her, and she didn't have the heart to disturb him.

Later that morning, after a brief half-hour nap on Jessica's bed, Truman walked into the Dodge House Hotel and took a seat at his regular table. He felt like he hadn't slept or eaten in days. He leaned back in his chair, surveying the dining room. Too early in the day for cowboys. The only people around were the good folks, and he recognized every face.

"Morning, Sheriff," Mrs. Brown said, approaching his table. "The usual?"

"Thanks, that'd be real nice. And add a slice of cherry pie to that, too, will you please?"

"Hungry today?"

"You bet."

She disappeared into the back kitchen while Truman stared out the window. He couldn't forget the look on Jessica's face an hour ago when he opened his eyes to find her lying beside him on the bed, resting her cheek on her hand, watching him with those sleepy and seductive green eyes.

She'd probably thought it mighty strange—how he rose to his feet and left the room so fast. Hell, he had no choice, really. When he woke up and looked at her with her wild chestnut hair spilling over her shoulders in an alluring, uncombed mess—certain parts of his body arose for some earnest horseplay.

If he'd stayed, he would have done more than just kiss her up against a whorehouse door. He would have flipped her onto her back and planted himself fervently between her sweet, luscious thighs, and that would have been some seriously dangerous territory to slide into.

A few minutes later, a plate of food appeared in front of him. He hadn't even seen Mrs. Brown coming. "There you go, Sheriff. Piping hot, the way you like it."

Yeah, he liked it hot, all right.

Thankfully, the succulent aroma of spicy roasted chicken distracted him from his degenerate thoughts, and he picked up his fork and dug in.

He ate his lunch and thought more about Jessica—and worked real hard to keep those thoughts strictly professional.

Maybe he should take her away for a while, just until the gang got bored and gave up. He could lose them. He'd lost a number of men hot on his trail before, but as he began to consider a plan to do just that, he shook his head. Ideas like that didn't come from anything professional. Truthfully, all he wanted to do was be alone with Jessica for a few days and quench his pent-up lust.

After he finished and paid for his meal, he left the dining room and walked out onto the boardwalk. Old Jimmy Clay was sitting on an upturned barrel, smoking a pipe. "Howdy, Sheriff. Swell day."

Truman settled his hat on his head and tipped it forward to shade his eyes from the blinding sun. "Certainly is. You just get here, Jimmy?"

"Been sittin' for about five minutes. Just came from Ham Bell's Livery. All kinds of commotion over there."

"Such as?"

"They had some ruffians in there last night. They were askin' about Junebug Jess. Threatened to drop a lamp in a haystack if no one fessed up."

Truman's blood began to boil in his veins. "Why didn't anybody tell me?"

"Tellin' you now."

Truman pounded down the steps and took off down the dusty street. Hell and tarnation, he was mad enough to swallow a horned-toad backwards.

By late afternoon, Jessica, growing restless and weary of the same four walls, sat forward in the rocking chair when a knock sounded at her door. "Who is it?"

"Truman."

She rose and crossed the room to unlock it. "Come in."

He entered, wearing the same clothes as the night before, but now they were coated in dust. He looked exhausted and was in bad need of shave.

"Any luck?" she asked, knowing the answer before he gave it.

"Afraid not."

"Don't tell me I have to stay here again another night."

"I don't want to risk moving you," he replied. "The streets are filling up and you'd be seen."

She returned to the chair to sit down. "Can I at least have a visitor? I'm bored to tears."

Removing his hat, he hesitated as he studied her face for a moment. "Well, it just so happens you're gonna have company tonight. All night as a matter of fact."

"Really? Who?"

He put his hat back on. "Me."

Jessica's heart began to race, as Truman turned and headed for the door.

"Wait a minute." She sat forward in the chair. "Where are you going?"

"To get a bath and a shave."

Jessica smiled at him flirtatiously. "You don't have to smell pretty on my account."

He turned the knob and opened the door. "Who said I'd be doing it for you? My horse is beginning to give me the cold shoulder."

He glanced back and winked at her, sending a wonderful shudder of anticipation through her body.

# Chapter Sixteen

That evening, after a few hours of mental preparation and soul searching, Jessica jumped when a knock rapped at her door. "Is that you?" she asked.

"Yeah," Truman replied.

She'd been reading a book about potatoes, and at the sound of his deep-timbered voice, she accidentally dropped the wildly stimulating piece of literature on the floor.

"Come in," she called out, picking up the book and opening it at random.

Truman walked in and removed his hat. His hair was wet and slicked back, and he wore a clean white shirt and black vest, along with a pair of freshly laundered trousers. "Are you hungry?" he asked. "Because I just told Rosie to bring up a couple of plates."

He crossed to the window, as he did every time he entered the room and pulled the curtain aside with one finger. Outside, it had begun to rain. "Kind of dark in here for reading."

He casually glanced down at the book on her lap.

Jessica admired the way his holster hung loosely at his hip. The leather was soft and well used.

"You're right," she managed to reply as she gladly closed the book.

He moved to the bedside table and scraped a match along the wall. It flared and illuminated his face as he lowered the flame to the wick of the kerosene lamp.

"Truman...."

"Yeah?" He glanced at her only briefly as he moved across the room.

"Why are you staying here tonight? Did something happen?"

He withdrew his revolver and checked the chamber for bullets. "I paid a visit to Ham Bell's Livery today and found out that Lou's gang doesn't plan on leaving Dodge until they find you and take what's rightfully theirs."

She bristled at the subtle note of accusation in his voice. "Does anyone know what they want from me?"

"No one seems to have the faintest idea. Funny, isn't it?"

Jessica, growing frustrated, met his stare. "You sound like you don't believe me again."

Truman moved toward her and lifted her chin with one finger. "Whatever this secret is that you're keeping, are you ever going to share it with me?"

She hesitated while she imagined how he would react if she told him the truth. Would he think she was off her rocker? "I might, one of these days..."

"Does it have anything to do with Lou's gang?" he asked, studying her intently.

"I already told you—no."

He backed away. "Well, if you don't have whatever it is they want, who does have it?"

"How should I know? I wasn't a close, personal friend of Lou's. All I know is that he was an unlucky brute."

Truman fell silent for a moment and sat down at the foot of the bed. "Back to your earlier question. I'm staying because I reckon they'll be looking everywhere for you. It might get rough tonight."

A knock sounded at the door, and Truman drew his gun. "Who is it?"

"Rosalie."

He holstered his weapon and went to open the door.

Rosalie entered with supper on a large tray. "Hey, Truman. I brought you and your lady some grub."

"She's not my lady."

Jessica squirmed inwardly at the cool tone of rancor in his voice.

"Either way," Rosalie said, setting the tray on the table, "there's enough food here to keep both of you busy for a while. When you're done, you can set the tray out in the hall. One of the girls will get it eventually."

"Thanks, Rosie," Truman said.

She ran her hands over her skirt. "I'll be right back."

"This looks delicious," Jessica said, looking at the plate of roast beef, baked potatoes, corn, and gravy. A fat buttered roll sat squarely on top of the beef, its bottom soaked with the dark brown sauce.

Rosalie knocked again, but Truman drew his gun just to be sure.

"It's only me."

He opened the door, and she swept in carrying two plates of chocolate cake and a bottle of wine. "I'll be next door if you need anything."

"Rosie?" Truman said.

"Yeah?"

He spoke quietly in her ear. "Try and keep it down tonight, if you can manage it."

Rosalie leaned out from behind Truman to peer at Jessica, who shrugged with casual indifference.

After the door clicked shut behind Rosalie, Truman locked it and sat down to eat. Silence followed, interrupted only by the clinking of forks against plates, the occasional squeaking of the bed when Jessica shifted around, and the rain pelting on the slanted roof above them. About halfway through the meal, Jessica rose and popped the cork on the wine bottle. She splashed some into a glass and raised it to her lips.

Truman looked up, but spoke too late. "Uh, careful...."

Good God! This wasn't wine! It tasted more like petroleum gasoline! "What is this stuff?" she asked, half choking on the words.

"I tried to warn you."

"No, you didn't!" She waved her hand in front of her open mouth, trying to fan the flames on her tongue.

He laughed quietly. "Yes I did. And it's moonshine from Ol' Bob Stafford. You gotta sip that stuff slowly."

Jessica made her way back to the bed with as much dignity as she could muster. Sitting down again, she lifted her fork and continued eating, using her meat to swab up the thick pool of gravy. That liquor must have seared her taste buds. She couldn't taste a thing.

Truman finished, licked his lips, and leaned back on the wrought iron bed frame. Self-consciously, and fully aware of his eyes on her, Jessica stuffed the last bite into her mouth and took another drink of the high-spirited alcohol. When the scorching sensation passed, she smiled crookedly. "I'm getting full." She dabbed at her lips with the napkin.

"I hope so. The town paid well for it."

"The town paid?" She felt her eyebrows lift involuntarily, and thought back to the night she'd seen him hand money to Rosalie. "At the dance?"

"Yeah."

"I thought you were..."

"You thought I was what?"

She shook her head, feeling like a complete fool. "I thought maybe you were paying for other types of services."

The smile in his eyes contained a sensuous flame. "I don't ever pay for that, Junebug."

"Ah—then I stand corrected." She reclined leisurely on the bed.

He stood and brought two slices of chocolate cake from the table, setting one down in front of Jessica. "Besides, women like Rosalie don't do much for me."

Trying not to react too strongly to this intriguing piece of information, Jessica took another gulp of the moonshine. "What about your wife?" she asked curiously. "What happened to her, if you don't mind my asking?"

He hesitated. "Consumption."

Jessica set down her glass. It was a one-word answer, yet there were still so many things she wanted to know.

"How long were you married?"

"Less than a year, but we knew each other since we were kids. Grew up in the same town, went to school together. My pa was a farmer. Her pa owned the dry goods store."

"You must have been very close, then," she said. "Very much in love."

How she envied that woman.

"I'm sorry that you had so little time with her," she added.

He nodded. "Yeah, it all happened pretty fast, especially the getting married part."

"How so?"

He kept his gaze lowered as he ate the cake. "I left home when I was sixteen. Wanted to work and earn my own way in the world. Then I came home ten years later when my pa died, and he left me the farm. I hadn't seen Dorothy in all that time, though she wrote me on occasion. When I saw her at my pa's funeral, she was already sick. She knew she was dying, and all she wanted was to be married before she left this world."

"So you stepped up to the plate…."

He finished his cake and nodded, while the rain came down harder on the roof. "Yeah, I guess you could say that."

"You must have loved her very much."

"She was a good woman."

A gust of wind rattled the six panes of glass in the window frame, and a draft slipped between the creaky, unpainted wallboards.

"Maybe this weather will keep Lou's gang home tonight," Jessica said, staring up at the wood ceiling and trying to mask the contentment she felt from being alone here with Truman, learning about his past, even though it was a painful one. "This seems strange," she sighed.

"What does?"

"Us. Being here. Doing nothing, just waiting for them to find us. It's like we're sitting ducks."

"I don't see it that way," he said.

"No? How do you see it?"

He tilted his head to the side. "I'd call it an ambush."

Jessica laughed. "An ambush?" She poked her cake with her fork. "Sheriff, I admire your confidence."

Truman swung his legs down and stood, causing the bed to squeak and bounce. Jessica watched him cross to the window.

Thunder boomed and the light flickered in the lamp. Then he looked at her. Deep in the blue of his eyes, a heated expression lingered—one she had not seen before.

She blinked slowly, as all the hazy hours and minutes leading up to this moment smudged together in her mind like a shifting fog.

Jessica swallowed and inched forward to touch her feet to the floor. Rising, she moved slowly toward him and stood before that shiny star on his lapel as it reflected the lamplight. Then she reached out and ran a finger lightly across the engraved letters.

"Careful," Truman said in a low voice. "I'm not made of steel."

She looked up at his face, disregarding everything else. "I don't want you to be."

"Are you sure about that?"

Their eyes locked for a full ten seconds before he stroked her cheek with the back of his hand, the gesture inflaming her desires to a shocking level of intensity. She ached to touch him, to kiss those soft full lips.

Turning her cheek into the warmth of his hand, she kissed his palm and sighed with pleasure.

"I've got to stay sharp," he whispered. "I can't be distracted."

He stopped talking all of a sudden. Then his lips covered hers in a hot and devouring kiss that took her breath away.

# Chapter Seventeen

Truman's hands on her body and his mouth playing upon hers smothered the last shred of self-restraint Jessica possessed. She burned with desire as he swept her into his arms, carried her to the bed, and laid her softly onto the mattress. Their mouths met briefly. Then he came down beside her, his hand roving the length of her body.

"Jessica..." His breath was hot and moist against her cheek, and it sent a flurry of delicious sensation through her. "I can't protect you this way."

"No... please, don't stop. I'll die if you do."

He shut his eyes. "I've tried to get you out of my head, but I can't. Every time I close my eyes, there you are, and all I want to do is find you and touch you. Do this to you."

He rolled on top of her and settled his hips closer to the warmth of her jean-clad legs.

Jessica moaned, unprepared for the immediate intimacy as he kissed her deeply.

In a swift and smooth movement, he reached down and unbuckled his gun belt and tossed it onto the bedside table with a heavy clunk.

Down he came again, lowering his full weight upon her, thrusting, stroking, groping. They kissed roughly and tugged at each other's clothes, while the passion sparked and flared into something unmanageable. There was no turning back now. She simply had to have him.

Truman reached to unfasten her jeans, but stopped in confusion. "What's this?"

Jessica lifted her head off the pillow. "Nothing. It's a zipper."

"How does it work?"

"Like this."

With crazy impatience, she unzipped them herself, and he slid his hand inside. She gasped with pleasure at his touch, while the fevered pounding of her heart sent her body over the edge.

"Take them off me…"

Needing no further bidding, he sat back and helped her tug the tight jeans down over her hips, while she unbuttoned her shirt with fumbling, trembling fingers.

He stared at her black bikini panties for a second or two, but thankfully disregarded whatever he was thinking and quickly removed his vest and shirt while he watched her remove hers.

He gazed with heady desire at her black lacy bra.

"It's something new," she explained. "It unhooks in the front. See?"

In a flash it was gone, tossed to the floor.

With equal haste, he unfastened his trousers and pushed them down over his hips, then settled himself between her parted thighs, looking down at her with sweltering, potent desire. "It's been a long time since I've—"

She laid a finger over his lips. "Shh…. It doesn't matter."

For a quivering moment, their bodies clung hotly together.

He lingered there, driving her mad with anticipation, kissing her neck and breasts, until she couldn't take it any longer. She needed him inside her and thrust her hips forward.

Truman let out a moan of pleasure as he entered and filled her in a single, perfect thrust. Time stood still. She could feel his heart beating against her chest. Then at last he began to move smoothly and steadily within her.

Jessica gripped the hard muscles of his lower back. Suddenly, she no longer felt displaced. This was exactly where she was meant to be in this moment, in this time. Here in his arms, connected to him. It didn't matter that they were born a century apart. They were together now, and that was all that mattered.

"I'll be careful," he whispered. "I'll stop before it's too late."

She understood that he was concerned about getting her pregnant.

"No, please don't stop," she replied. "There's nothing to worry about. You can't get me pregnant."

Because she was wearing an IUD.

"How do you know?"

"I just do. I promise, it's fine."

Truman kissed her lightly on the lips, then gazed into her eyes as he began to move. For a long time, he made love to her with great care and deliberation. Soon, she couldn't keep the passion at bay. Her body tingled and pulsed. Tossing her head back, she shuddered just as a mighty release found her and left her weak and sated with rapture.

A moment later, Truman thrust deep into her as he climaxed. He let out a rugged moan and collapsed onto her in exhaustion.

Soon, their breathing slowed to a matched pace, raindrops pelted against the window, and the wind rattled the panes. Jessica ran her fingers lightly up and down his smoothly muscled back, damp with perspiration.

"Are you all right?" he whispered. "Did I hurt you?"

"Not a bit." She wrapped her legs around him. "I loved every minute of it."

Sometime after four in the morning, when Truman was certain the saloon had cleared out, he rose from bed and got dressed. After a long and appreciative moment admiring the smooth curves of Jessica's exquisite naked form, he stroked her hair away from her face and disciplined himself into remembering what he was here to do. His job.

He pulled the quilt up to cover her shoulders and left quietly, closing the door behind him and locking it.

Bracing both hands on the railing outside Jessica's room, he watched the barkeep sweep a broom across the floor below, and thought about what had just happened.

Making love to Jessica had unraveled every tight coil inside him, coils he'd spent the last two years working hard to keep tightly maintained.

Hell, the closest friend he had was Deputy Dempsey, but the kid didn't know the first thing about Truman's personal life, which left Truman on his own most of the time. Jessica was the only person in Dodge who knew anything, and for the first time in two years, he felt an emotion emerge from somewhere deep down, a place he thought he had conquered. It was a place that knew pain.

A place that remembered....

Sweeping those thoughts from his mind, Truman walked down the hall. The scent of stale beer and cigar smoke stunk up the saloon. He'd be half glad when winter arrived. At least the cattle drives would be finished for the season, and things would quiet down to a milder type of living.

When Truman reached the downstairs, Lenny crossed both hands over the broom handle. "Can I get you something, Sheriff?"

"Any food out back?" he replied.

"Try the kitchen." Lenny whistled a tune and returned to his work.

A moment later, Truman came out of the kitchen with a plate of sugar cookies. He took a seat at a table, as a woman's sultry voice reached him from across the room.

"I always knew you had a sweet tooth."

He turned to see Rosalie meandering through the saloon, her hips swinging back and forth. The closer she came, the more she swung that skirt.

"Evening, Rosie. You done workin'?"

"Looks that way." She reached his table and lifted a foot up onto the chair next to his, to re-tie the laces on her heeled boot. "Slow night. For some of us, that is."

Truman picked up a cookie while Rosalie dropped her skirt and sat down with one hand on her thigh, an elbow perched on the tabletop. "This is the first I've seen of you tonight. Where have you been?"

"Around."

Rosalie let out a throaty laugh. "You've been around all right. You've been all around little Miss Junebug." Rosalie peered into Truman's face. "You're not in love, are ya'?"

"You know better than to ask me that, Rosie."

"Oh, that's right. You don't like folks poking their noses into your personal affairs." She rotated a half circle on the chair and stood. Sauntering around the bar, she scooped up a bottle and two glasses. "I feel like a drink. What'll it be?"

"Nothing for me."

"Why, because you're on duty? You gotta learn to have some fun, sweetheart. That girl up there...she don't deserve all that devotion."

Truman pushed the plate of cookies away. "And what makes you think I'm devoted?"

"Oh, I just have a feeling, that's all. I also have a feeling she's bad news."

Rosalie poured whisky into one glass, but Truman placed his hand flat across the top of the other.

Rosalie paused with the bottle suspended horizontally in the air. Then she set it down, picked up her own glass, tossed the whisky back, and swallowed it in one gulp.

Turning away, she headed for the stairs. "You're a damn fine thing to look at, Truman. Finest lookin' man in Dodge. Anytime you want to come see me, it'll be on the house." She disappeared into the darkness, but called out in a throaty voice. "You remember that offer, now. I have a feeling after Junebug leaves town – which she will, no doubt about it— you'll be needing to take the edge off."

\* \* \*

Jessica woke to a ray of light piercing through the window. Outside, a pack of dogs barked ferociously.

She sat up and stretched her arms over her head, then winced in agony.

Oh, the headache. How much of that moonshine did she drink? She lifted the bottle to inspect it, sloshed the remains about inside, and collapsed in horror onto the pillow.

A few minutes later, an aggressive knock sounded at her door. Jessica sat up. "Ouch…geez." She cupped her forehead and massaged gently. "Who is it?"

"It's Truman. Open up."

Wrapping her reprehensible naked self in the quilt and vowing not to do anything like this again, she padded in her bare feet to the door, and opened it. Truman stood in the hall, washed and shaved, and dressed in black again, looking like a sexy hero out of a classic spaghetti western flick.

Yet no fictional hero on the big screen could ever do what this man had done to her last night. Her head was still spinning from the shocking and wicked impiety of it—and that particular commotion in her brain had nothing do with Ol' Bob Stafford's atrocious moonshine.

"Get dressed," he said without ceremony. "We're leaving."

Recognizing the urgency in his tone, she froze. "Why? What happened?"

"Just do as I say. I'll be back in five minutes." He started to go, but spoke over his shoulder. "Wear your trousers."

With that, he walked away, leaving Jessica naked under the quilt, still standing at the door.

She quickly shut it and dropped the blanket onto the bed, wondering if she had imagined the grouchiness in his tone. Was he trying to put distance between them because of what happened last night? Or did something terrible happen? Something to do with Lou's gang?

As soon as she was dressed and everything was packed, Jessica sat on the edge of the bed waiting.

Another knock sounded. She rushed to the door and flung it open.

"You should've asked who it was before you opened it," Truman said, walking in.

"I think I know the sound of your boots by now," she replied.

He moved fully into the room, carrying a brown slicker and cowboy hat. "Put these on." He tossed the hat onto the bed and held the coat up for her. "I don't want anyone to recognize you."

Studying his expression in those spark-like seconds, listening to the impatient tone in his otherwise patient voice, Jessica turned her back on him and shoved her arms into the sleeves of the slicker. He eased the coat onto her shoulders and turned her around to face him. He tugged at her lapel to tighten the collar around her neck and rolled up the long sleeves.

"I can dress myself, you know," she said.

"I'm sure you can." He picked up the hat and rotated it in his hands, while looking at her long tousled hair. "Can you pin that up?"

She dug into her leather bag to retrieve the pins from the bottom and swept her hair up in a messy twist on top of her head. Pulling the hat on, she tucked up all the loose strands.

"How's that?" she asked, raising her hands.

"Fine," he answered.

"Fine?" she replied, feeling a bit testy from the after-effects of the moonshine. "That's all you have to say to me? Can we at least please mention the elephant in the room?"

He faced her and frowned in confusion. "What elephant?"

She shook her head in disbelief. "We had sex last night. Seriously dirty sex. Want me to describe it to you?"

The room went suddenly quiet.

"No. I remember. Now, come on." He scooped up her bag and led her out of the room, along the railing toward the stairs.

Jessica followed him down to the front door and stopped there.

"Don't say a word to anyone," he said. "Just get in the wagon out front. The driver will take you to a safe place."

She placed her hand on his forearm. "Are we okay? This feels weird, and I don't want to leave here if we need to talk about stuff."

He looked at her strangely. "If I'm going to protect you, I need to keep my mind on my job, not the dirty sex. And I certainly don't want to talk about it. Now off you go."

He handed her the bag and shuffled her through the swinging doors into the blinding morning sunlight. Stopping on the boardwalk, she squinted and shaded her eyes, feeling more turned on than she'd ever felt in her life.

A wagon was parked out front. She walked around the back of it, climbed up and sat down. The driver slapped the reins and whistled, the mules began to walk, and the bumpy ride began.

"Angus?" she whispered. "Is that you?"

"Just look straight ahead," he replied, "until we're out of town."

She did as she was told, lowering her chin so no one would see her face beneath the brim of her hat.

Leaning back and folding her arms, she wondered where in all this expanse of flat windy prairie they were going to go, and how long it would take to get there.

Outside of town, the golden prairie opened up and the blue sky spanned one horizon to the other. "What's going on?" she asked. "Why was Truman in such a hurry to get me out of there?"

Angus glanced over his shoulder to make sure they weren't being followed. "Lou's gang's been asking questions about you. They were searching everywhere last night, and Truman said it was only a matter of time before they got to the whorehouse."

"So where are we going?"

"Truman heard from the Russells that the gang searched their place last night."

"Who are the Russells?"

"They own a claim out that way." He pointed eastward. "Mr. Russell said the gang searched everywhere—the house, the barn, even the outhouse. All the while, they kept him and his wife at gunpoint."

"That's terrible. Was anyone hurt?"

"No, but Mrs. Russell insisted they leave and visit relations in Caldwell, so I agreed to milk their cow and feed their chickens for them. The house will be empty for a while, but we'll sleep in the barn. Truman figures, if the gang was there only last night, they won't go back again tonight. They'll be looking elsewhere."

"I hope he's right about that." A gust of wind blew across the prairie. Jessica placed a hand on top of her hat to keep it from flying off, while the mules shook their harnesses and plodded on.

"I meant to tell you," Angus said, "Wendy and I ate dinner together last night."

"Really?"

"Yes, and I'm growing quite fond of her."

"That's wonderful," Jessica replied, touching him affectionately on the shoulder. "Does she feel the same way about you?"

"I don't know."

Jessica watched his profile as he slapped the reins again.

"How does a man know?" he asked.

"Does she blush when she sees you?"

"A little, but it might just be shyness."

"Does she smile and giggle a lot?"

"Wendy's not much of a giggler."

"Have you kissed her?"

"Heavens no."

Jessica removed her hat and held it on her lap. "Maybe you should."

"No, I couldn't possibly. What if she didn't want me to? It would be very embarrassing."

"Sometimes you have to take risks," she told him, as she gazed across the prairie where meadowlarks sang and swooped low over the grass. "If you really want to love someone, you need to be able to share everything with them."

Last night, Truman had made love to her as if in a dream, and this morning, she had felt the raw ache of being torn away from him.

Yet, he still knew so little about her.

While she stared down the long road that stretched before them, she knew it was probably time to heed some of her own advice. She was going to have to tell Truman about her time traveling eventually.

Maybe tonight would be the night.

# Chapter Eighteen

It was six o'clock in the evening by the time Truman returned to the jailhouse to check in before leaving for the Russell's claim. He had spent the entire day searching for the gang while fighting an exhausting need for sleep, which he'd have to continue resisting, at least until he reached Jessica.

He walked into the law office, where Deputy Dempsey was seated at the desk with his cheek on his hand, reading another dime novel.

Truman removed his hat and raked his fingers through his hair. "Did you hear anything about the gang?"

"No, Sheriff." Dempsey quickly closed the book. "I asked all over town, though. Even went out to the Jones Ranch. They ain't anywhere."

"They have to be somewhere." Truman's spurs jingled as he crossed the room and looked over a few new police court dockets on his desk. Seeing nothing unusual, he pressed his palms over his bloodshot eyes and rubbed. Then he blinked a few times.

Dempsey looked up at him as if waiting for instructions.

"You'll need to stay here," Truman said, heading for the door. "In case anybody comes forward with information about the gang. All of Dodge knows we're looking for them. I'm sure somebody will see or hear something."

"You should get some sleep, Sheriff. You look like you were run over by a cattle drive."

"I'll sleep later."

"Where are you going now?" Dempsey asked.

"I'm gonna get a quick meal at the Dodge House, then head out to watch over Miss Delaney. I won't tell you where, though. Best to keep that secret."

He opened the door and stepped out onto the front porch, feeling more impatient to reach Jessica than he could ever have anticipated.

After Truman ate a quick supper at the Dodge House, he rode out of town toward the Russells' claim, checking over his shoulder every so often to make sure he wasn't being followed. The sun was low in the sky, and since riding into it was hard on his eyes, he kept his head low, shaded by the brim of his hat.

He was halfway there when he saw an overturned wagon up ahead, and the blurry image of a man. Truman slowed Thunder to a trot and approached.

The man was waving his arms over his head.

Truman dismounted. "You all right? Is anyone hurt?"

"Yes. My wife." The man stood on the other side of the wagon, looking down.

Truman walked around the wreckage to help the injured woman, but stopped dead when four Winchesters all cocked at once.

Staring at the four surviving members of Lou's gang and kicking himself for being so foolish as to let down his guard, Truman raised his hands in the air.

"Keep yer hands over yer head, Wade," Bart said, reaching into Truman's holster and confiscating his gun. The gang slowly surrounded him, and the wind roared over the wagon, spinning its wheels.

"Now, you're gonna tell us where you been hidin' that little lady of yours. She has something that belongs to us." Bart jabbed him in the ribs with the barrel of his rifle, while his forefinger flexed at the trigger.

"If you wanna see the sun come up tomorrow," Corey added, "you best tell us where she is."

Truman spit off to the side.

"Where is she?" Bart demanded. "And if you don't answer me soon, I swear on my mother's grave, I'll blow your brains out."

Truman glared at Bart, his ugly face not six inches away. "Sounds like things are going to get messy, then," he replied, "because I ain't telling you shit."

Bart's eyes clouded over with rage. "You're gonna be sorry you said that." Then he swung his Winchester through the air and struck Truman sharply in the head.

As time ticked by in the Russells' hayloft, Jessica found it increasingly difficult to ignore the worries that were niggling at her.

"It's been dark for at least an hour," she said to Angus. "He should be here by now."

"I'm sure everything's fine."

The remainder of the evening dragged by slowly. Jessica passed the time reading under the lantern while Angus napped. Hours later, the flame flickered and the barn creaked in the wind like an old ship.

Wondering what time it was and what had become of Truman, she rose to her feet and walked to the other side of the loft. She perked up for a moment when the dog barked. Maybe Truman was coming…

Hearing only the incessant howl of the wind, she gave up on the notion.

She returned to where Angus slept and tried not to wake him as she lifted the watch out of his pocket to check the time. Eleven thirty.

Damn. Truman had said he would be there before dark. Something must have happened.

Leaning forward on one knee, she shook Angus. He twitched, and then he awakened with a jolt.

"Angus, wake up. It's eleven thirty, and Truman's not here yet."

Angus sat up. He rubbed his head and smoothed his thinning hair. "Maybe he's at the house watching from there."

"I need you to go check."

"Of course. You stay here."

He made his way down the ladder.

A few minutes later, the barn door squeaked open, and Jessica rose to her feet. "Did you find him?" she asked.

Angus shook his head.

Jessica pounded a fist against the post. "Something's wrong. I can feel it. We have to go look for him."

Angus hesitated. "We can't do that. I promised to keep you here. And what if he arrives, and we're gone?"

She considered it a moment. "Here's what we're going to do. I'll stay here while you head back into town. Find Dempsey, and tell him that Truman never arrived. Learn whatever you can."

"The sheriff's probably locking that gang up right now," Angus replied, as he gathered up his coat.

An hour later, Jessica was just drifting off to sleep for the briefest of moments, when a bandanna was shoved into her mouth, and ropes snaked around her wrists and ankles. Flinging her arms about, thrashing on the blanket like a caged animal, she fought the waves of fury that slammed over her.

Someone tied her wrists behind her back while another roped her ankles together. When she tried to scream, she inhaled the sour tasting, sweat-drenched essence of the soiled fabric that filled her mouth, and her enraged plea was reduced to a pitiful moan.

"Your lawyer friend led us right to you," Bart said, smiling diabolically at her. "He came rolling in off the east road, and there are only so many ranches in this direction."

One of the others laughed. "And they say lawyers are supposed to be smart."

"Get her up, boys."

Jessica grunted when Corey lifted her like a sack of grain and flung her over his shoulder. Her hair fell forward over her face.

"How am I gonna get down from here?" Corey complained, standing at the edge of the loft.

Jessica heard Bart's deep, sardonic voice behind them and saw the glare of the lantern he held. It swung dangerously close to her face, and she shrank back defensively.

"Throw her down, Corey," Bart commanded. "Throw her into that haystack."

"What if I miss?"

"You won't miss."

"I'm not a very good thrower."

"Just do it, ya sissy."

He paused there, looking down.

"Do it, Corey!"

The third voice came from below, and the encouragement was all he needed. Jessica struggled and fought right up until the last second. Then Corey threw her over the side.

She hit the hay, and the wind blew out of her lungs.

Before she had a chance to suck in a breath, she was picked up and hurled over someone else's shoulder, her head bobbing up and down as she was carried outside.

She was thrown like an old blanket onto a horse, her hands still tied behind her back. Corey mounted behind her and held her firmly, so she wouldn't fall off.

As soon as they gained some distance from the Russells' farm, Bart trotted up next to Jessica. Her position made it impossible to see his face, but she could hear him laughing.

"Don't fret, little Missy," he said. "There ain't no Junebugs where you're goin', so you won't be tempted to shoot anyone by mistake."

"I highly doubt it," she mumbled through the dirty bandana, wishing she had a gun right now.

# Chapter Nineteen

Jessica lay on the damp dirt floor of a root cellar, struggling with the prickly bonds at her hands and feet. Her wrists burned under the coarse rope hair; the corners of her mouth stung against the bandanna's gritty abrasion. A few times on horseback she had gagged, but that was only when she stretched her body and arched her back to see the sky. By finding the North Star, she had established that they were heading west across the prairie.

She could only hope the information would prove useful.

Directly above her, a kerosene lamp hung from a hook on a beam. She squinted into the light. Then she looked all around, considering a possible way out.

The cellar foundation was constructed of stones. There were no windows. To the right, wooden barrels lined the wall. The steps were steep like a ladder, and she was grateful Corey hadn't simply tossed her down like he'd done at the Russells' barn.

Closing her eyes, she searched her mind for a plan, but a brilliant escape strategy failed to materialize.

Jessica strained to listen for anything that might give her some ideas. Above her, the lantern hissed and sputtered.

And someone on the other side of the cellar was breathing.

She struggled in a panic to comprehend the possibilities—perhaps this anonymous breather was one of the gang members guarding her. Or maybe it was the owner of the house, the poor soul. Or a huge, ferocious dog that hadn't been fed in days....

Eventually Jessica summoned her courage, and then she inched her way on her back across the dirt floor.

The sound was coming from the other side of the cellar, behind the thick stone support wall in the center. She wiggled her way around the wall, where it was much darker. Slowly her eyes adjusted, and she focused on a man, but it was too dark to see his face. He was tied to a chair and slumped forward.

Jessica nudged her shoulder against his leg. She tried to speak, but only grunts and gibberish broke through the gag. Bumping and prodding, she uttered words as best she could. "Wake up, wake up!"

Suddenly, the man jerked wildly like a bucking stallion. It was a fit of anger, the likes of which Jessica had never seen. She flipped over and rolled across the floor to escape the unpredictable path of the thrashing chair.

After a moment, he went still, seemingly spent of energy. Jessica lay there in fear, listening to the violent rush of the blood in her veins.

The man seemed unaware of Jessica's presence on the floor not three feet from his boots. He began to tug against the ropes that bound him. Sitting up again, Jessica uttered a sound as best she could to let him know he wasn't alone.

There was a pause. Silence. Then, "Jessica?"

She recognized the voice. It was Truman's.

Dizziness swarmed in her head as she rose up onto her knees and touched her forehead to his chin. He nudged her with his face, burying his nose into the crook of her neck. "Thank God you're alive," he whispered. "Did they hurt you?"

"No."

The ropes at her wrists and ankles felt like shackles now. She tugged and pulled, ignoring the chafing pain.

"Wait," he said. "Try to get behind me and untie my hands."

She nodded and inched along the floor, so they were back-to-back. She then wiggled her cold fingers to find the ropes in the dark. She felt the leg of the chair, but she was too low to reach his hands.

Jessica grunted as she pushed upward with all her might. She used Truman's weight as leverage, balancing as best she could. The ropes around her ankles pulled tightly as she tried to stand.

She fumbled as she untied the knots at his wrists. After a considerable struggle, she loosened them, and Truman pulled a hand free. He untied the rest of the knots, and then released her as well.

They each untied their ankles, and Jessica rose to her feet. In one swift motion, she was in his arms. "I didn't know what happened to you."

"I was on my way to you, and they caught me off guard. I was tired...I should've known better."

His mouth covered hers. He crushed her body to his and pulled her close. His lips were warm and moist as he kissed and caressed her, and she sighed with a pleasure that seemed impossible under these circumstances, but there it was. They were together. Nothing else mattered.

He drew away and whispered faintly, "I was in hell today. It was all I could do to keep from following you after you left Rosie's. Then when they ambushed me, I didn't know if I'd ever see you again."

Jessica took his hand. "Come over to the lamp, so I can look at you." He followed, but when she caught sight of him, she gasped, a sharp sound in the bleak silence. "Oh, God."

He was black and blue, one eye swollen shut. Blood matted his hair close to his temple. The skin over his cheekbone was cut. Blood stained his black shirt and dripped down his neck.

"Oh, Truman." Jessica reached to touch his face, but he jerked away.

"Don't," he said.

She wanted to pound the disgusting thugs who brought them here. "How could they do this to you?"

"They're cowards. They knocked me out before they took their punches. I don't remember any of it."

Jessica wished there was something she could do to clean his wounds, but they didn't even have any water.

"I need to get you out of here," he said, looking around. "Do you know where we are?"

"About a half-hour ride west of the Russells' place."

He frowned. "That's not good. If they let you see where they were taking you, I doubt they plan to let us out of here alive."

She shut her eyes and tipped her forehead against the solid wall of his chest. "This really sucks."

He gathered her into his arms again, and Jessica knew that while he held her, he was thinking and plotting.

"We have to find out what it is they want from you," he said, "then tell them you have it, but not with you. We'll try to bargain."

"Will it work?"

He gazed down at her. "I don't know. They seem pretty ruthless."

"I can be ruthless, too," she assured him.

If one of them came down here now, she was quite sure she would beat him insensible with her own hands.

"Maybe Dempsey will find us," she said, working hard to restrain those feelings of aggression—at least for now. "Angus told him you were missing. Soon, he'll discover I'm gone and…"

She watched Truman beneath the orange glow of the lamp, thinking back on everything that had brought them here and wished in vain that she'd never stopped to fight with that Junebug.

Truman looked at the stairs. "Have you tried the door?"

"No."

He brushed by her and climbed the cellar steps. He listened at the top and jiggled the latch, but the door was bolted shut. When he heard nothing from the other side, he began to slam his shoulder against it.

A voice shouted. "Give it up, Wade! It's locked tight with a few extra boards nailed on just to be sure."

Truman uttered an oath and stepped back down.

The voice called down to them again from behind the locked door. "You two might as well relax. Bart'll be down in the morning to have a little chat with you." His footsteps started away and then stopped. "Oh," he added, as if he'd just thought of something clever. "Enjoy your last night together."

Jessica listened to the heartless laughter and felt breathless with rage. Then she began to tremble. If only she would wake up in her own bed with Truman beside her and find the television on....

Footsteps pounded across the floor overhead; bedsprings creaked and bounced. Then silence.

"I guess we're stuck here until morning," Truman said. "Do you have any idea how late it is?"

"It must be after three. Maybe four."

"We should get some sleep." He unhooked the lamp, carried it to the other side of the cellar, and found an old blanket from behind one of the crates. "You can lie down on this."

Jessica glanced up at his bruised face. "We'll share it. How about over there?" She pointed toward the far corner where they would be out of sight if anyone came down the stairs. Truman set the lamp down and spread the blanket on the ground.

"I don't want this to be our last night together," she whispered as she lay down.

"It won't be."

Curling up beside him on the blanket, she hid her face in his shoulder while he stared up at the ceiling, blinking.

"What if tomorrow...?"

Truman leaned up on his side and draped one arm across her stomach. "Everything will be fine."

"You always say that, but what if it isn't? What if tonight really is our last night?"

He touched a finger to her lips.

"Make love to me," she said.

His expression grew strained. "Jessica...."

"Why not? I'm in love with you. There, I've said it." Relief flooded through her, but his reaction crushed it instantly. His eyes turned cold, and his voice was dark and almost threatening.

"I don't want you to love me."

"Why?"

Lying back, his hand slipping from her stomach onto his own, he said, "There are things you don't know about me. Things no one knows."

She wanted to tell him that it didn't matter. There were things he didn't know about her either, like the fact that she came from another century and still wanted to return home. She felt torn, yes...because of how she felt about him, but this was not her world, and when the time came – if it came – she would leave him. It would kill her inside, but she would do it.

If only she could take him with her, but would he even want that? Would she? How sensible or realistic would it be to bring a lawman from the Wild West into the twenty-first century? How would they ever live?

She leaned up on an elbow and looked into his eyes. "You can tell me anything," she said, "because I have secrets, too. Things you wouldn't believe."

He touched her cheek. "I've always known that, since the first moment we met." Abruptly, he sat up. Then he stood and rested his forehead on a low timber beam.

Jessica rose and approached him. "Tell me everything. I want to know all your secrets. Then I'll tell you mine."

A vein pulsed at his temple. "I don't know if I can. The words are like poison on my tongue."

He moved into the shadows and sat down on the chair. Jessica picked up the lantern and set it on the dirt floor at his feet.

He leaned forward with his elbows on his knees, his hands locked together in front of him.

"Why don't you want me to love you?" she boldly asked.

He lifted his eyes, and the malice was there again, reflecting in the lamplight. "Dorothy loved me," he said, "and I wish every day that she hadn't."

"Are you afraid I'll get sick and die, like she did?"

He pinched the bridge of his nose. "No, it's not that."

"What is it, then?"

There was a long pause. "It was my fault that she died."

Jessica knelt down and took his hands in hers. "She was sick, Truman. You can't blame yourself. It was no one's fault."

He glared at her with dark and brooding hostility. "You're wrong about that."

"How?"

The flame in the lantern sputtered and hissed. "Because I shot her."

# Chapter Twenty

A cold wave of shock moved through Jessica as she digested Truman's words.

"What happened?"

He sat forward again, rested his elbows on his knees, and looked her in the eye as he spoke.

"She was sick—that much is true—and we couldn't run the farm. We needed money, so I set out to collect what I thought would be an easy reward. There was an outlaw they called Big Dog. He knew I was looking for him, and by that time, folks knew my aim was good, and I didn't miss my mark often. I reckon he wanted to get to me before I could get to him, so he came to the house."

Jessica swallowed over the sickening lump of dread that rose up in her throat.

"When Big Dog walked in my front door," he continued, "I drew my weapon. Big Dog shot me in the shoulder, and I shot him at the same time. He dropped his gun but stayed on his feet, while I fell back onto the floor. He was wobbling, and I figured he'd go down any time. So I lay there with my six-shooter aimed at his head, not even knowing if I had any bullets left."

Sitting back in the chair, Truman kept his eyes trained on Jessica's. "That's when Dorothy came out of the bedroom with my shotgun. I didn't see her. She was so quiet on her bare feet. Big Dog saw her though. He made a move for his gun, so I fired. Dorothy stepped between us right then and took my bullet in her back." His quiet voice shook. "She thought Big Dog shot her, and I never told her the difference. She died right there in my arms. The last thing she said was, 'I saved you.'"

Jessica got down on her knees in front of him. "I'm very sorry, Truman."

"I buried her on the hill," he continued, "and everyone in town thought..." He looked down. "I told them Big Dog shot her. Then I took the reward money, sold the ranch, and left town for good."

"It was an accident."

"But I should have told people. I should have told her folks. They were good people, and I lied to them."

"You'd been through hell, dealing with the worst kind of guilt. You were in no state to think clearly." She ran her fingers down his arm, searching for the right words.

"I killed my wife," he said, shaking his head. "I'll never forgive myself for it, and I don't want to lose you like I lost her."

"You will forgive yourself," she said. "I'll make sure of it. And you won't lose me."

A chill shivered up her spine. Could she really promise him that?

Suddenly, in a rush of movement, he stood up, pulled her to her feet, and smothered her next words with a deep, open-mouthed kiss that left her burning with love and desire.

She knew she had to tell him the truth about where she came from, but he needed her now. He needed this, so she would confess her secrets later. Besides, morning would be here soon, and they'd done enough talking....

His lips seared a path down her neck, and she threw her head back, opening herself to him completely.

"I need to make love to you," he growled in her ear, and just the sound of his voice fired a tremor of relentless passion into her blood.

Jessica slid her hand down his firm thigh and wondered how he had endured the past two years without intimacy, hiding his secret from the world. "Yes...."

In a reckless flurry of movement, she unfastened his trousers and slid her hand inside. He responded with a groan of pleasure, while she touched her lips to the fine curve of his collarbone, tasting the delicious salty flavor of his skin. Nipping gently, her lips followed her trembling fingers as she undid the buttons of his shirt and kissed his chest. He pulled his shirt off over his head, and her lips found the firm, smooth corded surface of muscle at his stomach.

Next, with clumsy fingers, she unbuckled his empty gun belt and dropped it onto the ground beside them.

"Come to the blanket," he said, taking her hand and leading her into the shadows. "We'll be more comfortable there."

She followed him away from the lamplight into the darkness where he had laid their bed. Barely able to see him, she reached out to touch him instead, her impassioned senses shifting away from sight and becoming alert to smells, sounds, and textures. Locked together, they sank onto the blanket.

Truman uttered a husky murmur and lowered himself on top of her. She wrapped her legs around him, unable to get close enough, wanting, craving everything she knew he was going to do with her.

His lips blindly sought the sensitive flesh at her neck. Warm kisses journeyed to her shoulder as he slid a hand inside her shirt. He released each button and slid the shirt off her, covering her with his hot, sensuous weight.

"You feel good," he whispered, reaching down to unfasten her jeans.

She wiggled out of them. He removed his, and as soon as he was naked beside her, she rolled onto him. "Lie back." She pressed her palm to his chest and guided him down. "Relax."

"That's not possible." His tone was low and laden with desire.

His fingers found her breasts and inflamed her swirling senses as she eased herself down onto him, melting around him. Slowly she moved with controlled effort. The hard swell of him filled her with soaring pleasure.

"God," he moaned, his hands trailing down her flat stomach and around her hips to guide her in the directions that pleased him. Jessica tipped her head back, swaying to his rhythm.

She went where he moved her, learning what he liked and what worked for her. Then she needed more, so she thrust faster, impatiently, until she was drained of strength, her body depleted of its power to thrust any harder.

Truman sat up and rolled them over onto the woolen blanket. "I wish we could do this forever," she heard herself say in a cloud of pleasure, aware that she was denying the dangerous reality that faced them.

"We will," he replied.

Within moments, his hips were grinding against hers, deeper each time as she arched her back. His name spilled from her lips, begging, pleading for more—more of his blinding, plunging desire.

Then, just as she began to believe there was no ecstasy more perfect than this, her body gave way, and she bit her lip to suppress the urge to cry out his name. All the sensual pleasures of life came to her at once, until she was spent, collapsing upon him, her arms falling open to the ground.

The bed above them had creaked and squeaked during the night, giving Truman something to pay attention to outside of his own thoughts and regrets.

Nestled beside Jessica, who slept contentedly on his shoulder, he stared up at the blackness above him and wondered how he could ever live his life from this day forward without her.

He simply couldn't. He was devoted now, for the rest of his days. That's the kind of man he was. When he loved, he loved forever. It was not something he took lightly. He loved from the deepest reaches of his soul. Not even death would keep him from her now.

Brushing the tip of his thumb over the soft, creamy skin at her neck, he recalled the sounds she had made when she'd shuddered beneath him. The bliss of that moment had consumed him so completely, he had imagined their predicament was all a bad dream.

Lying here now, he knew that to be a sad hallucination.

Truman shifted. His arm was falling asleep, but he didn't want to wake Jessica. Her breathing had grown steady quite some time ago, and she had not stirred except for a slight twitching of her cheek where it was snuggled against his shoulder. Her heavy hair lay across his chest, tickling him each time it fluttered against the light breezes of her sweet breaths. He touched her lightly, but noticed the back of her arm seemed cold. He covered it with his hand.

A few moments passed. In the quiet, he felt her awakening, by the change in her breathing and the subtle movement of her head as she swallowed. Then a sweet whisper floated into his consciousness. "Do you think we'll be all right tomorrow?"

Truman hugged her. "Yes."

They had discussed their escape strategy in great detail after they'd made love.

If only he had his gun. The sorry events of the day before made him want to lash out and smack that overhead beam. He'd been foolish to ride up to that wagon without thinking. He should have slept at some point. He shouldn't have believed he could stay alert.

Pins and needles tingled up his arm, so he tried to move. Jessica, so incredibly attuned to his needs, lifted her cheek, sat up, and watched him roll his shoulder to get the feeling back.

"Maybe we should get dressed," she said.

"Yeah. It must be almost dawn." He reached across her and picked up her clothes, holding them out to her. "Do you remember what to do?"

"I think so," she answered, wiggling into her jeans.

He stood to pull on his clothes. "It would be best to let me do the talking."

He buckled his empty gun belt and shook his head at the foolish comfort he took from the ritual.

"What should we do now?" Jessica asked, combing her fingers through her hair.

"There's not much we can do but wait."

Truman looked into her eyes and wondered how they had come to this. "I'm sorry," he said. "I promised I'd protect you, didn't I?"

Just then, the cellar door burst open.

A shot of panic fired into Jessica's blood as she was blinded by the bright sunlight cascading down the cellar steps. Reaching for Truman's hand, she knew this was the moment that would decide their fate.

He squeezed her hand, then moved protectively in front of her. Two dirty boots stepped into view and stomped down.

"Howdy," Corey grunted, sucking on a cigar. He pulled it from his thin lips and tapped ashes onto the dirt floor.

Jessica wanted to dash forward, throw her body into him, and punch him repeatedly in the head, but one look at the revolver in his belt told her that would not be a wise move.

Truman spoke daringly. "What do you want, Corey?"

"You know exactly what I want." He placed the cigar between his teeth and walked into the shadows. "You two have been spending an awful lot of time together lately."

Jessica bit her lip, wondering how in the world they were going to make their plan work.

"Get to the point," Truman demanded, his eyes narrowing.

"Bart wanted to kill you, Wade, but I told him not to. I knew you was worth keeping."

Calmly, Truman removed his hat and ran his fingers through his hair. "Why's that?"

Corey pointed his cigar toward Jessica. "It don't take a fool to see that you and this little lady are workin' together, maybe even enjoying a little naughty business on the side."

"What's your point?" Truman replied.

"Well," he said, tapping more ashes onto the floor. "That makes things easier. You see, if one of you was to be in a whole lot of pain—"

"Touch her, and you're a dead man," Truman ground out.

Jessica felt the heat of his fury in the pit of her stomach and was glad she wasn't on the receiving end of it. She took one look at Corey and guessed he felt the same way. He cleared his throat nervously, and then continued as if he hadn't been interrupted.

"If one of you was in pain," he continued, "maybe the other might think more carefully about givin' us what we want. Love is funny like that, ain't it?"

Jessica touched Truman's shoulder. "Maybe we should give it to him."

He shook his head. "No, because he won't let us live anyway. If we're going to die, we'll die together—right here."

Jessica's hand dropped, certain that her contribution to the discussion had moved things along. It was a good thing, too, because she sure as hell was tired of wasting time, and she wanted to beat this ass to a pulp.

Truman looped one thumb through his gun belt. "Even if we did agree to give it to you, do you think we'd be fool enough to keep it on us?"

Corey smiled, his mouth curving in a manner that made Jessica wonder if he knew anything of human kindness. "No," he said, sardonically. "I've never taken you for a fool, Wade. You either, Junebug. That's why I came down here. I figured it's time I cashed in on some of those smarts of yours."

# Chapter Twenty-One

Corey paced back and forth, pondering what to do. "I figure," he said, "if two people have a common enemy, that just about makes them partners, don't you think?"

Truman leaned at his ease against a post. "Tell me more."

Smoke spiraled upward as Corey took a deep drag off his cigar. "Bart's been vexing me lately. He's been gettin' too big for his britches, acting like he should be the new leader of this outfit."

Jessica noticed Truman's patience wearing thin; he was tapping his thumb on his empty leather holster.

"So what do you plan on doing about it?" he asked.

"Them boys left me here while they went into Dodge for some ladies. But the way I see it, when they come back, you and me will have developed a proper friendship, and you'll be takin' me to where you hid that little piece of paper."

Jessica felt a spark of adrenalin. Their plan was working, progressing as it should, yet what they possessed was only a small shred of the information they needed to save themselves.

"If you don't consider me your friend," Corey continued, "I won't take too kindly to that. I might just shoot you right here. The lady'll be more obliging, I'm sure, when she sees how ugly a man can be when blood's drippin' down his face."

Truman looked down and kicked at the dirt with the toe of his boot. "I think we can work something out."

"Good. Now, the bank'll be open soon, so why don't you tell me where you hid that combination?"

Jessica sucked in a quick breath as everything began to make sense. Lou must have had the bank safe combination in his possession when he was shot.

She slid a glance at Truman, wondering what he was going to do next, when all of a sudden, he grabbed her by the elbow and roughly pulled her closer.

"You're gonna have to ask the lady," he said. "She hasn't told me yet, and I've been romancing her night and day. Maybe you can kiss better than I can."

Jessica gasped in horror, struggling. "Truman!"

His fingers bit into her flesh.

Corey smiled and took a step forward. "A kiss sounds good."

Light from the lantern swept across his stubbly face, deepening the shadows under his craggy features. Jessica could smell him now—the stale odor of his filthy body, the fetid stink of his breath. She shrank back in disgust.

Corey puckered and stepped forward. "No!" she screamed, struggling and hoping that Truman would not let it happen. She wanted to follow his lead, but she was also certain that at any moment, she was going to fight this.

All at once, Truman let go of her, punched Corey in the face and kicked him off his feet. He fell against the stone wall, hit his head, and collapsed to the ground with a tremendous thud.

Dropping to his knees, Truman seized his gun and checked it for bullets. He clicked it shut, grabbed Jessica's hand, and without another word led the way up the stairs.

"You were going to let him kiss me!" she pointed out, none too pleased about it either.

"No, I wasn't."

"Yes, you were! He was only inches away!"

Truman stopped at the top of the stairs and looked around at the small, deserted house. "Just be glad, love, that he was so slow on the draw."

They ran outside to the barn. Finding Thunder still saddled from the night before, they mounted together and galloped up the road toward town.

*Three hours later*

Eating breakfast with Angus did little to calm Jessica's fears. Consuming an entire pot of coffee didn't help matters either. Her mind became a stampede of disoriented worst case scenarios, while she explained everything to Angus and waited for Truman to return. He had ridden off to fetch Dempsey and arrest the gang, who had spent the night at Rosalie's whorehouse.

She'd have to get used to worrying, she supposed, as she rolled up her sleeves to wash the dishes. It wasn't easy loving a lawman – in this century or any other.

She pressed down on the pump handle and rinsed the plates with the cold water that gushed out and splashed onto her shirt.

While she stared at the sparkling drops, an agonizing question nagged in her brain. She and Truman were from different worlds, and she still hadn't told him where she came from. When he learned the truth, would he even believe her? Would he think she was insane or lying to him again for some reason?

If she did end up staying here, she certainly wasn't going to stay home and embroider all day. She'd want to start up a business, and maybe a running club. Or she could become an inventor and strike it rich with everything she knew about industry and technology. At the very least, she would open a pizza shop with delivery. She really missed pizza—with extra cheese and pepperoni and bacon and hamburger.

Once she laid the dishes out on the counter to dry, she went into the parlor to see Angus. He was reading by the window with a silver pistol resting on the cushion beside him. Jessica stared numbly at the weapon. When had she become so indifferent to guns and bullets, and even death? Did life mean so little here?

They both looked up when they heard hoof beats approaching. Angus reached for the pistol while Jessica pushed the white lace curtain aside with one finger, but relaxed when she discovered their unexpected guest was Deputy Dempsey.

Please, let Truman be safe.

She watched Dempsey hop off the horse, tie the reins to the front railing, and dig into a saddlebag. She stayed indoors while Angus walked onto the covered porch.

"Deputy Dempsey, I hope things are well?"

Dempsey removed his hat and climbed the steps. "Couldn't be better. The gang's behind bars, and we've notified the bank about the stolen combination to the safe. We'll be following up on that in the next few days."

Jessica, hearing the good news, exhaled a long-held breath. She walked out to the porch. "Is Truman all right?"

"He's fine. Looking pretty black and blue, though. The doctor's checking him over now. I brought this for you." Dempsey held out her satchel. "It was in the Russells' barn."

Jessica reached out and took it from him. She looked inside to find her red shoes still tucked beneath her gowns.

"I just thought I'd come out here and let you know," he added. "Sheriff Wade said he was gonna do everything in his power to make sure the people of Dodge learn to forget those rumors about Junebug Jess. He said he knows there ain't no such person, and he wants you to feel that you can stay in town if you want to." He tipped his hat. "Well, I better be getting on my way." Turning, he stomped down the steps, mounted his horse, and galloped away.

Jessica stared after him.

Angus laid a hand on her shoulder. "Looks like somebody wants you to stay in this century."

Strangely, however—despite everything Jessica had gone through with Truman, and no matter how desperately she longed to be with him—something deep inside her told her that this was not where she belonged.

The heels of Jessica's shoes clicked along the dry, boarded sidewalk while a familiar cow-scented breeze blew into her face and whipped up a torrent of light dust in the street. It whirled in a circle, and then settled down just as a horse-drawn wagon rolled by and stirred it into a pirouette again.

When she reached Zimmerman's Hardware Store, Jessica looked through the window, wondering if the storeowner had sold her necklace yet. Not that it mattered. Liam was long forgotten. Their relationship had been as fake as its stone. She was better off without the necklace, so she started down the boardwalk again.

She stopped a second time, however, when another thought struck her. That necklace was a piece of the future. Something told her she should have it. She turned back toward Zimmerman's and nearly collided with a dog who must have been following her.

There, gazing up at her with big brown eyes and an eager panting smile, was a white Jack Russell terrier very similar to George, her dog back home.

A pain squeezed her heart as she remembered how George used to sit on the floor between her legs to wait for supper while she would stand with her feet braced apart, opening a can of something. God, she missed him. She hoped her parents were taking good care of him.

She knelt down and scratched behind the dog's ears. "Hi there, cutie. Where did you come from? You look just like my dog back home."

"Hello." Those familiar black boots stepped into her range of vision.

Jessica immediately stood. She hadn't seen Truman since they parted after escaping the gang's hideout, and for some reason, there was a strange awkwardness between them now. "Hi."

Just then, the dog nudged his nose under her skirts and sat down between her feet.

"This a friend of yours?" Truman asked, looking down.

Jessica laughed. "No, I've never seen him before, but this is exactly what my dog does." She lifted her skirts to let him out from under her petticoat and knelt down again to pat his head. "Does he belong to anyone?"

"Yeah, the Peterson's. His name is Leo."

Jessica continued to ruffle Leo's ears while he licked her chin. "Too bad, because I would have loved to take him home with me."

A young boy called out from across the street. "Leo! Come on! We gotta go!"

Leo looked at Jessica and hesitated.

"Go on," she said, waving a hand as she rose to her feet. "He's calling you."

Only then did the dog dash off toward the Peterson boy.

For a long moment, she watched them run together down the boardwalk and felt a deep ache of longing in her chest.

"Care for some company?" Truman asked. "I'd like to walk you home."

"That would be nice," she replied, "but I need to go into Zimmerman's. Will you come in? I'll just be a minute."

"Sure." He opened the door for her, and the bells jingled.

Jessica walked in and approached the clerk at the counter while Truman waited at the window, watching the street.

"Can I help you?" the clerk asked.

"Yes. Do you still have that necklace I sold you?"

"The diamond? Yes, just a minute." He went out back, and returned after a few seconds. "Here it is."

She admired the large sparkling stone, which dangled from his fingers like a pendulum.

"I was thinking of making it into a ring," the clerk mentioned.

Jessica cleared her throat. "How much are you asking for it right now as a necklace?"

"Forty dollars."

"But it's not a real diamond."

"Looks real to me."

She dug into her purse, counting what she had. "Would you take thirty-eight?"

"It's forty dollars."

"I see." She paused a moment, thinking about the irony of it—that Liam probably hadn't paid much more than that for it back in the twenty-first century.

The merchant seemed to be waiting for her to agree to the price, but unfortunately, she didn't have enough money with her. The rest of her reward was at Angus's house. "Could you hold it for me? I'd like it just as it is."

"I suppose I could do that. Only a couple of days, though."

"Thank you." She moved toward Truman who was watching her with curious eyes.

"Ready?" he asked.

"Yes."

He opened the door, nodded a thank you to the clerk, and escorted her out. As they stepped onto the boardwalk, a voice called out from a few doors down. "Hey, Junebug!"

Truman and Jessica stopped and turned.

"I'd watch out for that sheriff if I were you!" It was Virgil Norton and his gang of rowdies. "He ain't gentle like I am!" They roared with laughter from a bench outside the Long Branch Saloon.

"That man," she said, irritably, "lacks refinement."

"Just ignore him," Truman drawled. "He's drunk, and he's more gurgle than guts." He placed a protective hand on her arm and guided her away. The other hand rested on his gun.

She and Truman walked past the storefronts and saloons until they came to the end of the boardwalk and stepped into the dusty street.

"Careful," Truman cautioned, as he guided her around fresh evidence that this was a cow town.

"Thank you." She had become quite adept at spotting these things, but today, her mind was elsewhere. It was time, she knew, to tell Truman the truth about where she came from. If she ever expected to feel genuinely close to him, to end this persistent awkwardness, there could be no more secrets. He needed to understand why she talked the way she did, and why she had very modern ideas about feminist issues.

Truman's spurs chinked as four chickens ran past them. "Must be a fire in the coop," he commented.

When they reached Angus's house, they stopped at the front gate. "Would you take a walk with me out onto the prairie tomorrow?" she asked, feeling nervous about the whole thing. "I think it's time we spent some time together and had a talk – about that secret of mine."

Truman eyed her speculatively. "I was wondering when you'd ask. I figured you'd be ready to tell me, eventually."

Jessica looked down at her feet.

"I'll come by around noon," he said.

He left her there at the gate, and she wondered uneasily if this would turn out to be a mistake. Maybe she would be wiser to keep her extraordinary secret to herself and just try to fit in.

But no. She couldn't live like that.

She had to tell him.

The following day, Jessica stood in front of the mirror in her bedroom, gliding a brush down the length of her hair, wondering how Truman was going to react when she told him where she came from.

What would he think about microwave ovens, movies, and space travel. Would he even believe it? And what if she were able to find a way home? If she could take him with her, would he come?

She was imagining all that when the sound of hoof beats approached the house. A moment later, a knock sounded at the front door.

"Jessica!" Angus called up the stairs. "Sheriff Wade is here to see you!"

A thrill moved through her. Taking one last look in the mirror, she quickly twisted her hair up into a knot on top of her head, pinned it and tucked the stray locks in as best she could. She smoothed out her dress, picked up her purse, and headed downstairs.

When she reached the parlor and her gaze fell upon Truman standing in front of the fireplace, she could go no further. Their eyes met and locked, and her heart turned over in her chest.

Before she entered the room, Angus donned his hat and told them he was heading into town to run a few errands, but Jessica knew he was simply giving them some time to be alone.

"Good morning," Truman said after the door swung shut behind Angus.

"Good morning." She strode into the room. "Do you want to sit down?"

Truman hesitated. He turned his hat over in his hands. His voice was heavy with what sounded like an apology, and Jessica felt a sudden twinge of discomfort.

"I'm afraid this isn't a social call," he told her.

"But I thought we were going to spend the day together."

He shook his head. "Not today."

Her stomach began to churn with a sinking dread. "Why not?"

"Because Virgil Norton was murdered last night."

"What!" Jessica exclaimed, her heart suddenly racing. They had seen Virgil only yesterday. "How? What happened?"

"That's what I'd like to know. I came to ask you where you were last night. Some time after eleven."

Her mind refused to register what he was implying. "You can't possibly think...."

"I don't think anything," he replied. "Just answer me."

She sat down. "I was here, sleeping. You don't seriously think I did it."

"Did you?" he asked.

"Of course not!"

He looked down at his boots, as if he didn't know what to believe. "I had to ask," he said coolly. "I'm the sheriff, and it's my job."

Jessica could feel her mood veering sharply to anger. "I thought you knew me better than that by now."

He gave no reply, and she noticed the muscle at his jaw was twitching. "I'm sorry, Jessica," he said, "but you're going to have to come with me."

She scoffed in disbelief. "What are you saying?"

"Just until we get everything straightened out. It's for your own protection."

"My protection? Why?"

He hesitated, his eyebrows pulling together in frustration. "Because if I don't bring you in, I might have a riot on my hands. There was another article in the paper this morning, and it said there was a witness who saw you do it. The folks of Dodge won't stand for any more of this. I just can't guarantee your safety."

She massaged her temples with two fingertips. "But I didn't do it. You can't lock me up because of a sensational story in a newspaper, just to keep people happy. It's not right. And who is the witness?"

"We don't know yet. That information wasn't printed in the paper, but we're working on it. That's why I need to take you in. Until I find out who killed Virgil, you're the only suspect, and I can't even prove you're who you say you are."

Jessica was tempted to spill everything out there and then, but she resisted the urge because he'd never believe it – not under these circumstances. He'd think she was crazy, and it would only make her appear guiltier.

"I was going to explain everything to you today," she said, "but I doubt you'd even believe it now."

"It doesn't matter what I believe," he replied. "It only matters that you come with me now, because if you don't, you might have to face a lynch mob – and that's the last thing I want. You should know that better than anyone."

He didn't say the words, but when she looked into his tormented eyes, she understood his meaning. He had already lost a wife. He didn't want to lose her, too.

Rising to her feet, she wrapped her arms around his neck and whispered, "Then I'll go peacefully."

He held her for a long moment, and she was astonished by the euphoria she felt, knowing that he cared for her so deeply.

It wasn't until much later—when he locked her up in the jail cell to be guarded by Dempsey—that she experienced an almost crushing urge to escape from this place and return to her own time.

# Chapter Twenty-Two

The jail cell was humid and hot. It smelled of heavy sweat and alcohol left over from the burping, hungover cowboy that Dempsey had recently let go. Sitting on the cot and feeling itchy beneath her ridiculous corset – a truly perverse instrument of torture—Jessica wondered what was going to happen next.

A number of times she asked to see Angus, but was told no one could find him, and as the day progressed, she grew increasingly worried.

It was dark when Truman finally returned to the law office. "You can go now," he said to Dempsey. "But keep an eye on things in the streets. Make sure your gun is loaded."

They both glanced at Jessica. Truman's eyes were frigid, icy blue.

The young deputy stood and headed for the door. "You can rest easy, Sheriff. I won't put up with any shenanigans. See you in the morning."

Truman walked to his desk, never meeting Jessica's gaze. His cool indifference made her wonder if he had somehow grown to detest her in this one, short, traumatic day.

He paused in front of his desk with his hands on his hips, as if thinking. For a tense moment, he stared down at all the papers and writing utensils on the desktop. Then he leaned forward in a sudden fit of rage and swept everything onto the floor. The jar of pens and the inkwell went flying. They crashed into the wall and flew everywhere.

Heart suddenly racing, Jessica rushed forward to the cell door.

His dangerous eyes focused in on her. Then he approached her and gripped the bars. "God, Jessica," he whispered, closing his eyes.

The agony in his voice caught her by surprise, and a wave of apprehension coursed through her. "Tell me what happened."

When he looked up, the dark rage was gone, but deep lines of regret were creasing his forehead. "Folks in town want to hang you."

Jessica backed away. "You're not serious."

"I won't let them do it."

"How can you stop it? If a judge says—"

"It won't come to that. I'll take you away before it does."

"You'd help me escape?" she asked, not sure she'd heard him correctly. "And you'd come with me?"

He didn't nod or say yes, but his eyes answered the question.

"But I'm innocent," she insisted. "Angus will help me prove it in court. Have you found him yet?"

He reached a hand through the bars and touched her cheek. "No. He's been missing all afternoon. But it doesn't matter. I'm going to get you out of this. No matter what it takes."

The words came to her in a light whisper, and she closed her eyes, almost drowning in relief. He did trust her. Even without knowing her secret, he knew she would never kill a man.

He drew her into his arms and pressed his mouth to hers. Jessica leaned into the cell door, savoring the velvet warmth of his kiss, barely able to believe she could feel so happy when her whole world was falling to pieces around her.

Truman pulled away and went to lock the front door, then returned with the jingling keys. He let her out of the jail cell, swept her into his arms, and carried her to the stairs.

Taking two steps at a time to the top, he kicked his bedroom door open with his boot and set her down on the floor.

Jessica, her mind swimming, backed all the way inside and hit the bed. "Thank God, Truman. I couldn't bear to be away from you another minute."

He unbuckled his gun belt and tossed it to the floor, then took off his shirt to reveal the most magnificent naked chest she'd ever seen in her life, and strode toward her. He cupped her face in his hands and kissed her deeply.

Jessica ran her palms over his deliciously smooth, contoured chest and down to the rippled muscles of his stomach. He flinched, but a faint murmur of encouragement prompted her to continue. He kissed her again, his hands roaming urgently over her dress.

All she knew in that moment was a need to feel his skin next to hers, a need to feel his lips and hot breath caressing her.

He unfastened her bodice and slid it off her shoulders. His lips were demanding, and his tongue probed her mouth in a slow, intoxicating rhythm.

Truman unbuttoned the top of her skirt and petticoats and let them fall gracefully to the floor at their feet. His fingers touched her corset, and he stepped back, leaving Jessica wobbling with impatient desire. Focusing closely on the task, he unhooked each hook. Soon, the tightness gave way, and she could breathe again. At last. The corset dropped to the floor, landing quietly on top of the skirts.

His arms came around to massage her back in a tight embrace, his breath moist against her neck and shoulder.

Flames of impatience licked within her. Truman guided her gently onto the bed. She sank into the soft, feather mattress, then inched back toward the pillows. Truman came upon her, moving. His hand wandered down her side, over her hips and to her leg, still covered by the cotton drawers.

"Take these off," he whispered.

She eagerly untied the ribbon at her waist, delighting in the cool air dancing across her skin, as Truman slid the drawers down her legs, then slowly rolled each stocking from her uplifted knees, dropping open-mouthed kisses down her thighs and calves. A deep, sensual ache enthralled her—a need to feel him inside her, to feel the sudden, shocking pleasure of his entry. "Please," she murmured.

Truman rolled away from her, kicked off his boots, and removed his trousers. Soon, as if in a dream, he was upon her.

"I can't wait anymore," he said.

She groaned as he filled her. All sense of time and place left her, and she could barely remember anything of her life before this exquisite moment. All she knew was the glorious feel of Truman driving into her again and again. Her former existence was consumed by the pleasure that rolled over her.

Together they reached an explosive climax and released everything to each other. He shuddered in her arms. She arched her back and drew in a deep breath.

In that wild, raging moment, Jessica knew that she would never—in all this peculiar, entangled eternity—be able to leave him. Nothing could take her away from him now. She belonged to him. This was meant to be.

She understood it now.

It's why she was sent here.


Later, still wrapped in each other's arms, Jessica and Truman resisted sleep. Outside, distant saloon pianos played over the faint laughter and rowdy hollering from the street. Closer to their window, crickets chirped in the darkness, smothering the cruel realities that faced them.

"What's going to happen next?" Jessica asked, as she rested her cheek on his shoulder.

"Everything will be fine," he whispered.

"You always say that."

"I've been right so far, haven't I?"

A quiet moment passed as Truman's thumb brushed over her shoulder, back and forth...until she felt almost hypnotized by it.

Yet still, that relentless ache in her chest persisted—the ache that came from wanting two different things at the same time. Now that she had surrendered to the love she felt for Truman, she would have to accept, once and for all, that she would never see her family again, or her dog, George. Her life in the twenty-first century was lost to her now, and she couldn't help but grieve for it.

Nevertheless, she couldn't imagine leaving this new life behind—most important...this love she'd found. Or rather, the love that had found her.

She never dreamed she could feel so close to anyone, that she could love a flesh and blood man with more than just her heart and body. They were connected somehow in a soulful, profound way, and the connection was beyond physical. It was not something she could touch or feel, yet it was very real. More real than anything she'd ever known back home. The depth of her love for Truman Wade ran too deep to even understand.

If only she could live two parallel lives.

If only she had all the answers and knew what was happening right now, at this very moment, in the future. What had become of her life there?

Did her parents believe she was dead?

"Truman?"

"Mmm?"

She rolled on top of him, laced her fingers together on his chest, and rested her chin on top of them.

He threw an arm up under his head like a pillow. "You look like you want to tell me something, and I really hope that's the case, because I've been waiting a long time."

"I do. I've wanted to tell you this since the first night we met, but I was too afraid."

"Afraid of what?"

She rubbed a finger over the smooth, warm surface of his chest. "That you wouldn't believe me. Or that you'd think I was crazy."

"I'd never think that."

She tried to smile, to make light of this, but it was impossible. "You might change your mind about that after you've heard what I'm about to say."

He frowned with some concern.

Lord. This was harder than she thought it would be.

"It's about where I come from," she said at last.

"Whatever it is, it can't possibly be any worse than the things I've told you."

"It's not like that," she said. "It's not something I've done. It's something I had no control over, and....well....brace yourself."

"I'm braced."

She leaned forward to kiss him. His lips were soft and moist. As she withdrew, he put his arm around her and coaxed her to lie beside him. His warm hand swept the locks of her hair across her shoulder.

Preparing herself for his shocked response, Jessica drew in a deep breath, and finally confessed the truth.

"I'm from the future."

# Chapter Twenty-Three

From where Jessica lay with her cheek on Truman's chest, he did not seem shocked. But of course, he was a cool-headed gunslinger.

Alert to any reaction, she waited nervously, but observed only that he continued to breathe at the same pace he'd been breathing before she'd dropped the bomb. His heart, which beat inside him directly below her ear, did not quicken. He simply lay there, twirling his index finger around a lock of her hair, staring at the ceiling.

"I traveled through time to get here," she continued, when she felt ready to reveal more.

Still, he failed to react as she imagined he would.

Bewildered, she began to ramble. "I was born in 1981. In Missouri. I don't know what happened to get me here, but here I am."

His hand stopped moving through her hair. At last he said, "I don't understand what you're saying."

"I don't understand it either." Jessica rolled off him and sat up. "When I came here—it was the night Lou was killed—I was driving to my mother's house." She glanced down at him. "I was driving in an automobile. You don't have them here. They're like wagons without horses, but they go much faster and run on gasoline. I was traveling at a speed of sixty miles an hour. It's very fast. You'd really like it."

His eyebrows lifted.

"The road was wet, and I hydroplaned and flipped my car. I'm not sure how it happened, but lightning struck, then suddenly I was here. I have no explanation for it. I certainly didn't know anything like this was possible. Not even in the future."

Truman held her hand. "Jessica, I really want to believe what you're telling me—"

"I know it seems impossible. I couldn't believe it myself at first, but you have to trust me. I'm not making this up."

"I do trust you, but—"

"No buts." She squeezed his hand. "Think back to that first night."

Truman said nothing for a moment or two. Then he sat up beside her. "I remember you were confused and disoriented. You talked about walking from a car wreck. I thought you meant a train."

"No. It was red hatchback."

His eyebrows pulled together in a frown. "And the things you wear under your trousers..."

"Panties."

"And that...zipper thing."

"All from the future. But there's so much more."

He looked at the window, opened his mouth to say something, but didn't.

Jessica said a silent prayer that he would believe her. If he didn't....

She simply couldn't bear to think about that. She needed him in her life here. He was her rock in this century. Her only anchor.

His expression stilled and grew serious. "It's the craziest story I've ever heard."

"I know."

He scratched his head. "Time travel...."

"Yes."

"It sounds insane."

"I know, but it's true. How can I prove it to you?" She paused, staring. "Look. See how perfect my teeth are...how straight they are?"

"They're very nice."

"Thousands of dollars to straighten them. Imagine that, will you? Braces."

"Never heard of them."

"That's because they're not invented yet. We also have cell phones — little communication devices that people carry around everywhere. Some people carry their BlackBerries in a holster like yours, but it's a phone, not a gun. We can take our phones anywhere, and punch in a number and call someone, or text a message to them, like a letter that gets delivered that second. And medicine... I wouldn't even know where to begin. Surgery has come a long way, let me tell you. People are going under the knife to get their noses changed or their double chins removed. They call it a facelift. And there's air travel, too. You wouldn't believe it."

He stared at her, and the amusement in his eyes faded away.

Jessica said nothing more. She waited uneasily, watching as everything settled into his mind.

Maybe she shouldn't have mentioned the face lifts.

"It almost makes sense," he said.

She regarded him with hopeful surprise. "It does?"

"Yes. I knew you were odd, and I haven't been able to find you in any town records. I put the word out everywhere. No one has ever heard of you."

"That's because I never existed before the night Lou was killed." Jessica sat nervously, watching his expression change as he stared at her.

He sat up abruptly and pulled her into his arms. After a moment, he drew back and looked her in the eye. "Will you be going back there?"

"You believe me?"

He blinked slowly, his gaze uncertain. "I don't know." He paused. "That day, out on the prairie...."

"I was trying to find a way home," she explained. "I thought if I spun around very quickly...but it didn't work."

He sat in silence. Jessica knew he was remembering everything he'd ever seen her do or say, and he was putting the pieces together.

"You still haven't answered my question," he said, leaning back with both arms propped behind him.

Jessica combed her fingers through her hair. "Even if I wanted to go home, I don't know how to get there. I've been trying to figure it out, but I don't even understand how this happened in the first place. If I knew, I might be able to duplicate it."

"I don't want to lose you."

She looked into the blue depths of his eyes. "I don't want to lose you either."

They shifted onto the blankets, Jessica on her back and Truman leaning down.

"I haven't always said the right thing," he told her. "I didn't trust you when I should have. I kept things from you about Dorothy and what really happened, but I trust you now. You're in my blood."

Jessica kissed his soft lips, and soon the urgency of the kiss mounted.

"Stay," he whispered into her hair. "Don't go back."

Jessica squeezed him. "I wanted to go back before, but now I'd rather die than leave you."

He pulled her roughly, almost violently to him.

"But what are we going to do about Virgil's murder? What if the judge sentences me to hang?"

"We'll leave Dodge."

She swallowed, nervously. "We'd be outlaws."

"Yeah, but we'd be alive—and together."

Jessica considered that, hesitating before she made any suggestions that could change the course of their future.

"Wouldn't it be better," she asked, "to locate Angus and get him to defend me and try to find the real killer? I didn't do anything wrong. There's no real evidence against me, other than that newspaper article which is all lies. It's just because I have a reputation. That's why people believe I did it, but that won't hold up in court."

Truman ran a hand over her shoulder and down the length of her arm. "We need to find out who provided the information for the articles."

Jessica nodded. "Yes, but I asked Mr. Gordon about it when the first article came out. He said he wouldn't reveal his sources."

Truman kissed the hollow at the base of her throat. "I'll ask him about it in the morning."

She squirmed with pleasure and moaned softly with ecstasy as he rolled on top of her and began to lay scintillating kisses down the side of her neck. "And what makes you think he'll tell you?"

"What makes me think that?" Truman's head drew back with surprise, then he smiled a wicked grin. "How about the overwhelming size and thrust of my six-shooter?"

It was enough to bring a swift end to the discussion.


The morning sun poured through the jailhouse window, landing a decorative square of light on Truman's paper-strewn desk. Outside, a small herd of cows was driving by, their clamoring hooves and constant moo's a distraction for Jessica, who was walking into the jail cell again. Truman guided her in, then swung the cell door shut on its squeaky hinges until it came to a final, clanging close.

"If anyone comes in here today," he said, "tell them I guarded you all night. Act like you know nothing about the hanging." He turned the key, and it clicked. "I'm sorry to have to do this."

"It's necessary. I'll be fine."

"I'll bring you some breakfast, then I'll try to find Angus. I'll also head over to the newspaper office to talk to Gordon. If I can't learn anything or get a retraction, we'll leave here tonight."

She reached through the bars to take hold of his hands. "I trust you."

"I'll be back soon." He kissed her one more time, and left.

When the door closed behind him, Jessica sank onto the crackly straw mattress on the cot, tipped her head back against the wall, and stared at the cobwebs near the ceiling.

A short while later, the front door opened, and Jessica leapt to her feet.

Angus, appearing out of breath, walked straight in. "Jessica?"

She hurried to the bars. "Oh, thank God! Angus! Where were you? I'm so glad you're back. You wouldn't believe what's happened."

"I know all about it," he said. "Where's Sheriff Wade?"

"He's gone for breakfast. What have you been doing? You look like you know something."

He crossed the room and stopped in front of the bars. His brown eyes sparkled with excitement. "I have wonderful news. I've figured out how to get home."

Jessica took an abrupt step back. "What do you mean?"

Angus reached into his pocket, searching for something. "It's this. It's as good as any plane or train ticket."

Jessica stood staring, her heart racing like a runaway wagon. With trembling fingers, she reached out to touch the shiny object in his hand. "You found my watch," she said.

"Yes. Isn't it amazing?"

To see this golden object that had once been a part of her old life, sent a prickle up her spine. "But what does this have to do with anything?"

"I'll tell you." He reached into his pocket and dug around some more. "I finally found my belongings from the twenty-first century, and I remembered my watch was missing, too, just like yours had been. So I went to the place on the prairie, where I traveled through time, and searched for a while, and there it was—in the grass." He held out his own watch. "I searched further, and I found yours, too, only a few feet away."

"Mine is still ticking," she said, holding it up to her ear.

"Yes, but look at the date."

"July 19th, 2011. That's a month after the day of my accident."

"Yes. It's incredible isn't it? It's a piece of the future, the only thing we have that connects us to it. According to this, time in the future is still rolling along, parallel to our existence here."

"But how will this get me back?" she asked.

"This may sound far-fetched to you—"

"Believe me, nothing at this point will sound far-fetched."

He nodded knowingly. "After I found our watches, I walked around on the prairie for a while until I stepped on a piece of ground that looked like it was wet, but it wasn't wet at all. There was a glimmer on the grass, almost like dew, and when I stood on it, I felt a tingling sensation all over."

Jessica felt her eyes widen. "What happened? Did you pass through a tunnel or something? Is that where you were? Did you go home and come back for me?"

"No, nothing quite so dramatic as that. It was nothing more than the tingling. So I marked the spot and went home to think about everything. I tried to remember what happened when I passed through the tunnel the first time ten years ago."

"And?"

"I was driving, just like you, and lightning struck the car as I drove over that spot on the highway. Time seemed to stand still for that instant while the car was sizzling with light. Then I began to spin through the tunnel. At the far end, I could see brown prairie grass, and I felt like I was going to crash into it. But before I came out of the tunnel, my watch came off. It didn't rip off either. It just came unclasped, almost gracefully. I watched it float along beside me, and then I thought: 'I can't lose my watch. I have an appointment.' But then I fell out of the tunnel and landed on the prairie—in 1878."

Jessica shook her head skeptically. "I still don't understand how this can get us home."

"I'm not finished explaining. As I said, I went home to think about everything and wondered what would happen if I stood in that spot again, dressed as I was ten years ago— with everything I had in my possession when I traveled through time. I put on my suit—and believe me, it wasn't easy to get into. I've put on a few pounds."

Jessica waved her hand. "Continue…"

"Yes, yes… So I put everything on and went and stood in that spot, but again, nothing happened, except for the tingling sensation, until I looked at my watch and realized it had stopped ticking years ago. The battery had run out. So I reset it for the correct date, ten years later, which took a few tries. I wasn't sure exactly what the date would be—but when I found it, I was sucked up into some kind of vortex."

"You're full of it!"

"No."

"But why are you still here? Didn't it work?"

Angus sighed heavily. "It would have, I believe, if I'd let it. But I panicked. All I could think about was Wendy."

Jessica paused. "You changed your mind?"

"Yes. I ripped the watch off and flung it away, and the next thing I knew, I was lying on the prairie again, staring up at the sky. Here in 1881, feeling very relieved."

Jessica squeezed the bars. "I have to sit down." She moved to the cot and sank onto the mattress.

"Are you all right?" Angus asked.

"I'm fine."

But that was a lie. Until this moment, she felt she had no choice about remaining here in the nineteenth century. It was easy to choose Truman. The fact that she loved him made it simple.

But suddenly it wasn't so simple anymore. She did have a choice. Did she want her old life back? To see her parents again? Her friends, her dog? To have indoor plumbing and cell phones and the miracles of modern medicine?

Or did she want Truman, and life as a renegade outlaw?

"Will you go back?" Angus asked.

Jessica thought about it. "What if I try, and I end up in the wrong time? There would be no point to that. No point at all."

"I'm sure your date of arrival is right here." He pointed at the watch.

Jessica stared at it, ticking away as if it really were July 19, 2011.

"Jessica...."

She looked up.

"Do you know what might happen to you if you stay here?"

She gazed back down at the watch. Her stomach began to lurch and roll. "Yes, but we could defend me in court. You're a lawyer."

"But things are different here. There's a reason they call it the Wild West. There's a lawlessness here that you just don't understand. I really think you should leave. As soon as possible."

"What if I don't want to go back?"

He shook his head at her. "But it was all you ever talked about. What about your family?"

God, she felt so disloyal to them right now. "Angus, I've found something here that I just can't leave behind."

He breathed deeply. "I see, and I understand."

"I can't leave him."

"Does he know where you come from?"

She nodded.

"Did you tell him about me, too?"

"No."

The door opened just then. Truman walked in with breakfast, but stopped abruptly when he saw Angus. "Morning. Good to see you back."

Jessica took one look at him—so darkly handsome in the doorway, with his black hat and long slicker, his steel badge and leather gun belt. Sensual memories of the night before flooded her mind and body, and she wondered how it was possible to desire someone as much as she desired Truman. What in the world was she going to do?

"I brought breakfast," Truman announced. He noticed Jessica's panicked expression and knew immediately that something was afoot. "Care to join us, Angus?"

Jessica gave Angus a pleading look that seemed almost desperate.

"That would be delightful," he replied.

Truman set the crate on the desk and removed a pot of hot coffee, a bowl of eggs, and some cornbread. "Compliments of Dodge House."

He served Jessica first, and took her plate into the jail cell. She gave him a polite, yet distracted smile that didn't help to ease his suspicions that something was amiss.

The three of them ate and made small talk. When they finished, Jessica brought up the subject of her arrest.

"Is there any way you can help us, Angus?" she asked. "You know I didn't kill Virgil. There's no concrete evidence."

He wiped his mouth with a cloth napkin. "What have you found out about it, Truman?"

"To be quite honest, sir, it doesn't look good."

"Why is that?"

"Virgil was shot between the eyes, just like Lou. And after that article in the paper about Jessica, and the fact that she accepted the reward for Lou's death—"

"But I didn't kill him. We all know that. Someone else did. I assumed they'd come forward for the money, but they didn't. I only took it because I had none. And then, when Lou's gang showed up, I was too busy worrying about what it was that they wanted."

"Which was?" Angus asked.

"They wanted the combination to the bank safe, which I knew nothing about." She took another sip of coffee.

Truman leaned back in his chair. "Jessica and I think there might be something to those articles in the paper. Henry Gordon was pretty secretive about it."

"I'll tell you what," Angus said. "I'll pay Jessica's bail today to get her out of here. Then you two can see what you can find out."

"Angus, would you really do that for us?"

He leaned forward and placed his hand on hers. "Of course. If things don't go well, I don't want you to be locked up in here."

Jessica shook her head at him. Truman caught the exchange, witnessed the torn expression on her face, but said nothing. In light of what she told him last night, he thought it best to wait until he could talk to her alone.

Finally, Angus made a move to leave. "Truman, you should come with me. We'll head over to see the judge right now. He's a reasonable fellow, and he respects me. I'll tell him Jessica will be staying at my house. I'm sure it won't be a problem."

Truman rose and shook Angus's hand. "Thank you, sir."

"My pleasure." He turned and kissed Jessica on the forehead, then left the office to wait for Truman outside.

Truman turned to face Jessica. "What's going on?" he asked.

"Nothing," she replied too quickly. "Everything's fine."

Truman hooked a thumb through his gun belt. It wasn't his style to feel this uncertain. Hell, it wasn't his style to feel much of anything at all. "You'll be here when I get back?"

"Of course. We'll talk then."

"It sounds important."

"It is, but Angus is waiting. You should go."

He stared at those moist ruby lips and wondered what she wanted to discuss, and hoped it wasn't going to be something he didn't want to hear.

He stroked a loose tendril of hair away from her face. "I have a bad feeling today."

"What kind of bad feeling?" she asked.

"I don't know. I can't explain it. I just feel like things are going to take a turn, and not for the better."

She backed away from him. "Are you afraid I'll hang?"

He gazed into her eyes for a long moment, then shook his head. "I can't say for sure. I don't know why, but I feel like we're going to be separated."

Jessica rested her palms on his chest. "I don't ever want to be separated from you," she told him. "I promised I'd stay here, and that's what I intend to do."

Her words should have eased his mind, but for some reason he couldn't explain, every muscle in his body tightened with apprehension.

# Chapter Twenty-Four

Truman agreed to meet Angus at the county courthouse immediately after he had a word with Henry Gordon, the newspaper editor—but when he reached The Chronicle office, the front door was locked. Wrestling with his growing impatience, he faced the street, thumbed his hat back off his head, leaned a shoulder against a post, and waited.

He thought about Jessica and what she'd told him last night. Perhaps the strangest thing about it was that he believed her, even though it was the most outrageous tale he'd ever heard.

But when he remembered how she was dressed the first time he saw her—with her hair long and loose about her shoulders, wearing red shoes and britches that looked like they were designed to fit a woman's shapely hips, and that bizarre zipper contraption – it all made a strange sort of sense.

Truman shifted his weight to the other foot and glanced up and down the street. Five minutes passed and still no one showed up to open the newspaper office. Unusual for a Tuesday, he thought, as he pushed away from the post. He might as well go and meet Angus, then he'd try Henry Gordon at home.

His spurs chinked as he headed down the boardwalk toward the courthouse.

"Truman!"

He turned to see Angus waving from across the street. Truman waited for a wagon to pass, then headed in that direction.

"I paid the bail," Angus said when the met. "You can let Jessica out, but Judge Whittier wants her to stay in Dodge."

"What if she doesn't stay?" It was half question, half warning. "You'll lose your money."

Angus shrugged. "I won't miss it."

Truman nodded and gave Angus a light slap on the shoulder. "Thank you."

"My pleasure. Here you go." He handed over the bail certificate and leaned in to speak quietly. "I presume you'll take her away?"

Glancing around to make sure no one was listening, Truman nodded.

"Where will you go?" Angus asked.

"Don't rightly know. Somewhere they won't find us. Maybe north. Maybe even as far as Canada."

Angus considered this, then relaxed his shoulders. "With any luck, you won't have to leave town at all. Did you talk to Henry Gordon?"

"Not yet. The newspaper office was locked up tight."

"Did you try his house?"

"That's where I'm heading now."

Angus and Truman walked down First Avenue to the corner, then stepped onto the boardwalk in front of Kelley's Opera House. A pack of hounds tore by, barking all the way, stirring up a cloud of dust.

"How well do you know Jessica?" Truman asked, wondering how much Angus knew about what was really going on.

"Quite well," he replied. "Why do you ask?"

Truman paused. "Do you know where she comes from?"

Angus stopped on the boardwalk. "Yes, as a matter of fact, I do." He lowered his voice. "I understand she told you."

Two ladies carrying parasols walked by, and Truman tipped his hat at them. "Nice morning," he said casually.

As soon as they passed, he continued. "She told me everything. Kind of hard to believe, don't you think?"

"Yes, it most certainly is."

"Do you believe her?"

Angus hesitated. "Do you?"

Truman hesitated for a moment as he thought about it. "I love her, Angus. So I guess that means I'll believe just about anything she tells me."

Angus smiled and laid a hand on his shoulder. "Good. Because it's true. Every last word."

They started walking again.

"Has she talked to you about her family?" Truman asked.

"Yes. At first, it was all she talked about—getting home to them—but as time moved on, she spoke of them less and less, and began to talk of other things. You, for one."

Truman looped both thumbs through his gun belt. "Will she be happy here, do you think?"

"Two weeks ago, I would have said no. She was determined to get home, no matter what it took, but now I believe she wants to stay. Even though we finally know how to get back."

Truman stopped in his tracks. "You know how to get back?"

Angus gazed uncertainly at him. "Oh, dear. Perhaps I shouldn't have said anything."

"She told me there wasn't a way."

"There wasn't, before today, but last night I figured it out. I believe, if we do everything just right, she can go back anytime she wants."

Truman swallowed over the peculiar dread and apprehension that had been eating away at him all morning. He tried to make sense of everything, to understand where he stood in all this.

"Can she travel back and forth?" he asked. "I mean, could she go there, and then come back here? Like, on the stagecoach?"

Angus wrinkled his nose. "I don't think so, not without risking her life. She was lucky to have survived the first time."

Truman's gut began to churn. "Could she take someone with her?"

"I'm not sure. I don't think so. But you could always try."

Truman suspected Angus's was just being polite.

All at once, his mood darkened. He knew the town wanted to hang Jessica. Was it selfish of him to keep her here? To help her break the law, ride out of Dodge, and turn her into an outlaw?

Maybe she was destined to go home. Maybe Angus figured this out yesterday for a reason.

"So, how does it work?" he asked, facing Angus. "How can she get home? I want to know everything."

On the way to the jailhouse, Angus explained it—from the car crash to the missing watch. Truman listened carefully to every word.

"She has to wear exactly what she had on when she arrived?" he asked.

"Yes, I believe so. The watch had been missing, but now we have it. I don't think there's anything stopping her."

Truman turned away, leaving Angus in front of the jailhouse. "Tell Jessica I'll be back soon. There's something I gotta do."

Jessica paced back and forth in the cell, while frantic thoughts bounced around in her head. She surprised herself sometimes. All along, she had dreaded making the decision of whether to stay or return home, but now the answer was clear. The dread was gone. She was going to do what her gut was telling her to do. She was going to stay, no matter what the cost.

Of course, she would always miss her old life and her family especially, but surely in time, it would get easier. At least she had Truman to help her through it.

Moving to the cell door, she rested her chin on one of the bars, and thought about how handsome he was the night before, when the moonlight had shone through the window and illuminated his face.

He filled the empty place in her heart, the place where a little voice had always insisted that something was missing from her life.

She had never been truly happy. She'd always wanted what she didn't have, what was beyond her reach, what was one day ahead. She spent days, week after week, seeking something better, working harder at her job, dreaming of something that would change her life and finally satisfy and her allow her some peace from the little voice.

Even when she thought she was in love with Liam, she wasn't happy. Something had been missing, and she foolishly believed that once they were married, she would stop dreaming and longing for whatever it was that remained so vague in her mind. Now at last, she understood what it was.

Contentment, peace, and fulfillment. Today was a better day. Even with all the danger and uncertainties, she was happier now than she had ever been, and she truly believed that everything would work out for the best. She was innocent of the crimes. The truth would come out.

And Truman loved her.

Just as she closed her eyes to rest for a moment, the front door opened.

"I'm back." Truman stepped into the office and removed his hat. "And I have good news."

"You found out who killed Virgil?"

"Well, not that good." He reached into his pocket and removed a set of keys. Crossing the room toward her, he jingled them. "Angus paid the bail and you're free, at least until the trial. That'll give us some time to do some investigating."

"What about the lynch mob?"

Truman unlocked the door and swung it wide open. Jessica walked out, straight into his arms.

"Don't worry. I'm not letting you out of my sight."

"Thank God," she murmured.

He kissed her deeply, with superb skill and relentless passion, and she came away, dizzy with longing, locked in his gaze, touching her fingertips to his lips.

He laid soft, moist kisses on her palm. "There are things we need to do," he said. "We shouldn't be standing here wasting time."

"You call this wasting time?"

He smiled, and the seduction in his eyes was an exhilarating balm to her senses that left her reeling with desire. "We need to go."

"I'm sure you're right," she breathlessly replied, but she couldn't seem to make her body move in any direction – not when he was dropping hot, sweet, tender kisses up her arm and sending her into a heated pool of sensual yearnings.

"We need to stop this," he said with a devilish grin, "before it gets out of hand…"

A moment later, after no shortage of wicked fits and starts, he led her out the front door of the jailhouse, and locked it behind them.

"We'll start by riding out to Henry Gordon's place," he said, "to ask a few questions."

He freed Thunder from the hitching rail.

They mounted, and Truman sat behind her.

"I get to sit in the saddle this time?" she asked.

"I reckon that's the best thing. That way, I don't lose sight of you."

"You're giving me goose bumps," she said huskily, as his breath tickled her ear.

He turned Thunder toward the edge of town. Soon they were out on the prairie, talking about their plans for escape should it come to that.

Later, the bright sun in Jessica's eyes and the swaying motion of the horse, plodding slowly along, weighed heavily upon her eyelids. She had slept only a few hours the night before, waking every hour or so to make love. She tipped her head back upon Truman's shoulder and closed her eyes.

It was not long before she encountered the sweet sensation of drifting off...into another dreamy existence, where she stood outside a hospital emergency room, peering through a round window, watching a doctor's back as he leaned over an unconscious man.

In her dream, she was home again in a modern and familiar world. Electronic devices beeped and florescent lights hummed. She heard footsteps hurrying behind her and turned to see two nurses approaching.

Jessica moved aside to let them pass. They pushed through the door without acknowledging her—as if she weren't even there—and she watched through the window as the doctor leaned over the patient.

"What are the vitals?" he asked one of the nurses, his back to Jessica.

The nurse wrapped a blood pressure band around the patient's arm and pumped air into it. "One-seventy over eighty."

Another nurse said, "Pulse is ninety-six."

The doctor leaned over the body and lifted the patient's eyelids, one at time, while he shone a penlight into his eyes. "Patient has a blown left pupil."

He paused, staring at the far wall. He reached a hand up and combed it through his hair, as if frustrated.

The nurse walked toward him. "Doctor, are you all right?"

He nodded, but stood motionless, as if he had seen a ghost. "Yes. I need a stat Chemstrip, and order blood work, and start an I.V. right away. Lift the bed so he's sitting up. Get him ready for intubation, and someone call neurosurgery. This guy's gonna have to go to the O.R."

When the doctor moved aside, and the head of the bed slowly lifted and came into view, Jessica sucked in a quick breath.

The man on the bed was Truman.

"Doctor, are you all right?" a nurse asked again.

"I'm fine."

"You don't look fine. You look pale."

From the door, Jessica watched him shake his head, though he still stood with his back to her.

"Something's not right here," he said. "I have a bad feeling. He's not going to make it."

Just then, the doctor turned around and looked directly into Jessica's eyes. Their gazes locked and held through the window. Her whole body began to tingle. It wasn't possible.

The doctor was Truman, too….

She jerked out of her sleep. "Where are we?" she asked, her heart pounding wildly in her chest. She felt Truman's hand on her stomach and said a silent thank you when she discovered they were still on the Kansas prairie.

"We're almost there," he said. "You fell asleep."

"I know." She licked her dry lips. "I dreamed I was back in the future."

"Did you see your family?"

"No. I saw you. Only it wasn't you. You were in a hospital. You were the patient, but you were the doctor, too."

"A doctor? Me? That's comical."

"Why?"

She felt his body heave with a sigh. "Me, saving lives. All I've ever done is take them."

Jessica turned in the saddle. "That's behind you, now. All that matters now is the future. You can be anything you want to be."

He tightened his grip around her stomach, nuzzling the hair at the back of her head. "I love that you have such confidence."

"More than anything." They rode in silence, while Jessica imagined Truman being something different than a lawman. "You could go to school, you know. There's a future in medicine. So much to learn." She turned her cheek to nuzzle his. "I could help you."

Then she realized what she was doing...

Listen to yourself, Jessica. Do you really want to change him? Is that what real love is about?

He smiled. "Let's take one day at a time. First, we need to prove your innocence."

Jessica inhaled deeply. Then she remembered the dream.

Truman, unconscious on the operating table, just like her brother, Gregory....

Thank God it was just a dream, she thought, looking down at the strong hands resting on her stomach.

Touching the rough, sun-bronzed skin, she imagined those hands pulling a trigger to kill a man.

Six men.

A shiver ran through her.

"Will you ever do it again?" she asked.

"Do what?"

"Kill someone."

He was silent for a long moment. "I hope not," he softly replied.

"I wonder about it sometimes," she continued. "It's a side of you I don't know."

She sensed his unease as he gazed across the prairie.

"It's a side of me I hope you don't ever have to see," he said. "I can't erase my past, Jessica. It happened. It's part of who I am." He paused. "Sometimes I...."

A hawk soared above them—a dark, ill-omened figure against the bright blue sky. "Sometimes you what?"

"Sometimes I wish I didn't have a conscience. I wish I didn't feel regret, but it's there in my head, constantly."

Jessica rubbed his hands. "I'm glad. It makes you human."

"It's not something I'm proud of," he continued, "killing those men. Every time I think about it, something inside me aches, like an old wound on a rainy day."

Thunder swung his tail to slap at a fly, and a gust of wind blew Jessica's hair away from her face.

"The first time I killed someone," Truman told her, "I did it for the reward. I was seventeen. After it was done, I sat under a tree and drank half a bottle of rotgut whisky. Then I had to drag a stiff body across the dirt and lift him onto my horse."

Jessica squeezed his hand tighter.

"I didn't sober up for days," Truman continued. "I had a saddlebag full of cash from the reward, and I spent most of it on booze. I can't remember much else about it. Afterwards, I got numb. I didn't think much about what I was doing. I just pulled the trigger and got paid for it. But when Dorothy...." He paused. "When that happened, everything changed."

Jessica reached back and touched his cheek. "I hope you never have to do anything like that again."

"I just wish I could make up for it somehow."

"You are making up for it," she told him. "As Sheriff of Dodge, you protect people. You're a good man, Truman. I know you don't think so, but it's true. And I intend to keep telling you that for the rest of my days—until finally, God willing, you believe it."

# Chapter Twenty-Five

Henry Gordon was a loner. He lived in a small rented house on the side of a hill, overlooking a narrow, winding creek.

When Truman and Jessica trotted into the yard, the curtains were drawn. The door was shut.

There was a goat tied to a post out front, complaining with a noisy bawl.

Truman dismounted and helped Jessica down. "Maybe we missed him. He's probably at the office by now."

They climbed the steps to the small, covered porch and walked to the front window. "Try knocking, Jessica."

She raised a fist and pounded on the door. "Mr. Gordon? Are you home?"

Only insistent complaints from the unhappy goat filled the silence.

"He must have left for work," Jessica remarked.

"Looks like it."

"And we wasted all this time coming out here."

Just then, the front door ripped open. Mr. Gordon reached out, grabbed Jessica by the wrist, and hauled her inside.

Truman drew his gun and was aiming by the time she whirled around in the open doorway to face him. But Gordon was shielded behind her, holding a gun to her head.

"Drop your gun, Wade, or I'll shoot her!" he shouted. "I swear on my life! I'm scared enough to do it!"

Truman was only four feet away, but in Jessica's eyes, from where he stood, it seemed more like a mile.

Her heart was pounding so fast, she could barely breathe.

Truman gave her that apologetic look. His voice was low and dangerous. "Drop it, Gordon."

"No, you drop it, or I'll kill her!"

Truman shut one eye to look down the long barrel of his Colt .45. "Drop it, I said."

Jessica felt Henry begin to hyperventilate behind her. "I'm gonna shoot her!" he said. "I swear! I can't take it anymore. I'm gonna shoot her!"

"No! Please!" Jessica screamed. "He'll do it, Truman!"

The little man flicked his gun around. "You heard her! Drop your weapon."

Jessica met Truman's gaze. She saw helplessness in his eyes—a look she'd never seen before.

It spooked her.

Like death.

His forehead creased with silent rage, then slowly, he lowered his six shooter.

No one said a word for a full ten seconds.

Henry nodded his head. "That's better. Now drop it and kick it behind you, down the stairs."

'I don't give up my gun,' Truman had once said.

Jessica's breath caught like a stone in her throat.

Then slowly…carefully…Truman bent down and set his weapon on the porch floor.

Jessica felt her hopes sink as he kicked it away. It clattered down the steps and landed not far from the goat.

"Let her go, Gordon," Truman said.

"Not yet."

Truman raised his hands. "What do you want? We can talk about it."

Jessica suspected this was the first time Truman had ever tried to handle a situation like this, without shooting first.

He was doing just fine.

Henry's arm tightened around her neck.

Jessica struggled to breathe.

Suddenly, another gun cocked. Jessica's gaze darted toward the sound, as Rosalie came around the side of the house aiming a rifle.

"What a sight," she purred. "Sheriff Truman Wade with his hands in the air. I'll never forget it as long as I live."

"What are you doing here, Rosie?" he asked.

She scoffed. "What does it matter? It's me you want to talk to, not Henry. That's all you need to know."

Jessica squirmed in Henry's arms, but he pressed the revolver tighter against her temple.

"Is that really necessary?" she protested.

Rosalie laughed. "Truman, that lady of yours likes to complain. I don't know what you see in her."

"What do you want, Rosie?" His voice was deep and controlled—a clear sign that he was angry enough to do serious damage.

"I want you, Truman," she flirtatiously replied. "I always have. You know that."

"Rosie?" Henry whimpered. "What do you mean? I thought—"

"Shut up, Henry," she snapped.

An edgy grumble escaped him, but Jessica was the only one to hear it.

Rosalie kept her eyes locked on Truman's. "I just wasn't good enough for you, was I? I was beginning to think you weren't even a real man, until Miss Junebug came to town." She glanced over at Jessica. "How'd you do it, anyway? How'd you get him to wake up finally?"

Jessica didn't respond, but deep down, she could feel her anger kicking and bucking, as if it had a personal, dangerous aim of vengeance all its own.

"Well, look at that. She's shy," Rosalie teased, while she flashed a bitter look at Truman. "Not that it matters, because I'm gonna shoot her anyway. After we're finished."

Jessica struggled in Henry's tight grip. "If you kill me," she said, "he'll hate you more than ever."

Truman held his hand up to hush her. "It's not about me, is it, Rosie?"

Rosalie smiled maliciously. "You're smart, Truman. That's why I always liked you."

"If you're looking for the bank combination," he said, "she doesn't have it."

Rosalie smirked. "I know she doesn't have it, Truman, because I have it. It's safely hidden in my corset, and has been all along. You're welcome to come search for it, though. I won't mind. In fact, I'd quite enjoy it."

Jessica clenched her fists in an effort to control her rage.

"What are you doin' out here anyway?" Rosalie asked. "This wasn't in the plan, but you made things a lot easier by coming. Saved us from breaking into the jailhouse."

Truman said nothing, and Jessica knew he was studying Rosalie's grip on that rifle.

"You don't get it, do you?" she said to Jessica. "Henry and I have been planning this ever since you came to town. I killed Lou. I wanted that safe combination, so I shot him. And when people thought you did it, the idea came to me. That's when Henry suddenly became real attractive." Rosalie looked at Truman. "I had him write those stories to keep folks thinkin' she was an outlaw. So naturally, when the bank gets robbed tomorrow, and the sheriff's found dead with a bullet between his eyes, folks won't be lookin' for me. They'll be lookin' for the notorious Junebug Jess. But unfortunately," Rosalie added, "they won't find her, because she'll be six feet under."

"What about Virgil?" Truman asked. "Why'd you kill him?"

"Everybody knew she didn't like him. They all saw what happened that day, and when folks started to forget about her reputation, I wanted to freshen up their memories. It worked didn't it? They want to hang her."

"You won't get away with this, Rosie."

"Won't I? Who's gonna stop me?"

All at once, Truman whirled around and grabbed the revolver out of Henry's hand.

Henry fell backwards against the house. Jessica screamed and ducked. A shot rang out, echoing off the barnyard buildings.

"I'm hit!" Rosalie yelled. "God help me, I'm hit!"

Everything was quiet except for the ring of a gunshot fading into the distance. When Jessica opened her eyes, Henry Gordon was standing over her, pointing. "Uh..." he stuttered.

"Truman!" Jessica fought for breath. He was halfway down the stairs, sprawled on his back with his hand on his chest. The front of his black shirt was drenched in blood, which was seeping through his fingers.

Jessica skidded down the stairs to his side and lifted his head onto her lap. "Oh my God, what happened?" she asked, realizing with horror that both guns had gone off at once.

His breath came in short gasps. "Dammit," he whispered, struggling to sit up.

Rosalie was lying on the ground at the bottom of the steps, moaning. "Truman? I...I didn't mean it!"

"Don't even speak to him!" Jessica screamed. She cradled his head, pushed the hair away from his face. He tried again to get up, but she held him down. "Lie still."

She hoped he didn't hear the fear in her voice as it cracked hideously on the last word. Tears flooded her eyes as she opened his shirt and examined the wound – a bullet hole in the chest, not far from his heart, bleeding profusely. She tugged her skirt up to cover the wound and staunch the flow of blood.

She thought of her brother, Gregory...

"Jessica...my pocket."

"What?" She could barely speak.

"My shirt p-pocket." He was panting now.

She lifted the flap and reached inside, where she found something that belonged to her. The diamond necklace.

"You need it to get home," he whispered.

"I won't leave you."

"I'm sorry," he said, coughing and panting.

His blood was all over her hands now and staining her skirt. Tears rained down her cheeks.

"Please, don't go," she sobbed, cradling his head in her arms.

"You can go back to your family now," he said.

"I don't want to go back." She bent forward and kissed him on the mouth.

"Yes, you do. I'm sorry. I wanted more time with you."

"Please hold on." She looked up at Henry. "Don't just stand there!" she shouted. "Get a doctor!" Henry took off down the stairs toward the barn.

"It's too late," Truman whispered.

"No, it's not. Try and hold on."

"I can't."

She kissed him on the forehead. "I love you," she told him. "I love you."

"Forever," he whispered.

His eyes fell closed.

Jessica's whole body shook uncontrollably with grief and rage. "Oh, no. Please wake up, Truman. Don't leave me."

Rosalie rolled over, clutching her leg. "Someone help me. I'm hurt."

Jessica ignored her. It can't be true. You aren't dead. You said everything would be all right.

She laid her hand on his chest where his shirt was soaked with blood. Please, let there be a heartbeat.

There was nothing.

Jessica bowed her head and wept. Shivering, she buried her face in Truman's shoulder. His hand fell limply off his stomach onto the step, but Jessica reached for it and drew it to her cheek.

Holding it there against her skin, she let one knee slip down a step so she could lie beside him.

"I love you, Truman." Forever.

Clouds moved in front of the sun, and a gust of wind blew across the prairie.

From that moment, time stopped completely for Jessica. There was no difference between past and future. She didn't care whether she went home or stayed in the past. Nothing mattered outside of her grief.

And yet, her heart continued to beat, and blood still moved through her veins....

# Chapter Twenty-Six

*Two weeks later*

"Baby? Can you hear me?"

Yes, she could hear things – the steady beeping of a heart monitor, voices in the corridor, water running from a tap— but her body simply wouldn't respond. All she could do was lay there, paralyzed, listening to that familiar voice.

"Jessica…you're safe now. You're in the hospital. Please wake up."

At last, she managed to open her eyes. "Mom?"

"Yes, I'm here. William! Come quick! She's awake."

Jessica squeezed her mother's hand as her father stepped into view.

"Oh, thank God," he said.

A terrible grief ripped through her heart, but she didn't really understand it. She couldn't seem to remember much of anything. What was she doing here?

Her mother leaned forward and hugged her. "We were so worried about you, but we never gave up."

Jessica looked around groggily, while intense but ambiguous emotions clouded her thinking. Everything was foggy. "What happened to me?"

"You had a car accident."

"A car accident," she repeated in confusion. "Am I okay?"

"You're fine, but you had us very worried."

Whispers of memories flashed in her mind—images of wide-open prairies, horses and wagons....

It was all so vague. She shut her eyes and fought to remember. She felt dizzy and nauseous as she grasped for a clear image of something, anything, but her stomach churned violently, and the faint smell of food from a wheeled cart in the hall made her want to wretch.

Jessica touched her throat. "My necklace. Where's my necklace?"

"Don't panic. The nurses had to remove it. I have it in my purse."

"And my watch?" She didn't know why these items mattered so much to her, but the need to ensure their existence seemed imperative.

"I have that, too."

Jessica needed to lie back. Her mother fluffed the pillow, while her father went to the corner table to turn on a little transistor radio. As he adjusted the tuning, static blared on and off until he found music.

Oh, Susanna. Don't you cry for me...

Jessica bolted upright. "That song."

"What about it?" Her mother frowned with concern.

"I remember it was playing in my car when I crashed." Fleeting images of rain and mud and Junebugs flashed before her eyes, and she rubbed hard at them while the music seemed to overlap into some other world, some other existence that tore at her heart and filled her with grief and despair. What was going on?

"Sweetheart, do you remember what happened?" her mother asked. "We need to know."

Her father moved closer. "Martha, give her time to recover. We can ask her later."

"Ask me what?"

Her parents regarded each other warily. They hesitated for a long moment before her mother finally spoke. "Jessica, where were you?"

221

Her heart began to beat faster, and her father glanced with concern at the monitor.

"What do you mean?" she replied. "You said I had a car accident."

"Yes, and we found you at the crash site. But before that, you were missing."

"Missing?"

"Your accident happened more than a month ago. We found the car, totally flattened—there was no way you could have survived in it—but you were gone, as if you'd vanished into thin air."

A tense silence weighed heavily in the room. Jessica tried to think, but her brain was in a stress-induced haze. "How did I end up here?"

The last thing she remembered was hydroplaning on the road and spinning around and around in the car.

But there was more. So much more.

She'd been to a funeral. Memories began to clog her brain. She'd been sick, so sick...throwing up from the grief.

A funeral. She'd lost him....

"A driver spotted you this morning in the same place we found your car," her mother said. "You were lying unconscious on the side of the road."

"How can that be?"

"Martha, stop," her father said. "Are you all right, Jess? You look pale."

Jessica stared blankly at him. "Could I have a glass of water?"

"Of course." Her father went to the tiny bathroom and turned on the tap.

"Do you remember anything at all?" her mother asked.

Her father returned with a white paper cup and a straw. He helped her to sit up and take a drink. When she lay back down on the pillow, a man's image appeared in her mind as clearly as if he were standing at the foot of the bed.

He wore a black hat and white shirt with a dark vest, and he was strikingly handsome with mesmerizing blue eyes.

"Jessica?"

"Yes?"

"Do you remember anything?"

She began to tremble. Maybe she shouldn't have swallowed the water so fast. "No. I feel sick. I think I need to...."

Her mother grabbed a silver pan, held it under Jessica's chin, and she retched into it. When she finished, she sat back on the bed and tried to take deep breaths. "What's wrong with me?"

Her parents said nothing.

"Why are you looking at me like that?" she asked.

Her father broke in. "Martha...."

Jessica's gaze shot toward him. His forehead crinkled with concern.

"Mom, Dad, there's something you're not telling me."

"Just try to remember where you've been," her father said. "It's very important."

"Why?"

Her mother lowered her gaze for a moment, then looked up again. "Jessica, I don't know how to tell you this, but I suppose there is no right way to say it. You're pregnant."

Good God.

All at once, memories flooded her brain, and she burst into tears, sobbing and laughing at the same time.

"Are you all right?"

She covered her face with her hands, unable to explain why she was so distraught, so grief-stricken, and yet so happy at the same time – about a man whose identity was still a mystery to her.

"Baby, what happened to you?" her father asked.

She shook her head. "I can't talk about it now. I need time to remember everything, and to understand it. It seems like a dream."

Her parents looked at each with alarm.

"I just need to be alone for a while," Jessica said. "I'm tired. I'll tell you more later, I promise."

They nodded reluctantly. "We'll come back after dinner." Her parents gathered their raincoats and headed for the door.

"Mom? Dad?" Jessica called, just before they left.

"Yes?"

"I love you."

They both smiled. "We love you, too dear. We're so glad you're home." The door swung shut behind them.

Jessica turned onto her side and stared at the radiator under the window. A bouquet of daisies and pink carnations were set in a vase on the sill, but they did little to elevate her spirits.

She'd never see him again. The man in the black vest.

His name was Truman.

It was all so misty. If only she could remember more...

She was carrying his child, and she would never be able to tell him.

A lingering grief washed over her. Heaven help me.

He died without knowing he was going to be a father.

Jessica lifted her wrist, examined the plastic hospital bracelet with her name on it, then dropped her arm onto the white sheets. Rain pelted against the window and an ambulance siren wailed outside.

For a long time, she lay alone in her hospital bed, longing for the sounds of wagons and the beating of hooves. Then slowly, more memories returned, until she was certain her heart was lost forever. Lost somewhere else in time.

She knew this familiar world couldn't replace what she'd found there. Her parents couldn't cure the pain she felt.

Where are you? If there's a heaven, and you're there, please wait for me.

With that prayer, she drifted off.


Jessica spent only one day in the hospital after the doctor examined her. He called it a miracle. Considering the damage done to her car, which had been crushed and mangled, it was astounding that she had survived.

"Your star was shining that day," he said, pressing a cold stethoscope to her back.

Yes. That shiny star crafted of steel....

She had not yet told anyone where she had been. How could she possibly explain that she believed traveled through a doorway in time to the year 1881? She'd sound insane, and maybe she was.

So—after promising to see a therapist to help her remember the forgotten month—Jessica returned home.

As the hours and days passed, and she settled into her familiar routine, it all began to feel like a dream, as if it never really happened.

But it must have happened, she kept telling herself, because she was pregnant.

On the third day, Jessica decided to do some quiet investigating on her own. Her first destination was the State Archives at the Kansas Museum of History.

"Excuse me?" she said, approaching the reference desk. A young woman looked up from her work. Her brown hair and freckles reminded Jessica of a friend she had made – a friend named Wendy. "Do you have newspapers from the 1800s?"

"Yes. We have most of them on microfilm."

"Could I look at some?"

"Certainly. I'll just need you to read our researcher policy, and I'll need a photo ID."

A few minutes later, the woman showed Jessica how to find the microfilm roll numbers using the card catalog. "Is there any particular date you're looking for?"

"I'd like to see June and July of 1881. The Dodge City Chronicle."

"You're the second person to come in here for those dates. Are you doing some kind of project together?" The young woman searched for the correct rolls, while Jessica tried to contemplate what she had just said.

There was someone else?

"No, I'm not working with anyone," she replied. "Do you know who this person was?"

"I don't know his name, but he was very handsome. He's been here a few times. He didn't say what he was working on. Maybe he's writing a book."

Jessica's mind began to sort through some interesting possibilities. Perhaps someone else knew about this doorway through time and was trying to learn more. Maybe someone had followed her back. "You're sure you don't know his name?"

She shook her head. "I'm sorry." The young woman handed her the rolls of microfilm, and showed her how to use the readers and make copies. "If there's anything else you need, let me know, and when you're finished, please return to rolls to the cart by the microfilm attendant's desk."

"Thank you." Sitting down, Jessica loaded the reel into place, pressed the forward button, and began to search for the proper date.

The papers were slightly out of focus, so she adjusted the knob and continued. Pages and pages of newsprint sailed by, and Jessica stopped it every second or two to check the dates. When she found a June headline, she stopped and refocused her eyes. Her stomach flipped over with disbelief.

JUNEBUG JESS KILLS LEFT HAND LOU.

Jessica slumped back in the chair. It was true. It really happened. She suddenly felt weak and dizzy.

How would she explain this? No one was ever going to believe it.

Sitting forward, she adjusted the knob on the machine, skipped ahead a month, and searched for the date Truman was shot. It was beyond hope, she knew, but a part of her prayed that it hadn't happened the way she remembered. Maybe, just maybe....

SHERIFF WADE KILLED!

The bold headline struck her agonizingly hard for the second time. The words were just the same as she remembered. Nothing had changed.

Jessica read the article, then rewound the microfilm and turned off the machine. She couldn't do any more research today. She needed to go home and think about all this.

She stood up, took the film rolls to the attendant, retrieved her purse and coat from the lockers outside the research room, and left the building. Outside, dark storm clouds swirled above and blew a strong, cold wind around her. She walked slowly toward her car, pushing away a lock of hair that had blown across her face.

Climbing into her rental car, she turned the key in the ignition. As soon as she was on the road again, she toyed with the cubic zirconia on her necklace, her mind a hundred years away.

Forever certainly didn't last very long.

When she returned to her apartment, George was waiting at the door, wagging his tail. "Hey, cutie." She shut the door behind her. George stood on his hind legs, reaching up to Jessica as if he wanted a hug. Jessica squatted down to have her chin licked, then rubbed behind his ears. "Calm down," she laughed.

Rising to her feet, she tossed her keys and purse onto the front hall table. The inside of her apartment seemed dark and dismal with the curtains closed, so she walked into the living room and flung open the drapes to looked out over the city. The wind was picking up, blowing the clouds across the sky at a clipped pace.

There was a time when she loved her view from the eighth floor, but these days, Jessica would have preferred a quiet neighborhood with a yard and a view of the prairie. She was quite sure George would prefer that, too.

She went to the kitchen and flicked on the overhead light. She plugged in the kettle and dropped a tea bag into her favorite cup. While she stood waiting for the water to boil, the telephone rang.

"Hello?" she answered.

"Hi. It's me."

"Oh, hi, Mom." Jessica sat down on the sofa.

"I just wanted to call and see how you're doing." There was a pause. "Would you like to come for dinner this weekend and stay a few days? I could put a roast in the oven and—"

"Thanks, Mom, but I think I'll stay home. I'm not really in the mood to drive anywhere."

"We could come and visit you."

Jessica gave no reply. She couldn't seem to get her mind off Truman. Sometimes it felt like a dream. Other times, it felt more real than anything she'd ever known.

Silence loomed at the other end of the line. "Are you sure everything's all right?" her mother asked. "You haven't been the same since you woke up in the hospital. You seem sad. I wish you could talk to me about what happened."

Tears pooled in Jessica's eyes, but she forced them away. "I'll be fine, Mom. Really. Just give me some time. I start therapy on Monday, so I'm sure that will help. I'll talk to you soon, I promise."

"Okay, honey. But remember, I'm here if you need anything."

"I know."

They said their good-byes and hung up. The kettle was steaming, so Jessica hurried to the counter to unplug it. When she tipped it to pour, the telephone rang again. She walked around the counter and picked up the receiver.

"Hello?" There was silence at the other end. "Hello?

A man's voice spoke up. "Jessica Delaney?"

"Yes."

There was a click, as if she'd just been taken off speakerphone. "Hi," he said. "I'm sorry. This may seem strange. We don't actually know each other, but we have something in common, and I'm wondering if we could meet to talk. I understand you just got out of the hospital."

Her heart began to race. "Who's speaking, please?"

"My name is Jake Spencer."

Jessica sat down on the sofa. George hopped up beside her. Stroking the soft hair under his chin, she tried to speak in a calm and steady voice.

"How do you know I was in the hospital?"

"I work there."

She paused. "Have we met before? Your name sounds familiar."

"Yes," he said, slowly. There was another long, drawn-out silence. "I'm the surgeon who operated on your brother last year."

Nervously, Jessica bit her lip. She wasn't sure what, exactly, was going on here, and why she felt like she was going to drop the phone. All she knew was that she wanted desperately to learn more about Dr. Spencer, and meet with him as soon as possible.

"What is it that you want to talk about?" she carefully asked.

His voice was husky and low. "Do you remember what happened to you after your car accident?"

Jessica sat forward, resting both elbows on her knees, while she grew more uneasy and restless by the minute. "How do you know about that?"

"It's common knowledge around here. Your parents conducted quite a search."

She glanced at George beside her on the sofa. The dog was trembling for some reason. "What do you want?" Jessica asked.

"I need to talk to you. Do you remember where you were while you were missing? Jessica? Are you still there?"

"Yes, I'm here."

"I need to know. Do you remember anything about what happened?"

She hesitated, afraid to trust anyone with this information. Fighting the urge to hang up, she decided to take a chance and answer. "Yes."

He said nothing for a long, tense moment.

"But I don't think I can discuss it with anyone," she added, losing her courage all of a sudden.

"Yes, you can," he replied. "I'd really like to talk to you about it. I've done some research on...." He stopped.

Jessica's heart thumped madly in her chest. "Go on."

"I've done some research on time travel, and I'd like to ask you some questions."

A wave of panic rolled over her. Did he know about the spot on the highway? Did he know how to use it? Could he help her go back and save Truman's life?

She'd tell him not to give up his gun when Henry demanded it. Or better yet, she'd never ride out to Henry's house in the first place.

Or if they did, they'd take a posse.

"When would you like to meet?" she asked.

"How about Wednesday morning? I can come to Topeka, if that's more convenient for you."

"No, I'll come to Dodge. I need to visit my parents anyway. Where should we meet?"

"How about the Boot Hill Museum? In the parking lot adjacent to the Visitor Center."

Jessica's palms were clammy. She was breathing very fast.

Did he know? Did he know about Truman?

"That would be fine."

"Ten o'clock?"

"I'll see you then." She hung up.

George rested his front paws on Jessica's lap and stared up at her, whimpering. "Don't worry. I'm not going away again."

She patted him until he stopped shaking.

A few minutes later, she stood and returned to the kitchen for her tea. Plugging the kettle in again, she leaned against the counter to wait.

Did Dr. Spencer know how it worked? Maybe the same thing happened to him. After all, she wasn't the only one. It happened to Angus as well. Who knew how many others?

The kettle began to steam. Jessica poured the hot water into her cup and plunged the teabag on its string.

While it steeped, she stared blankly at the wall, thinking about Truman and the child she was carrying, and how desperately she wished she could tell him about it.

The fact that she traveled through time to find him somehow made his death more difficult to bear. There were too many bizarre factors to accept it like a normal passing. Before her car accident, he had been dead for a hundred years, but she was still able to touch him, talk to him, fall in love with him. Death had no meaning, and for that reason, she just couldn't seem to let go. Hope still lived and breathed formidably within her.

If she could do it once—meet him after he'd already died a century earlier—why couldn't she do it again? Perhaps there was a way—a way to go back and change what happened that day.

Good God, if there was, no matter what it took, or how long, she was going to discover it.

# Chapter Twenty-Seven

Jessica pulled into the museum parking lot at 9:45 Wednesday morning, and found it nearly empty. Disappointed, and a great deal more nervous than she expected to be, she adjusted her sunglasses, walked to the Visitor Center, and waited.

She checked her watch. Ten minutes to ten.

"He'd better show up," she said, feeling slightly irritable, for she had tossed and turned all night, thinking about this moment, and she hated feeling so powerless and unsure of herself.

A few seconds later, a silver mini-van pulled into the lot. Jessica's nerves quivered with anticipation, but a woman got out.

Next, a blue Accord pulled in, but an older man climbed out.

Jessica checked her watch again. It was five minutes to ten. She paced back and forth in front of the entrance, her stomach burning with nervous butterflies.

She checked her watch one more time. It was ten o'clock. "Where is he?" she whispered, looking around.

Just then, a shiny black Mustang convertible with the top up drove in. She stopped pacing and squinted, but the sun reflected off the car's windshield, blinding her momentarily, so she couldn't see the driver. The Mustang pulled into a spot near her car.

No one got out.

She waited.

And waited.

Finally, the door opened. A dark-haired man wearing sunglasses, a white T-shirt and faded blue jeans, stepped out onto the lot. Before she could get a good look at him, he leaned into the car again to search for something.

She could still see his legs—clearly muscular and well-proportioned. She suspected he spent a fair amount of time keeping in shape. Or maybe he just looked like that naturally.

After a few seconds, he straightened and shut the car door. When he turned and walked toward her, he twirled and jingled his keys around on a finger, then dropped them into his pocket.

Jessica felt her insides zoom like a roller coaster. That walk. That twirl of the keys. It was just like....

No, you're imagining it.

She lifted a hand to shade her eyes, and watched him approach. Her heart was pounding like a big drum, faster and faster until she was sure it was pummeling her ribs.

The man walked straight toward her. Obviously there was no doubt in his mind who she was. Then he removed his sunglasses, and Jessica sucked in a quick breath. He looked so much like Truman, it was uncanny.

But he isn't Truman. He can't be. Don't even think it.

He smiled at her with that apologetic look Truman had given her so many times, but when he came closer, she saw subtle differences. This man's eyes were green, not blue, and the laugh lines around them were different—more pronounced. He was not quite as tall as Truman, and his hair was dark brown, not black.

He stopped when he reached her, and stared.

His gaze traveled down the length of her body to her black skirt and the same pair of red pumps she had been wearing when she first met Truman.

She stared right back at him. "Dr. Spencer?"

His eyes lifted. "Yes. It's nice to see you again, under better circumstances this time."

"Indeed."

They shook hands.

"Welcome home," he said.

His words penetrated her memory, curling around her emotions until she began to feel overwhelmed by them.

What did he mean…welcome home?

"Why did you call me?" she asked tentatively.

"I...." A woman passed by them, and he waited for her to enter the Visitor Center before he continued. "Let's take a walk."

"Sure."

He pressed his hand into the small of her back to guide her along. The simple gesture was so familiar, she felt hopes come at her from all directions. Perhaps it was cowardice, but she beat back those hopes as fast as she could focus her will-power.

"I know this may seem strange to you," he said as they walked across the parking lot, "but I've known you for a long time. Even before that day in the hospital with Gregory."

Goosebumps shimmied down her body. "I don't remember meeting you before."

"No, we hadn't actually met...well, not really."

Jessica squared her shoulders, gathering what strength she had left. "What are you saying, Dr. Spencer?"

"Please, call me Jake." He paused for a moment, staring intensely into her eyes. "I know what happened to you. I know you traveled back in time, and I know that you...that you miss someone."

None of this made sense. Her head began to throb as she fought to control the feelings she knew were illogical.

"And I know about Truman," he added.

All her attempts to stay calm, all her resolve to grieve silently for the man she loved, evaporated before her like water on a hot stove.

Jake brushed a tear off her cheek. "Please, don't cry," he said.

But she couldn't keep her voice from breaking. "How? How could you know about him?"

"Because...I am him."

Shock exploded within her. Before she knew what she was doing, she had turned and was walking away from him.

"No, it's not possible." She couldn't believe it. She couldn't risk another loss like that if he were lying.

His footsteps followed, tapping rapidly over the pavement. A familiar rhythm. Soon, his hand closed around her elbow and he turned her around to face him. "Jessica, it's me. You know it is."

"No, you can't be. " Tears ran down her cheeks and her heart felt raw. She couldn't take any more pain.

"Yes. It's me."

"But you're not the same," she said. "You look different."

He nodded. "I know, but you have to believe me. I was there. I was Truman, and I told you I'd love you forever. It was the last thing I said to you. Please remember."

Jessica stepped back, away from him. It was impossible for anyone but Truman to know that.

"How is this possible?" was all she could say.

They started walking again and paused in front of his car. "Truman died in 1881," he replied, "but somehow he...I...followed you here."

Jessica reached up and touched his face. "How?"

"I know I look different. I am different. Truman was born again in me, and he lived an extra thirty years since the day you last saw him."

"I don't understand."

"I didn't either, not until I was older. I always knew I was different – as a kid, I had an obsession with the Old West – but I thought the memories were just dreams or fantasies. Then it all started to seem very real to me. I began to research Truman Wade, and sure enough, I found him. I found photographs of him and newspaper articles describing things I'd already known about. And I found things about you."

Jessica felt unsteady on her feet. She was still having trouble believing all this. Or maybe she was afraid to believe it.

"Do you remember all of Truman's life?" she asked uncertainly.

He shook his head. "Not all of it. Only certain things later on. I remember Dorothy, and I recall things about bounty hunting, but most of all, I remember you."

Her heart warmed at the words. "You're a doctor now."

"Yes. I did things differently this time, and now my life makes more sense to me. You have to believe me, Jessica. I've been waiting such a long time for you to come back."

Suddenly she was filled with a hopefulness she never imagined she would feel again. "But if you've known about me for so long, why didn't you find me sooner? I've been right here in Kansas for years. I almost married someone else."

"I was afraid of altering fate," he replied.

She shook her head with disbelief. "How long have you known who I was?"

"About five years. I came to Dodge City when I finished my residency. To wait for you. But I didn't remember anything about you having a brother. I was shocked to see you that day, and I tried so hard to save him. If I could have foreseen what would happen to him, maybe I could have done something to prevent it, but you were all I saw."

Jessica touched his cheek and felt a lump form in her throat. "No more regrets," she said. "We can't change the past. I don't think we're meant to. All we can do is build the future."

Jake nodded and kissed the palm of her hand.

"When I first met Truman," she said, "I knew he looked familiar, but I couldn't place him. Now, I remember. He reminded me of you. I remember that day in the hospital. The day Gregory died. You knew my name."

"Of course I did."

"But," she said, pulling away so she could look at him, "what have you been doing all this time?"

"We have a lot to catch up on," he told her with a smile. "Now I save lives, instead of take them."

"Truman said that to me once," she replied. "I dreamed he was a doctor, but he laughed at the idea. I told him he could be anything he wanted to be."

Jake smiled. "I remember that, too. It was the last day we were together. We were riding on my horse. Maybe you planted the idea in me."

A horn honked somewhere. Such a modern sound.

"It is you, isn't it?" she finally said, in a quiet, shaky voice.
"Yes."

Without hesitation she wrapped her arms around his neck, laughing and crying at the same time. Could she believe him? Could she really trust him? Dear Lord...she had to. Nothing would ever mean anything to her again if she couldn't have this. Again.

Jessica's feet came clear off the ground as he lifted her and swung her in a circle.

"I love you," she whispered in his ear, astonished by how quickly she could utter those words to a man she thought she barely knew, but now it felt so right, and so comfortable.

"I love you, too."

When he set her down, he gazed into her eyes for a second, then pressed his lips to hers.

In that instant, Jessica knew it was true. His lips were the same. The kiss was the same.

He was Truman. Her Truman.

He brushed her hair away from her face. Jessica touched her necklace—the one Truman had returned to her just before he died.

The pain of that day still ached inside her, but as she looked at this man before her, she realized it was fading fast. Truman had indeed come back to her. He had promised her forever, and he had kept that promise.

She reached up and touched Jake's cheek. In his eyes, she saw the ageless connection they shared.

He held his hands out in front of him, turned them over and looked at his palms. "These hands...they've never held a gun, and they never will."

She trembled with joy. Everything that had happened made sense now.

"It's not going to be just us, you know," she said, grinning mischievously, resting her hand on her belly.

The news registered on Jake's face, and Jessica saw the faint memory of his own demons disappearing. "I know."

"How do you know?"

He gave an apologetic shrug. "I'm a doc. When they brought you in, I was involved. I followed your progress, but I couldn't say anything to anyone. And I knew I had to give you time to recover before I dropped this on you." He pulled her close and buried his face in her hair. "I'm so happy," he said. "This time, I promise, everything really is going to be all right."

A gentle sigh of a breeze blew across their faces, hinting at hope and contentment.

Jessica stepped back and nodded. "I think it's going to be better than all right."

Then her cell phone rang, and his BlackBerry vibrated at his belt. They reached for them quickly, then looked at each other and laughed.

"Let's shut these off," he said, moving close to her again. He slid his warm hand up under the hair at her nape and whispered in her ear. "It's high time we got out of here, don't you think?"

She glanced up at him flirtatiously as a delicious rush of desire shivered through her. "That depends. What did you have in mind, Sheriff? And dare I ask—will handcuffs be involved?"

He smirked and led her toward his Mustang. "I'm game if you are."

He opened the door for her and waited until she was comfortably seated on the leather upholstery before he shut the door, circled around the front, and got into the driver's seat. He slid the key into the ignition, started the engine, and pushed a button to lower the top.

"Do you remember Angus Maxwell?" he said, while the top retracted and folded away.

"Yes, of course. Why? Is there some news about him?"

Jake turned down the volume on the radio. "Nothing recent, but when I was researching I came upon some announcements in the old newspapers. He married Wendy Smith, and they had three children. All of his descendants are living right here in Dodge."

A tiny thrill moved through her. "Have you tried to contact them?"

He shook his head. "No, but I'll be willing if it's something you want to do."

Jessica smiled at him as a fresh breeze blew through her hair. "We'll have to think about that."

He revved the engine and adjusted the rearview mirror.

"Did you know I'm a writer?" she asked.

"Of course. I read your column religiously. I especially liked the one about how to train for the New York Marathon. I'm thinking about doing that."

"Yeah?" She sat up straighter as her passion for running sparked in her veins. "Me, too. But we'd have to qualify."

He shifted into reverse to back out of the parking spot. "I'm sure we could help each other out. You strike me as the competitive type. How early do you like to get up on a Saturday morning?"

"Very early," she replied, "unless there's a reckless consumption of moonshine the night before, which shouldn't happen too often, I hope."

"I'll try not to be a bad influence." He hit the gas and headed toward the exit.

"I'm also thinking about writing a book," she added.

He drove under the museum archway, pulled out onto the street, and shifted into second gear. "Really?" He looked her square in the eye. "That sounds amazing. What kind of book?"

"A romance novel," she replied. "Maybe a time travel."

Jake put on his sunglasses and grinned at her. "What would you call it?"

She slipped off one of her red stilettos and massaged her calf and arch while she thought about it. "Taken by the Cowboy," she said at last, "and I shouldn't have to do much research at all."

He chuckled softly. "That sounds like something I might like to read. Just make sure you work in those red stilettos, because they're really hot." He shifted into second gear and sped up the street. "Now let's go to the costume shop and see if we can rustle up a pair of handcuffs and a leather gun belt."

"And a hat," Jessica added with a smile as she leaned close and laid her hand on his gorgeous muscular thigh, "because there's just something about a man in a Stetson."

They turned a corner, and Truman shifted smoothly into third.

## -THE END-

*To stay informed about Julianne's current and future releases, personal appearances—or to learn about great contests and giveaways — please sign up for her email newsletter. It's a private list, and your email address will never be shared with anyone.*

*Julianne also invites you to visit her website to learn more about her writing life, and to view photos and watch videos about her books. You can even take a virtual tour of her home office. Julianne is active on Facebook and Twitter, where she chats with readers every day.*

*Excerpt from* THE COLOR OF HEAVEN
*By Julianne MacLean*
*writing under the pseudonym E.V. Mitchell*
*Copyright 2011 Julianne MacLean*

# Preface

A lot goes through your mind when you're dying. What they say about life flashing before your eyes is true. You remember things from your childhood and adolescence – specific images, vivid and real, like brilliant sparks of light exploding in your brain.

Somehow you're able to comprehend the whole of your life in that single instant of reflection, as if it were a panoramic view. You have no choice but to look at your decisions and accomplishments – or lack of them – and decide for yourself if you did all that you could do.

And you panic just a little, wishing for one more chance at all the beautiful moments you didn't appreciate, or for one more day with the person you didn't love quite enough.

You also wonder in those frantic, fleeting seconds, as your spirit shoots through a dark tunnel, if heaven exists on the other side, and if so, what you will find there.

What will it look like? What color will it be?

Then you see a light – a brilliant, dazzling light – more calming and loving than any words can possibly describe, and everything finally makes sense to you. You are no longer afraid, and you know what lies ahead.

# Chapter One

In this remarkable, complex world of ours, there are certain people who appear to lead charmed lives. They are blessed with natural beauty, have successful and fulfilling careers. They drive expensive cars, live in upscale neighborhoods, and are happily married to gorgeous and brilliant spouses.

I was once one of those people. Or at least that's how I was perceived.

Not that I hadn't endured my share of hardships. My childhood had been far from idyllic. My relationship with my father was strained at best, and there were certain pivotal events that I preferred to forget altogether – events that involved my mother, which I don't really wish to go into now, but I will explain later, I promise.

All you need to know is that for a number of years my life was perfect, and I found more happiness than I ever dreamed possible.

My name is Sophie. I grew up in Camden, Maine, but moved to Augusta when I was fourteen. I have one sister. Her name is Jen and we look nothing alike. Jen is blonde and petite (she takes after our mother), while I am tall, with dark auburn hair.

Jen was always a good girl. She did well in school and graduated with honors. She went to university on scholarship and is now a social worker in New Hampshire, where she lives with her husband, Joe, a successful contractor.

I, on the other hand, was not such a model student, nor was I an easy child to raise. I was passionate and rebellious and drove my father insane with my adventurous spirit, especially in the teen years. While Jen was quiet and bookish and liked to stay home on a Friday night, I was a party girl.

By the time I reached high school, I had a steady boyfriend. His name was Kirk Duncan, and we spent most of our time at his house because his parents were divorced and never around.

Before you pass judgment, let me assure you that Kirk was a decent, sensible young man – very mature for his age – and I have no regrets about the years we spent together. He was my first love, and I knew that no matter where life took us, I would always love him.

We had a great deal in common. He was a musician and played the guitar, while I liked to sketch and write. Our artistic natures gelled beautifully, and if we hadn't been so young when we first met (I was only fifteen), we might have ended up together, married and living in the suburbs with a house full of children. But life at that age is unpredictable. It's not how things turned out.

When Kirk left Augusta to attend college in Michigan and I stayed behind to finish my last year of high school, we drifted apart. We remained friends and kept in touch for a while, but eventually he began dating another girl, and she was upset by the once-a-month letters we continued to write to each other.

We both knew it was time to cut the cord, so we did. For a long stretch I missed him – he was such a big part of my life – but I knew it was the right thing to do. Whenever I was tempted to call him, I resisted.

I went on to study English and Philosophy at NYU, which is where I met Michael Whitman.

Michael Whitman. The name alone had a sigh attached to it…

He was handsome, charming and witty, the most perfect man I had ever seen. Every time he walked into a room, I lost my breath, as did every other hot-blooded female within a fifty-yard radius.

If only I knew then, when I was nineteen, that he would be my future husband. I probably wouldn't have believed it, but there's a lot I wouldn't have believed about the extraordinary events of my life. I doubt you'll believe them either, but I'm going to tell them to you anyway.

I'll leave it up to you to decide if they're real.

# Chapter Two

Michael was nothing like Kirk or any of the boys I had known in high school. His parents owned a corn farm in Iowa, but he looked as if he'd been raised by aristocrats in an English country house and had just stepped off the cover of GQ magazine.

Well-dressed and devastatingly handsome – with dark, wavy hair, pale blue eyes, and a muscular build – he had a way of making you feel as if you were the most attractive, witty, charismatic person on earth. And it wasn't just women who worshipped him. He was a man's man, too, with a number of close, loyal friends. His professors respected him. He was an A student and the class valedictorian at graduation. And then – big surprise – he went off to Harvard Law School on scholarship.

He was your basic "dreamboat," and though he spoke to me now and then on campus, like everyone else, I mostly admired him from afar.

It wasn't until four years after graduation, when I was interning in the publicity department at C.W. Fraser – a major publisher of non-fiction books and celebrity tell-alls – that I became the envy of every single young woman in Manhattan and beyond.

It was June 16, 1996. I was twenty-six years old, and had helped to organize a book launch party that Michael attended.

We saw each other from across the room and waved. Later that night, we went out to dinner, and when he escorted me home, I invited him inside. We stayed up all night, just talking on the sofa, listening to music, and we kissed when the sun came up.

It was the most magical, romantic night of my life.

One year later, we were married.

During our honeymoon in Barbados, Michael confessed something to me that he'd never been able to talk about before, not with anyone.

When he was twelve years old, his older brother Dean had died in a tractor accident. The vehicle slid down a muddy embankment, rolled over and landed on top of Dean, killing him instantly. Michael was the one who found him.

His voice shook as he described Dean's lifeless body, trapped beneath the heavy tractor.

I hadn't known about the accident when we attended university together. I don't think anyone did. Michael had always seemed so strong and dynamic. It seemed as if nothing bad could ever touch him.

As soon as I heard this, I understood that we shared something very profound – a common experience that left us both broken in unseen places, for I had lost my mother when I was fourteen.

I was still angry with her for leaving us.

Because that's what she did. She made a choice, and she left us.

I, too, shared these things with Michael, and we grew even closer.

# Chapter Three

When I mentioned earlier that I had once led a charmed life, I was referring to this stretch of time, which began on my wedding day and lasted for ten wonderful years.

Michael and I were crazy in love as newlyweds. He rose quickly at the law firm, and we both knew it was only a matter of time before he became a partner.

Things were going well for me, too. Six months after we began dating, I was offered a full-time, permanent position in the publicity department at C.W. Fraser, and with Michael's encouragement, I pursued my first love – writing – and began submitting stories to magazines. We dined out often and connected with all the right people. Before long, I was leaving my job in publicity to write for the New Yorker.

Everything seemed perfect, and it was. We made love almost every night of the week. Sometimes Michael came home from work with a Victoria's Secret box containing something lacy, wrapped in pink tissue paper, and we'd make love during Letterman.

Other times, he brought ingredients for chocolate martinis and we'd go dancing until midnight.

We were as close as two people could be, and just when I thought life couldn't get any better, the most amazing thing happened. I found out I was pregnant.

How effortless it all seemed.

Looking back, I sometimes wonder if it was all a dream. I suppose it was, because eventually I did wake from it. In fact, I sat straight up in bed, gasping my lungs out.

But let's not talk about that yet. There are still a few miracles to explore.

So let's talk about the baby.

# Chapter Four

Here's the thing about motherhood. It exhausts you and thrills you. It kicks you in the butt, and the very next second makes you feel like a superstar. Most of all, it teaches you to be selfless.

Let me rephrase that. It doesn't really teach you this. It creates a new selflessness within you, which grabs hold of your heart when you first take your child into your arms. In that profound moment of extraordinary love and discovery, your own needs and desires become secondary. Nothing is as important as the well-being of your beautiful child. You would sacrifice anything for her. Even your own life. You would do it in a heartbeat. God wouldn't need to ask twice.

\* \* \*

Our beautiful baby Megan was born on July 17, 2000. It was a difficult labor that lasted nineteen hours before ending in an emergency C-section, but I wouldn't change a single second of it. If that's what was required to bring Megan into the world, I would have done it ten times over.

For the next five days, while recovering from my surgery, I spent countless hours in the hospital holding her in my arms, fascinated by her movements and expressions. Her sweet, chubby face and tiny pink feet enchanted me. I was infatuated beyond comprehension by her soft black hair and puffy eyes, her sweet knees and plump belly, and her miniature little fingertips and nails. She was the most exquisite creature I had ever beheld, and my heart swelled with inexpressible love every time she squeaked or flexed her hands.

How clearly I remember lying on my side next to her in the hospital bed with my cheek resting on a hand, believing that I could lie there forever and never grow bored watching her. There was such truth in the simplicity of those moments.

Michael, too, was captivated by our new daughter. He went to work during the days, but spent the nights with us in our private room, sleeping in the upholstered chair.

When we finally brought Megan home, I came to realize that Michael was not only the perfect husband, but the perfect father as well.

He was nothing like my own father, who had always maintained an emotional distance. No... Michael changed diapers and couldn't seem to get enough of our baby girl. He carried Megan around the house in his arms. He read books to her and sang songs. A few times a week, he took her for long walks in the park so I could nap or have some time to myself, simply to shower or cook a meal. I felt like the luckiest woman alive.

Later, when Megan was out of diapers and had finally given up drinking from a bottle at the age of two, I began to feel that I was ready to start writing again.

Michael – always so generous and supportive – suggested that he take Megan to Connecticut every Sunday afternoon to visit his sister, Margery.

It worked out well. Margery was thrilled to spend time with them, and those happy day trips out of the city created an even stronger bond between Michael and Megan.

It wasn't long before I was submitting feature stories to a number of national parenting magazines. Always, in the back of my mind, however, was the dream of returning to the New Yorker, perhaps when Megan was older.

Sometimes I wonder if I would have done anything differently in those blissful days of new motherhood if I had known about the bomb that was about to drop onto our world. I believe I will always wonder that, and there will be no escaping the regrets, rational or otherwise.

# Chapter Five

When Megan was three-and-a-half years old, my father came to visit us in New York. It was the first time he had seen our house (we lived in a brownstone in Washington Square), and he mentioned repeatedly that he was sorry for not coming sooner. He said he was a "terrible grandfather."

"Don't worry about it, Dad," I replied as I passed the salad bowl across the table. "I've been terrible about visiting you, too. Life just gets so busy sometimes. I understand. It's hard to get away."

It was a lie, casually spoken, and we both knew it. Nothing had ever been easy between the two of us. There was an awkward tension that was obvious to everyone, including Michael, who was the one person in my life Dad actually approved of.

"You caught yourself a good man there," he gruffly said on our wedding day, then he patted Michael on the back and left early.

But of course he would love Michael. Everyone loved Michael. He was a handsome, charming, witty, Harvard-educated lawyer. A good provider and a devoted husband. As far as my father was concerned, Michael's small-town upbringing on a farm in the Midwest was the icing on the cake. I think Dad was still in shock that I had managed to marry such an amazing man.

We finished dinner and dessert, then Dad went off to bed at nine, not long after Megan fell asleep.

He planned to stay only twenty-four hours.

The following day, I worked hard to keep him busy and avoid any awkward silences or conversations about the past. Mom especially. It was not something we ever talked about.

Megan and I took him to the top of the Empire State Building, then we visited the Museum of Natural History, and of course, Ground Zero.

As he drove away, waving out the open car window, Megan slipped her tiny hand into mine, looked up at me with those big brown eyes and asked, "Will Grampy come back again?"

I hesitated a moment, then wet my lips and smiled. "Of course, sweetie, but he's very busy. I'm not sure when that will be."

We went back inside.

Michael was at work. The house seemed so empty and quiet.

"Want to make some cookies?" I cheerfully asked.

Megan gave me a melancholy look that will stay with me forever, because it was the first sign of the terrible nightmare that was about to befall our family.

I didn't know that then, of course. At the time, I didn't know anything.

"Okay," she replied.

I picked her up and carried her into the kitchen.

\* \* \*

The following morning, Megan didn't wake until 8:30, which surprised me, because she was usually climbing onto our bed at six a.m. sharp. She was more dependable than our digital alarm clock.

When eight o'clock rolled around and she was still sleeping, I assumed she was tired from our sightseeing trip the day before.

I was wrong about that. It was something else entirely – something I never imagined would ever happen to us.

That was our last day of normal.

# Chapter Six

Over the next seven days, Megan grew increasingly lethargic and took long naps in the afternoons. Her skin was pale and she slumped in front of the television without ever smiling – not even for Captain Feathersword.

By week's end, she was irritable and couldn't bear it when I touched her, so I made an appointment with our doctor, who told me to bring her in right away.

As I was dressing Megan for the appointment, I noticed a large bruise on her left calf and another on her back. I mentioned this to the doctor, who sent us to the hospital for blood work.

Everything happened very quickly after that. The results came back an hour later, and Michael and I were called into the pediatrician's office for the results.

"I'm so sorry to have to tell you this," Dr. Jenkins said, "but Megan is very sick. The tests have indicated that she has acute myeloid leukemia."

She paused to give Michael and me a moment to absorb what she had told us, but I couldn't seem to process it. My brain wasn't working. Then suddenly I feared I might vomit.

I wanted to tell the doctor that she was mistaken, but I knew it wasn't true. Something was very wrong with Megan, and I had known it before the blood work even came back.

"Are you all right, Mrs. Whitman?" the doctor asked.

Michael squeezed my hand.

I turned in my chair and looked out the open door at my sweet darling angel, who was lying quietly on the vinyl seats in the waiting area with a social worker. She was watching television and twirling her long brown hair around a finger.

I glanced briefly at Michael, who was white as a sheet, then faced the doctor again.

"I'd like to admit her through oncology for more tests," Dr. Jenkins said, "and start treatment right away."

No. It wasn't true. It wasn't happening. Not to Megan.

"Mrs. Whitman, are you all right?" Dr. Jenkins leaned forward over her desk.

"I'm fine," I said, though I was nothing of the sort. There was a crushing dread squeezing my chest as I imagined what was going to happen to Megan in the coming months. I knew enough about cancer to know that the treatment would not be easy. It was going to get much worse before it got better.

She was just a child. How was she ever going to cope with this? How was I going to cope?

"You say you want to begin treatment right away," Michael said, speaking up at last. "What if we don't agree? What if we want to get a second opinion?"

I glanced quickly at him, surprised at the note of accusation I heard in his voice.

"You're welcome to get a second opinion," Dr. Jenkins calmly replied, "but I strongly recommend that you allow us to admit Megan today. You shouldn't wait."

Michael stood up and began to pace around the office. He looked like he wanted to hit something.

"Is it that bad?" I asked. "Is there no time?"

There was an underlying note of confidence in the doctor's eyes, which provided me with a small measure of comfort. "Of course there's time," she said. "But it's important that we begin treatment immediately. It's also important that you try to stay positive. You're going to have a difficult battle ahead of you, but don't lose hope. The cure rate for leukemia in children is better than seventy-five percent. As soon as we get her admitted, we'll prepare the very best treatment plan possible. She's a strong girl. We're going to do everything we can to get her into remission."

My voice shook uncontrollably as I spoke. "Thank you."

I stood and walked out of the office in a daze, leaving Michael behind to talk to the doctor. I wondered how in the world I was ever going to explain any of this to Megan.

# Chapter Seven

There is nothing anyone can say or do which will ease your shock as a parent when you learn that your child has cancer.

Your greatest wish – your deepest, intrinsic need – is to protect your child from harm. A disease like leukemia robs you of that power. There is no way to stop it from happening once it begins, and all you can do is place your trust in the doctors and nurses who are working hard to save your child's life. You feel helpless, afraid, grief-stricken, and angry. Some days you think it can't be real. It feels like a bad dream. You wish it was, but you can never seem to wake from it.

The first few days in the hospital were an endless array of X-rays, blood draws, intravenous lines, and lastly, a painful spinal tap to look for leukemia cells in the cerebrospinal fluid.

Not only did Michael and I have to get our heads around all of those tests and procedures, we had to educate ourselves about bone marrow aspirations, chemotherapy and all the side effects, as well as radiation treatments and stem cell transplants. In addition, we had to notify our friends and family. Everyone was supportive and came to our aid in some way – everyone except for my father, who remained distant as always.

He sent a get well card. That was all.

I pushed thoughts of him from my mind, however, because I had to stay strong for Megan.

I promised myself I would never cry in front of her. Instead, I cried every time I took a shower at the hospital (I never left), or I cried when Michael arrived and sent me downstairs to get something to eat. During those brief excursions outside the oncology ward, I would take a few minutes in a washroom somewhere and sob my heart out before venturing down to the cafeteria to force something into my stomach.

It was important to eat, I was told. The nurses reminded me on a daily basis that I had to stay healthy for Megan because she would be very susceptible to infection during treatment, and a fever could be fatal.

So I ate.

Every day, I ate.

Michael had a difficult time dealing with Megan's illness. Perhaps it had something to do with the loss of his brother when he was twelve. Some days he wouldn't come to the hospital until very late, and a few times I smelled whisky on his breath.

One night we argued about what we should say to Megan. He didn't want me to tell her that the chemo drugs would make her throw up.

I insisted that we had to always be honest with her. She needed to know that she could trust us to tell her the truth and be with her no matter how bad it got.

We never did agree on that, but I told her the truth anyway.

Michael didn't speak to me for the next twenty-four hours.

\* \* \*

"I don't want my hair to fall out," Megan said to me one afternoon, while we were waiting for the nurse to inject her with a combination of cytarabine, daunomycin, and etoposide. "I want to go home."

I dug deep for the strength to keep my voice steady. "I know it's going to be hard, sweetie," I replied, "but we don't have a choice about this. If you don't have the treatment, you won't get better, and we need you to get better. I promise I'll be right here with you the entire time, right beside you, loving you. You're a brave girl and we're going to get through this. We'll get through it together. You and me."

She kissed me on the cheek and said, "Okay, Mommy."

I held her as close as I could, kissed the top of her head, and prayed that the treatment would not be too painful.

Megan's hair did fall out, and she was extremely ill from the chemotherapy, but within four weeks, she achieved complete remission.

I'll never forget the day when those test results came back.

Rain was coming down in buckets outside, and the sky was the color of ash.

I was standing in front of the window in the hospital playroom, staring out at the water pelting the glass, while Megan played alone at a table with her doll. I told myself that no matter what happened, we would get through it.

We would not stop fighting.

We would conquer this.

Then Dr. Jenkins walked into the room with a clipboard under her arm and smiled at me. I knew from the look in her eye that it was good news, and my relief was so overwhelming, I could not speak or breathe.

A sob escaped me. I dropped to my knees and wept violently into my hands.

This was the first time Megan saw me cry. She set down her doll and came over to rub my back with her tiny, gentle hand.

"Don't cry, Mommy," she said. "Everything's going to be okay. You'll see."

I laughed as I looked up at her, and pulled her into my loving arms.

# Chapter Eight

After a short period of recuperation, Megan entered a phase of post-remission therapy, which consisted of more chemo drugs to ensure that any residual cancer cells would not multiply and return.

I wish I could say that our lives returned to normal, but after facing the very real possibility of our daughter's death, I knew the old "normal" would never exist for us again. Our lives were changed forever, and some of those changes were extraordinary.

From that day forward, I saw more beauty in the world than I had ever seen before. I cherished every moment, found joy in the tiniest pleasures, for I understood this amazing gift called life.

I gloried in the time we spent together, knowing how precious and fragile it all was. Sometimes I would look up at the sky and watch the clouds shift and roll across the vibrant expanse of blue, and I wanted to weep from its sheer majesty.

We lived in a beautiful world, and I felt so fortunate to have Megan at my side. I had learned that I was stronger than I ever imagined I was, and so was Megan. She had fought a difficult battle and had become my hero. I respected and admired her – more than I ever respected or admired anyone. I was in awe of her.

In addition, friends and family offered us help and support, and I saw, through the eyes of my heart, how incredibly lucky we all were to be on the receiving end of all that generosity and compassion. It was something wonderful to witness, and I felt truly blessed.

It may seem an odd thing to say, but I sometimes felt that Megan's cancer, even though it was painful, had brought something good. It had taught us so much about life and love. I had grown – so had she – and I knew that this change in us was very profound and would affect both our futures.

Later I would learn how right I was.

For something both glorious and mystifying still awaited us.

# Chapter Nine

Over the next two years, I helped Megan through her post-remission therapy and cherished every precious moment with her, basking in the joy of our existence.

Michael reacted differently.

He was overjoyed, of course, when Megan achieved remission. We celebrated and went to Disney World for the weekend. But slowly, over time, as the weeks pressed on and there was still no end to the doctor appointments and pills and blood work, he began to withdraw.

Every evening when he came home from work, he poured himself a drink. Though he never consumed enough to become noticeably intoxicated, it was enough to change the core of the person he had once been.

He smiled less often (oh, how I missed his smile) and he left all of Megan's medical care to me. He didn't attend any of her appointments, nor did he stay informed about her medications at home. I administered all of them myself.

The Sunday trips to his sister's house in Connecticut fell by the wayside as well, along with my writing.

Not that I cared about that. Being with Megan was all that mattered to me – but perhaps that was part of the problem where Michael was concerned.

In the early days of our marriage, when we were passionately in love, he was the center of my world. Maybe he couldn't accept the fact that I had a new hero now, and there were things in life I revered more than his success at the firm or our expensive dinners out.

These were things he didn't understand.

"They're just clouds," he would say when I wanted to lay on the grass and watch them roll across the sky. He would frown at me as I shook out the blanket. "Don't be so emotional. It's ridiculous."

Or maybe that was the heart of the problem. Maybe he couldn't handle the complexity of his own emotions. We had come very close to losing our daughter, and sometimes it felt like we were still standing on a thin sheet of ice with a deep crack down its center.

What if it happened again? What if Megan relapsed? What if we had another child and the same thing happened? How would we cope?

It had been so difficult the first time. I couldn't imagine going through anything like that again.

I understood his fear. I felt it, too, but it didn't keep me from loving Megan or spending time with her. It only intensified our bond.

I wanted to be closer to Michael, but he was always too tired, not in the mood, or too busy.

Once, I suggested that we try therapy together – surely a child with cancer was enough to warrant a few sessions with a professional – but he was worried that someone at the firm might find out, and he was determined to stay strong. He was a partner now and couldn't afford to be weak.

His behavior saddened and angered me, and I regret to say that this wedge in our relationship only grew deeper over time. I felt more and more disconnected from the love we once shared.

Consequently, when the next bomb hit, our foundations were unsteady. As a couple, we were damaged and vulnerable, and it all went downhill from there.

# Chapter Ten

On a snowy late November afternoon in 2005, I was putting away the dishes, and Megan screamed in the bathroom. As soon as I heard the terror in her voice, I dropped a plate on the floor. It shattered into a hundred pieces on the ceramic tiles, and my heart dropped to my stomach.

Please, let it be a spider, I thought as I ran to her.

When I pushed the door open, I found her sitting on the floor with blood pouring out of her nose. She was slumped over, trying to catch it in her hands.

Quickly I grabbed a towel, held it under her nose and helped her up. "It's all right, honey. Mommy's here now. Everything's going to be fine."

But I knew it was not that simple. She was not fine. She'd been fatigued for the past week and had lost her appetite.

I don't know how I managed to think clearly as I helped her out to the front hall. All I wanted to do was cry or yell at someone, but I could do none of those things because I had to focus on picking up my purse, locking the door behind me, buckling her into the car, and driving to the hospital.


After two years in remission with normal blood counts and an excellent prognosis, Megan suffered a relapse in her central nervous system.

The doctor explained that this type of relapse occurred in less than ten percent of childhood leukemia patients, and that Megan would require frequent spinal taps to inject chemotherapy drugs directly into her cerebrospinal fluid.

I tried to call Michael on his cell phone, but he wasn't answering and the receptionist couldn't tell me where he was.

I was enraged. I remember thinking, as I stood at the nurses' station and slammed the receiver down, that I wanted to divorce him. Why wasn't he here with me? Why did I have to shoulder all of this alone? Did he not care? Didn't he love his daughter? Didn't he love me?

I sat down on a bench in the hospital corridor and struggled to calm myself before I returned to Megan's bedside, but my heart was throbbing in my chest and I was afraid I might, at any second, start screaming like a lunatic.

Why was this happening? Recently, I had begun to feel some security that Megan was going to be all right and live a long, happy life. She would go to high school, college, get married and have children of her own. I was certain that one day, all of this would be a distant memory, because we had fought hard and beaten it.

But the cancer was back. The treatments had not worked. The leukemia cells were infecting her blood again.

I stood up and ran to the nearest bathroom, where I heaved up the entire contents of my stomach.

Sometime after eleven that night, Michael arrived at the hospital. I had no idea where he'd been all day or why he hadn't answered his phone. I didn't ask. All I did was explain Megan's diagnosis in a calm and cool manner, because by that time, I had reached a state of numbness. Megan was sleeping and I couldn't seem to feel anything. I couldn't cry, couldn't yell. I couldn't even step into Michael's arms to let him hold me.

I suppose I had been enduring this alone for such a long time that I didn't need him anymore. I didn't need anyone – except for Megan, and the doctors and nurses who could keep her alive.

When Michael absorbed what I told him about the nosebleed and the fatigue over the past week, and the spinal taps and radiation she would require, he pushed me aside, marched up to the nurses' station, and smacked his palm down upon the countertop.

A nurse was seated in front of a computer, talking to someone on the phone. "I'll get right back to you," she said, then set the receiver down and looked up at him. "Is there something I can do for you, sir?"

"Where the hell is Dr. Jenkins?" Michael asked. "Get her out here. Now. She has a lot to answer for."

I rushed forward and grabbed hold of his arm. "It's not her fault, Michael. She's doing everything she can for Megan."

He roughly shook me away. "Everything? What kind of hospital is this? Why didn't anyone see this coming?"

"Keep your voice down," I said. "You'll wake Megan. She'll hear you."

A baby started to cry somewhere down the hall.

"I don't care if she hears me! She needs to know that at least someone is looking out for her."

My stomach muscles clenched tight. I could feel my blood rushing to my head, pounding in my ears.

"Someone?" I replied. "Like who? You? Pardon me for saying so, Michael, but you've done nothing for Megan over the past two years. I've taken care of her every minute of every day, while you find other more important things to do. So don't you dare pretend to be her savior tonight. I won't let you make enemies out of the very people who are trying to save her."

I gestured toward the nurse – though I didn't even know her name – and she slowly stood up.

She was a tall, broad-shouldered black woman with plastic-rimmed glasses and a fierce-looking gaze. "Is there going to be a problem here, sir?" she asked. "Do I need to call security?"

Briefly he considered it, then turned his back on her and faced me. A muscle twitched at his jaw as he spoke. "I told you we should've gotten a second opinion."

Michael reached into his breast pocket, pulled out a business card, and tossed it onto the counter. He pointed a threatening finger at the nurse. "See that? Yeah. You're going to hear from me."

He walked out and left me standing there with my heart racing, perspiration beading upon my forehead.

Not because I was afraid, but because it had taken every ounce of self-control I possessed not to punch Michael in the face.

I took a few deep breaths to calm myself.

"Was that your ex?" the nurse asked.

I glanced at her nametag. "No... Jean. We're still married."

Jean removed her glasses, pulled a tissue from the box on the counter, and proceeded to clean her lenses while she strolled out from behind the counter.

She approached me, slid her glasses back on, then laid a hand on my shoulder. "You look like you could use a Popsicle."

Not knowing what else to say, I simply nodded and followed her into the lunchroom.

-End of Excerpt-

# THE REBEL

*A Highland Short Story*

*By Julianne MacLean*

*Excerpt - Copyright 2011 Julianne MacLean*

*November 13, 1715*

On the field of Sherrifmuir, six miles northeast of Stirling Castle

At the sound of the bagpipes and the roaring command of his chief, Alex MacLean drew his sword and broke into a run, charging up the north face of the hill.

A wild frenzy of bloodlust exploded in his veins and fuelled his body with savage strength and determination, as he and his fellow Jacobite clansmen advanced upon Argyll's left flank. Their lines collided in a heavy clash of bodies and weaponry, and suddenly he was thrashing about in a red sea of chaos. Men shouted and lunged, shot each other at close range, they severed limbs and hacked each other to pieces. Blood splattered onto his face as he spun around and swung his sword at one soldier, then another. Adrenaline fired his instincts. The fury was blinding. His muscles strained with every controlled thrust and strike.

Keenly aware of all that was happening around him, he raised his targe to encumber the piercing point of a bayonet. Dropping to one knee, he dirked the offending redcoat in the belly.

Eventually, in the distance, beyond the delirium of combat, the Government Dragoons began to fall back, retreating through their own infantry. The fury was too much for them. Alex raised his sword.

"Charge!" he shouted, in a deep thunderous brogue. "For the Scottish Crown!"

He and his fellow clansmen cried out in triumphant resolve and rushed headlong at the breaking enemy ranks, while the Jacobite cavalry thundered past, galloping hard to pursue the Hanoverians into the steep-sided Glen of Pendreich.

Moments flashed by like brilliant bursts of lightning. The battle was nearly won. The redcoats were fleeing....

Before long, Alex slowed to a jog and looked about to get a better sense of his bearings. He and dozens of other clansmen were now spread out across the glen with precious space between them and clean air to breathe.

It was over. Argyll's opposing left flank was crushed. They were retreating to Dunblane.

Stabbing the point of his weapon into the frosty ground, Alex dropped to his knees in exhaustion and rested his forehead on the hilt. He'd fought hard, and with honor. His father would be proud.

Just then, a fresh-looking young redcoat leapt out from behind a granite boulder and charged at him. "Ahh!"

He was naught but a boy, but his bayonet was sharp as any other.

Rolling across the ground, Alex shifted his targe to the other hand to deflect the thrust of the blade. The weapon flew from the soldier's hands and landed on the grass, but before Alex could regain his footing, a saber was scraping out of its scabbard, and he suddenly found himself backing away defensively, evaluating his opponent's potential skill and intentions.

Blue eyes locked on his, and the courage he saw in those depths sharpened his wits.

Carefully, meticulously, they stepped around each other.

"Are you sure you want to do this, lad?" Alex asked, giving the boy one last chance to retreat with the others in his regiment. "I've done enough killing this morning. I don't need more blood on my hands. Just go."

But why was he hesitating? The dark fury of battle still smoldered within him. What difference would it make if he killed one more? All he had to do was take one step forward and swing. The boy was no match for him. He could slay him in an instant.

"I'm sure," the lad replied, but his saber began to tremble in his hands.

Alex wet his lips. "Just drop your weapon, boy, and run."

"No."

Alex paused. "You're a brave one, aren't you? Or maybe you're just stupid."

All at once, the young soldier let out a vicious battle cry and attacked with a left-handed maneuver that cut Alex swiftly across the thigh.

He gaped down at the wound in bewilderment.

Musket fire rang out in the distance. The morning chill penetrated his senses, steeled his warrior instincts.

The next thing he knew, he was whirling around with a fierce cry of aggression. He swung his targe and struck lad in the head. The young redcoat stumbled backward. His saber dropped from his grasp.

Then, as if it were all happening in a dream, the soldier's hat flew through the air, and long black tresses unfurled and swung about. The boy hit the ground and rolled unconscious onto his back.

Alex's eyes fell immediately upon a soft complexion and lips like red cherries. All thoughts of war and the Jacobite triumph fled from his mind as he realized with dismay that he had just struck a woman.

*-End of Excerpt-*

# About the Author

Julianne MacLean is a USA Today bestselling author of 15 historical romances, including The Highlander Trilogy with St. Martin's Press and her popular American Heiress series with Avon/Harper Collins. She also writes contemporary mainstream fiction under the pseudonym E.V. Mitchell, and her most recent release THE COLOR OF HEAVEN was an Amazon bestseller. She is a three-time RITA finalist, and has won numerous awards, including the Booksellers' Best Award, the Book Buyers Best Award, and a Reviewers' Choice Award from Romantic Times for Best Regency Historical of 2005. She lives in Nova Scotia with her husband and daughter, and is a dedicated member of Romance Writers of Atlantic Canada. Please visit the author's website for more information.

# Books by Julianne MacLean

## Harlequin Romances:

Prairie Bride
The Marshal and Mrs. O'Malley
Adam's Promise
Sleeping with the Playboy

## The American Heiress Series:

To Marry the Duke
An Affair Most Wicked
My Own Private Hero
Love According to Lily
Portrait of a Lover
Surrender to a Scoundrel

## The Pembroke Palace Series:

In My Wildest Fantasies
The Mistress Diaries
When a Stranger Loves Me

## The Highlander Trilogy:

Captured by the Highlander
Claimed by the Highlander
Seduced by the Highlander

## Writing as E.V.Mitchell:

The Color of Heaven

Made in the USA
San Bernardino, CA
09 March 2013